M000283050

# THE RELUCTANT DETECTIVE

## A C.T. FERGUSON PRIVATE INVESTIGATOR MYSTERY (#1)

### TOM FOWLER

WIDENINGGYREMEDIA

Do you like free books? You can get the prequel novella to the C.T. Ferguson mystery series for free. This is exclusive to my VIP readers. Just go here to get your book!

The Reluctant Detective, a C.T. Ferguson Private Investigator Mystery by Tom Fowler

Published by Widening Gyre Media, LLC. Silver Spring, MD

**Editing** by Chase Nottingham

**Cover design** by Earthly Charms

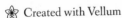 Created with Vellum

*For Lisa and Isabel*

My father tossed a section of folded newspaper at me. It landed on my parents' garish coffee table. "I'm sure *The Sun* appreciates you," I said, "along with their dozens of other subscribers."

"Open it," my father said.

I looked at the section he had thrown toward me. It was the classifieds. I knew what was coming and didn't want to open the paper.

"Page three," he said.

"You actually ran the ad," I said.

"You were supposed to do it." My father pushed his glasses up on his nose.

"Who still reads the newspaper?"

"We expected you to do more of this kind of thing yourself," he said, ignoring my reasoned objection. "Do you have a case yet?"

"No," I said.

"Have you even talked to anyone?"

"No."

"You'd better start."

I started by looking at the ad.

*C.T. Ferguson*
*Licensed Private Investigator*
*The P.I. who helps the little guy*
*Individual clients only (no corporations)*
*No fees: all services provided pro bono!*
*Office: 410.555.6733*

MY PARENTS HAVE a lot of talent when it comes to investing, playing the markets, inheriting money, and things like that, but they are devoid of both skill and taste when it comes to anything creative. Block letters, no graphics, plain text . . . I shuddered when I saw it. If my computer skills lay more with graphic design, I might have wept.

"What's wrong, son?" my father said.

"Two thousand two called and wants its half-page ad back," I said.

"It doesn't have to be flashy. It just has to advertise the business you said you'd start running."

I cringed at the tagline. "The PI who helps the little guy?"

"What?" my father said. "Everyone needs a slogan. I think it's catchy."

"So was the plague, Dad," I said.

"Coningsby, you shouldn't fuss so much," my mother said. "If you want any money from us, you need to do the work you said you'd do."

There she went, reminding me of our devil's bargain already. I had set the over/under at ten minutes. Pay the unders. "I know, Mom," I said.

"If you'd found something else to do. . . ."

"I volunteered at the Esperanza Center a few times."

"What did you learn?"

THE RELUCTANT DETECTIVE / 3

"Mostly how rusty my Spanish is," I said.

"You could just work with them, Coningsby. They could use the help."

"No," I said. "I need to do something that lets me use what I know. I need to do it my way."

"This could work out very well," my mother said, beaming. "This ad will allow you to help people who need it. Maybe we'll make a philanthropist out of you yet."

"I think I'd rather be a philanderer."

"Coningsby!"

"Just being honest," I said.

"Yes, well," my mother said, sniffing like she did every time I offended her sensibilities, "I think our publicity campaign is off to a wonderful start."

"I guess we'll see how many calls I get."

"I'm still surprised you settled on being a detective," my father said.

This would be good. "Why?" I said.

"Well, it seems . . . different than what you did in Hong Kong."

"I helped some people in Hong Kong, Dad. Now I get to use a lot of the same skills here. Hackers are the new detectives."

My father rolled his eyes. "You can't solve everything sitting at a computer."

"I'm sure I can't. But I think I can do a lot of the legwork there."

"What you're talking about is just as illegal here as it was overseas," my mother said. Her tone evoked the one she used to scold me as a child. "That crowd you fell in with had you do all sorts of criminal things."

I shook my head. "They were a useful crowd, Mom. You've told me before you think everything happens for a reason." She frowned at me but finally gave a nod. "Maybe going overseas and learning what I learned happened so I can be a detective now." I didn't know if my mother would believe that—I didn't—but if it placated her, it would be good enough.

"Getting you out of Hong Kong wasn't easy, son," my father said. "We just don't want to see you wind up in trouble again."

"I won't. Look, you both want me to get a job helping people. Hell, you're forcing me to. I need something to do after . . . after China. I can use my skills to help people in ways the police can't. There's value there."

"Richard doesn't see it that way," my mother pointed out.

Of course he didn't. My cousin Rich is a Baltimore police officer. I imagined he found the idea abhorrent. "He'll come around once I work some cases," I said.

"Are you sure?"

"I can't control what he thinks, so I'm not going to worry about it. I need to get back home. The media blitz continues."

"At least it's starting," my father said.

I looked at my parents. They hadn't aged much since I left after finishing my master's. My hair was the same dark brown as my father's, though gray encroached on his temples and the back of his head. It also infringed on his stubble on the rare occasions my mother didn't tsk him into shaving. My mother yielded to vanity years ago and dyed her hair blonde. It wasn't the exact shade I remembered from my youth, but it came close. They didn't decorate their house elaborately or have a live-in housekeeper, though they could afford both. They put a lot of their money into causes they believed in. I had become one of those causes, and an employee of their foundation. I owed them an honest effort, regardless of my feelings about this blasted new career.

"Maybe I'll get a case today," I said.

"Good luck, son," said my father.

With the ad they placed for me, I would need it.

* * *

THE LIGHT GLARED down at me, bright and hot, just like it had in the Chinese prison. Heat hit my face. I closed my eyes. A harsh voice interrogated me, asking me the same question over and over. My chest tightened. I took a deep breath and opened my eyes. Instead of Chinese prison guards, I saw Jessica Webber.

I pushed the lamp on my end table back a few inches, changing the angle. The tightness in my chest eased. Jessica looked at me with concern. "C.T., are you okay?" she said.

"I'm fine."

"You didn't seem fine a minute ago."

"Really, I'm good."

"I had asked you about China." Jessica looked at her notes. "You started talking, mentioned your arrest, and then . . . I don't know; you got a little PTSD on me there."

"I'm fine, Jessica," I said.

Jessica, a local reporter, constituted the second part of my parents' publicity campaign for my nascent operation. I told her I'd be glad to talk to her, both because I needed the publicity and because she had to be the prettiest reporter I'd seen since arriving back in the States. Maybe her easy charm compelled me to open up. Maybe it was the extra cleavage exposed by leaving a button undone. The clincher had to be the fact she got me talking about my favorite subject.

Myself.

We began the interview talking about the pro bono private detective service, as planned. "Got my credentials two days ago," I told her. The phone company just connected the land-line I expected not to use. If the media blitz stopped with

Jessica, I would be OK with it. Jessica had long blond hair, stood almost six feet tall in heels, and her legs suggested she wore heels often. She had curves but her sleek arm muscles revealed she knew her way around a gym. Once I started talking about China, something somewhere told me to shut up, but I didn't listen.

Thoughts of what happened after I got arrested assaulted me again. I pushed them down. I needed a breath. Hell, I needed oxygen a long time ago, and should have stopped then. But what's said is said. I took those necessary breaths and tried to forget my experiences with my Chinese jailers. Jessica kept looking at me for a few seconds before she spoke. "Were you scared?"

"Yes," I said after a few seconds. "I speak the language, but I didn't want them to know, so I just played dumb."

"You speak Chinese?"

"I lived there for three and a half years. I couldn't get by without speaking it. Besides, it makes the Chinese restaurant experience over here so much richer."

"What do you mean?"

I smiled at her. She smiled back. "Do you know what they say about you in the kitchen?"

Jessica gave a light, airy chuckle. "I don't think I want to," she said.

"You don't."

She nodded. "Back to Hong Kong, C.T. What happened after they hauled you off to jail?"

I focused on inhaling and exhaling. I felt I should tell her something but wanted to stop well short of everything. "They didn't care if I was an American from a wealthy family. I heard them say it enough times. My cell was dark, and they brought the same food all the time, so I don't know how long I was there. When I got sent before the judge, he ordered me held over for trial. When I finally got out, and they told me they were deporting me, nineteen days had gone by."

"Wow." Jessica leaned forward in the seat. I resisted the urge to inspect the cleavage her unbuttoned buttons invited me to look at. "That's almost three weeks."

"The longest almost three weeks of my life."

"And now you're here and setting up a free PI business."

"Yes," I said.

"I don't get it," said Jessica. "A doesn't really lead to B there."

I shrugged. "A man must maintain a little mystery."

"Your potential clients may not agree," she said.

I winced. Now I would pay for my love of talking about myself. "I did a lot of babbling," I said. "Some of what I said wouldn't help me if it found its way to print."

"Is that so?" Jessica flashed an amused smile. She had an angle here.

"I think it would reduce my potential client pool."

"I think you might be right."

"Can I talk you out of putting the information in your story?" I said.

She gave me her enigmatic smile again, but it lingered on her face longer this time. "We reporters don't believe in compromising the integrity of our stories, Mr. Ferguson."

"Is that so, Miss Webber?" I said.

"At least, not without a nice dinner," Jessica said. "And I mean a *nice* dinner."

"I know what a nice dinner means. When?"

"Tomorrow night. I'll come by at 7:30. We can discuss the terms of my omission of several important facts over dinner."

"And dessert."

She smiled again. "And dessert."

* * *

AFTER JESSICA LEFT, I switched on the ringer on my business line. I felt weird living in an apartment and having an office there. A house would come in time. Right now, I didn't have a spare hundred grand floating around. Asia can tax a fellow's resources, especially when said fellow is bankrolling a group of hackers, pirates, and thieves.

After I turned the ringer on, I got calls from two local TV stations. Someone opening a free detective service apparently counts as big news. Maybe the chill in the air accompanying Novembers in Maryland chased all the evildoers inside for a day or two, allowing yours truly a moment in the spotlight. The reporters surmised I hadn't answered the phone yet because I had already been working. I let them think what they wanted. I spoke to the reporters for a few minutes each, went out for dinner, and called it an uneventful night a few hours later.

The next morning, I woke up at the beastly hour of 8:40. I stepped over a few newspapers as I went out for a morning run in the brisk November air. Five days ago, it had been sixty degrees. Then the temperature plummeted by half in two days, and we got an early snow. Welcome to Maryland, where fall and winter live in sin. By now, all but the last bits of compacted black snow had melted. I made a circuit of the nearby Fells Point streets and ran alongside the Baltimore Harbor. I smelled coffee and pastries from nearby bake shops. Had I waited a couple hours, I could have started and ended my run with the smell of seafood. Just over a half-hour after I set out, I walked back to my building, picked up a paper, and went inside.

I saw my parents' ad as I perused the paper. If the bloody thing turned out to be effective, it would be worth it in the end. I cringed as I read the tagline again. I set the paper on my kitchen table and got a shower. When I wandered out some 20 minutes later, my business line rang. Could this be my first potential client? I hoped so. I felt an unfamiliar nervous tingle in my chest as I picked up the phone. "Hello?" I said in the most professional voice I could muster.

"Yeah, I saw an ad in the paper," a man said. He spoke in a voice barely above a whisper. I had to increase the volume to hear him. "Are you the guy running the free detective business?"

"I am," I said. "What do you need?"

"Someone's following me."

"Do you know who it is?"

"Yeah, man."

Were I the type to believe in regrets, I would have regretted asking my followup question. "Who is it?" I said.

"The government," he said.

"The government?"

"Yeah. And they spy on me through my TV, too. Saw it on the news. I had to get a really old one to stop that shit."

"You know TVs don't work that way, right?"

"The old ones don't."

"None of them do," I said. "They never have. The government isn't spying on you. They wouldn't waste the time."

"I know they have me on a list," he said.

"I'm sure they have you on several. Now take off your tinfoil hat and listen: I'm putting you on a list, too. It's called the do-not-call list. Stop watching X-Files reruns and get outside more." I hung up the phone before he could say anything else.

Of course, he called right back, then again, then again. I didn't answer. The government wouldn't waste time with him, and I decided to adopt the same policy. After four callbacks, he got the hint and stopped. Or the government found him and killed him. I had no preference.

A few minutes later, the phone rang again. I checked caller ID to make sure it wasn't that same idiot before I answered. "Hello?" I maintained my professional tone.

"Are you C.T. Ferguson?" a woman said. "The guy with the ad?"

"Speaking. What can I do for you?"

"I need you to find someone."

I pumped my fist at a legitimate call. "I'll give it my best shot. Who am I looking for?" I grabbed a legal pad and a pen.

"Her name is Muffins."

I had started to write, then stopped. "Is she a stripper?" I said.

"No, she's a Labrador," the lady said.

"You want me to find your dog?"

"She's a very nice dog."

"I'm sure she is. I like dogs, but I'm not here to find missing pets. Print out signs and staple them to telephone poles. If those don't work, walk around your neighborhood with a whistle and a cookie." She started to say something, but I hung up. I wondered if established detectives had to deal with crackpots, too. The advertisement of free services brought out the crazies. I hadn't wanted this gig to begin with, but if the signal-to-noise ratio didn't improve soon, it would be worse than I imagined.

Another few minutes went by, and the phone rang again. My professional voice started to crack under the weight of exasperation. "Hello?"

"Is this C.T. Ferguson?" the woman on the other end said.

"It is."

"I saw your ad. I . . . I think my husband is cheating on me."

I winced. Of course, now someone would call me and want me to poke around in some domestic matter. I wanted a juicy murder or at least an interesting burglary, not someone diddling the office secretary. How boring. I took a breath, shoved those thoughts aside, and summoned my professional voice again. "Why don't you come in, and we can talk about it?" I gave her my address, and she gave me her name and other basics.

"I'll be there in an hour," she said.

It would be a long hour.

CHAPTER 2

I SPENT SOME OF THAT TIME TIDYING UP. IN MY YOUNGER days, none of my imaginings of my future life included having an office. After spending nineteen days in the Chinese prison, I wanted to keep myself busy. Plus, if I wanted any of the family money—and I did—I had to get used to having an office and having clients in it.

I used my second bedroom. The apartment boasted one large and one medium-sized bedroom. As apartments went, the rooms were spacious. My office held a desk, a small refrigerator, a high-backed leather executive chair for yours truly, and two conference chairs for prospective clients. The desk was large enough to fit a pair of 24-inch monitors, a keyboard, a color laser printer, and still leave me space to doodle, take notes, or pretend to take notes while people droned on about infidelities real and imagined. I made sure the conference chairs faced the desk, and the overhead light and ceiling fan were on.

After I put everything in order, someone knocked on the door. I looked through the peephole. A woman stood on my welcome mat, bundled up more than she needed to be against the cold. Between her coat, hood, and wool hat, I could barely see any of her face. A few stray locks of black hair spilled onto her coat. I unlocked the deadbolt and opened the door. "You're Mrs. Fisher?" I said.

"Yes," she said. "May I come in?"

"Of course." I moved to the side and let her enter. She stopped, took a deep breath, and removed her gloves. I noticed she still wore her wedding ring. Years as a professional bachelor conditioned me to look for it, and it could have been important to the case. Once her gloves were off, Mrs. Fisher pulled back her hood and removed her hat. Her ovular face was rounded in the right places. It wouldn't launch a thousand ships, but I figured it good for a solid two-fifty. Her hazel eyes already had worry lines etched around them. Her hair was shoulder-length and straight. She wore dark blue jeans and a Ravens sweatshirt under her coat.

"I'll take your coat," I said. She handed it to me, and I hung it in the small closet. "My office is right down the hall." Alice followed me. I sat behind my desk and gestured to one of the conference chairs in front of it. She looked at me.

"Call me Alice," she said. I looked back at her. Alice was no taller than five-four, but possessed an above-average figure to match her pretty face. Her clothes hid a lot, but I guessed she frequented a gym—or at least a home treadmill. She didn't seem like a woman a man would cheat on, but I knew several fools who cheated on their very attractive wives with women they shouldn't have glanced at a second time.

Was I supposed to say something now? Alice came to me, so it made sense she should do the talking. On the other hand, she was a guest in my office, and I was the detective. Maybe I should ask her. Why didn't the state go over important matters like this? Alice solved my conundrum by talking.

"Like I said on the phone, I think my husband is cheating on me."

"Why do you think so?"

"The usual signs."

"Usual signs?"

"You know."

"Pretend I skipped cheating husband day at detective school," I said.

Alice sighed. "You know . . . he works late a few nights a week." Her eyes rarely focused on one thing for more than a second or two when she talked. Even if she looked right at me, she would glance away, then at something else, then back at me. The whole thing felt disconcerting. "That started a couple months ago. He doesn't always let me know in advance, either. Sometimes, I don't find out until I get home and call him."

"Did anything happen at his job around the time he started working late?"

"Like what?"

"Like a new secretary, new coworker . . . anything like those?"

"He didn't mention anything."

"Anything happen at home two months ago to drive him away?"

Alice shook her head. "No, nothing."

I nodded. "What else have you noticed?"

"He's usually evasive about where he's been, even if it's just work. He won't tell me the things he worked on. I can never reach him at his desk after hours, either; I always have to call him on his cell phone."

"So you think he's playing grab-ass in someone else's office."

"Yes, I do," Alice said with a frown. "I also noticed he had a black eye a couple weeks ago. He said it was an accident . . . someone knocked a machine door into him, or something like that."

"Did you believe him?" I said.

"I didn't press it."

I thought of ways a black eye could be indicative of an affair and kept arriving at situations where Alice's husband should have been hurt worse. "Do you know many of your husband's coworkers?" I said. "Especially the women?"

"I've met most of them at holiday parties, cookouts, things like that. Most of the women there are attractive. They're almost all friendly, too."

"Doesn't mean he's sleeping with them."

"I know." Alice's eyes welled with tears. "I just have this feeling he is. That after nine years, I'm not enough for him anymore." She wiped at her eyes with the outside of her index finger. "I need to know, either way." I realized although my desk had many useful things atop it, a box of tissues could not be included in that number.

"Do you want a tissue?" I said.

Alice nodded and sniffed, wiping at her eyes the whole time. I got up, left the office, and went into my bathroom down the hall. I grabbed the box of tissues from atop the vanity and carried it back. As I moved behind my desk, I held the box out toward Alice. She grabbed a tissue and dabbed at her eyes with it. "I'm sorry," she said. "I guess now that I'm talking to a detective, the reality is hitting me."

"Don't apologize," I said. "I'm sure it's a stressful situation."

"Have you ever been married, C.T.?"

I chuckled. "No."

Alice cracked a smile. "Yeah, you don't strike me as the marrying type." Alice dabbed at her eyes some more. I let her compose herself. Outside, a succession of horns honked. No matter the hour, someone drove badly in Baltimore, and three or more people had to react. Alice wiped her eyes again, blew her nose, and tossed the tissue into the wastebasket.

"Where was I?" she said.

"Telling me I wasn't the marrying type."

She smiled again, briefly. "Oh, right. My marriage has been great until now. This patch of uncertainty has taken a lot out of me."

"Has your husband noticed?" It occurred to me I didn't yet know the husband's name. I really had to get better at this whole asking questions thing.

"If he has, he hasn't said anything yet. I've tried to be a good wife and keep up the façade at home. Besides, he may not be cheating on me. I don't need to worry him over nothing."

"I should get some basic information from you." I took a legal pad and pen out of the top drawer. "What's your husband's name?"

"Paul. Michael Paul Fisher, but he goes by Paul."

I jotted it down. "Where does he work?"

"He works for Digital Sales. He's an account manager."

"Is he a glorified salesman?" I said.

Alice frowned. "I think salesmen report to him. I'm not a hundred percent sure, really."

"You said you've been married nine years?"

"Yes. Nine years last month, in fact."

"Where do you live?"

"We bought a house in Glen Burnie about ten years ago."

"How's the house holding value?"

"It's not." Alice's eyes continued flitting to anything in the room. "We've lost a good bit on it since we've owned it."

"So you're underwater?"

"Yes," she said.

I finished taking my notes. "All right, I guess I have all I need for now."

"You'll be in touch?" she said.

"When I know something," I said.

"What about updates?"

"I'm not going to send you status reports, if that's what

you're getting at."

"Why not?"

"Because you're not paying me, and I'm not paying a secretary. When I know something, I'll tell you."

Alice stared at me. "That seems irregular, but I'll trust your professional judgment. Have you worked a lot of cases like this before?"

I shook my head. "Can't say I have, no."

"Did you used to be a policeman?"

I winced. "God, no."

"How did you come to be a detective, then?"

"It fits my skills."

"I hope it does." Alice stood. "Thank you for taking the case. With the house situation, I don't have enough money to hire a real detective."

I would probably have to get used to the remark. Alice realized what she said because her eyes went wide, and she shook her head. "I didn't mean it like that," she said. "I meant I couldn't afford a detective who charged the going rate."

"I understand what you mean." I offered her a smile, which she returned. "I'll let you know when I know something."

"All right." I walked Alice out of the office and back to the foyer, where she fortified herself against the Alaskan winter not currently enveloping Baltimore. "I'll be in touch if anything else comes up that might be important, she said.

"OK," I said. "Take care."

"Thank you." Alice Fisher walked out of my apartment. I closed the front door behind her and locked the deadbolt. My first client. I had a case. A case about adultery, but maybe not, starring a man who just so happened to have pretty, flirty coworkers, and a wife who couldn't look me in the eye while she recounted her sob story.

What the hell had I gotten myself into?

CHAPTER 3

I SAT AT MY COMPUTER. THE VAST WORLD BECKONED. Alice Fisher wanted to know if her husband cheated on her. The answer was out there, and I would find it. I found a lot more sensitive information without ever leaving the comfort of my chair in Hong Kong. Finding dirt on the Fishers would be easy.

Or so I thought. I really didn't know where to begin. Between my computer classes, things I taught myself, and what my friends in China showed me, I felt confident I could hack the CIA and misdirect the operation to some ayatollah in Iran if I had to. How could I use those skills to help the average American married couple? This wasn't a Chinese database I was breaking into or a website we defaced for the laughs. These were regular people with regular problems.

I had the world at my fingertips and I didn't know where to begin.

This seemed so easy when I got my license. My cousin Rich laughed at me and told me I had no experience, and this would be harder than I imagined. I scoffed at him, but right now, I couldn't argue. I didn't know how to investigate a case of maybe-infidelity. I knew I didn't want to dangle out of a tree with a fish-eye lens and take pictures of Paul Fisher groping someone not his wife. All I had to do was find something worth doing in the meantime.

Alice told me a few things about her and Paul. I looked at my notepad. They lived in Glen Burnie. Home was as good a place to start as any, and didn't even require any hacking to get their address. She said they didn't have a lot of money by virtue of being underwater on their mortgage. A lot of people found themselves in that same situation when the housing bubble burst, and home values slid down a slippery slope. Years in, the recovery still hadn't happened for many people.

Finding out how much they paid for their house only took a minute. I learned the Fishers spent $259,000 for their house seven years ago. Because I'd rather dive into a freshly-dug grave than live in Glen Burnie, I didn't know how the figure jibed with the market, but it sounded reasonable. Recent comps confirmed the numbers. Now I needed their mortgage information. I wondered if American banks fortified themselves better than those in Hong Kong.

After a few minutes, I learned they didn't. Finding out which bank held the loan took hardly any time. From there, a firewall and an intrusion detection system presented flimsy roadblocks. An IDS sounds like a great thing, and many companies rely on them. But once a hacker knows which IDS is online (and there are myriad easy ways to figure it out), bypassing or tricking them is easy. Locks only stop honest people, and IDSes only stop stupid hackers.

I brought up the Fishers' loan. They had refinanced a year ago to take advantage of the lower rates. The loan looked normal to me. They still owed just over $236,000 in principal, made their payments on time, and could boast of a good interest rate. Why did Alice say they were underwater? Did the house lose its value? The appraisal performed for the refinance valued the Fishers' house at $256,000. Even if it lost 10% of its value in the intervening year, my estimate still put it around $231,000, which was close to their outstanding balance.

Alice Fisher lied to me about her and her husband's loan balance exceeding their home's value. The lie bothered me. If they couldn't afford a "real detective," it had nothing to do with their mortgage. I would have to dig deeper. I wondered if either of them had a rap sheet. If Paul got arrested for something and had to take a lesser job at work, it would explain things—and he may not have told his wife about the demotion out of pride. I wanted to see what the police knew about Paul and Alice Fisher.

I pursued the information in person.

* * *

"Are you serious?" Rich said, laughing.

So much for cooperation from the Baltimore Police and from my cousin in particular. I took a chance trying to catch Rich at his desk, and risked a bigger chance hoping he would throw me a bone. "I am," I said. "You can share information with me. I'm a licensed private investigator."

"Faking your background doesn't mean you know how to solve a case," Rich said. He looked at me with smug amusement. "If you did, you wouldn't be here." Rich's desk was the most Spartan in the place, which didn't surprise me. Only the essentials sat atop its medium cherry surface and nothing could be out of place. Rich and I both favored our fathers, so we looked a little alike, but he had a sharper, sterner face. His hair remained in the buzz cut he'd sported since before he enlisted in the Army, though some gray now mingled with the brown. His dark blue uniform looked like it had been pressed the moment before he put it on.

"I know enough to know I need more information," I said. "I need to see if the BPD has anything on these people."

Rich shook his head. "You're actually working a case," he said.

"This is my job now," I said.

"Yeah, sure it is. We both know you're doing this so your parents don't disown you."

"I don't see what my motives have to do with anything."

"Oh, come on, C.T.! You don't really want to do this job, so you're going through the motions enough to make your parents happy with you again. Then it'll be to hell with everyone else, just like it always is with you."

"Look, maybe helping people hasn't always been high on my list of things to do. But right now, it's what I'm doing, and I'm going to do it as well as I can."

"I'd like to believe you. Really, I would. Then I remember you're the guy who went overseas to help Chinese criminals with hacking and piracy." I noticed a few people looking at us now. Rich's desk sat against a wall on one side, but the other three were populated with people who had taken a sudden interest in the conversation.

"They might not have heard you in D.C.," I said.

"Whatever," Rich said. "Maybe after you've solved some cases and paid your dues, I'll let you see our files."

"Let me get this straight. Seeing your files would help me solve this case, and presumably others I get. But you won't let me see the files until I solve cases without benefit of those files."

"Exactly," Rich said.

"What is this, hazing? What happened to 'to serve and protect'?"

Rich narrowed his eyes. "You don't get to question me on my oath. You wouldn't know anything about it. You're just in it for the money."

"You've known me my whole life, Rich. OK, maybe I'm vain and—"

"*Maybe?*"

"So I am. Whatever, you know I finish what I start. Say what you want about me, but I'm not a quitter. When I start something, I follow through."

Rich looked at me for a few seconds and nodded. "I'll give you that much."

"Great. Can you also give me a file or two?"

He chuckled "Not a chance. Hey, I'm getting some coffee. You want any?"

"No, thanks."

Rich got up and walked into the next room. I looked around. People who had taken an interest in our conversation a minute ago now ignored me in favor of their work. I scooted my chair closer to Rich's desk and leaned across it. I minimized his email and opened a DOS prompt. I entered the command to get his IP and MAC addresses, jotted the info on a Post-It note Rich had on his desk, closed the DOS box, and restored Outlook. By the time Rich emerged from the other room with a cup of coffee in his hand, I had put the note in my pocket and moved my chair back to its original position.

"You're still here?" Rich said.

"Just hoping you'd change your mind," I said.

"Not going to happen."

"All right," I said, getting up.

"Wait, you're done?"

"What do you mean?"

"You're just giving up? What happened to that tenacity you were telling me about?"

"Right now, I have more productive things to do than get stonewalled," I said. I walked away before Rich could say anything else. I already had what I needed. With Rich's IP and

MAC addresses, I could get any file I wanted, and he wouldn't even know about it.

It ended up being a productive trip after all.

* * *

IN THE HACKING days of yore, folks like me used to engage in a practice called war dialing. The hacker would use a program to dial a bunch of numbers, eventually discovering which numbers belonged to the modem banks. This was easier when businesses used blocks of consecutive phone numbers. I did something similar in fingerprinting the BPD's network, discovering what services ran on which IP address. Rich's IP address gave me the starting point. I didn't need puny desktop computers used by jealous and embittered sergeants, though: I needed servers. It took me a while, but I found them.

From there, I made the BPD's network believe one of my virtual machines was one of its own computers. The MAC address helped here. It's a physical address, but virtual machines need them for networks to deliver data. The setup took me about two minutes. It probably should have taken one, but I double and triple-checked to make sure I didn't leave any e-footprints. With my computer accepted as part of the BPD's network, I now had access to all of their resources, including the files Rich didn't want me to see.

I searched for police files on both Alice and Paul Fisher. My computer crunched through records from throughout the state and returned a hit on Paul Fisher after about two minutes. He had a DUI arrest from six years ago. It led to his license being suspended for six months, but he remained on the good side of the law since then. Alice Fisher had never been arrested. I remembered her shifty eyes from our meeting earlier. Something had to cause her suspicious behavior.

I wasn't going to find any more answers in Paul Fisher's thin police report. Alice said he worked for Digital Sales. Maybe I could discover something on their site. Digital Sales had been in business for over 15 years and sold all manners of copiers, fax machines, printers, scanners, and other office technology. I saw a listing for Paul under Account Managers. The site didn't explain what an account manager did, leaving the duties as an exercise for the reader to deduce.

I considered hacking into Digital Sales' web server to see what else it may have said but decided against it. They were a big enough company to pay someone else to do their web work for them. Whoever designed and maintained it probably only knew Paul Fisher by his picture and title. If I wanted to know anything else, I would have to take a trip down there.

THE FIRST FLOOR of Digital Sales was a mass of hallways and cubicles. The receptionist smiled at me as I approached her desk. She was pretty in the hot librarian way, with her brown hair pulled back and half-moon glasses framing her pleasing face. Closer, I noticed she favored the Jessica Webber method of blouse buttoning. Maybe I had gotten used to the more conservative way women in Hong Kong dressed. Welcome (back) to America, C.T.; be sure to stop and admire the scenery. I returned her smile as I stopped at her large desk.

"I need to speak to someone with an impressive title," I said.

"Well," she said with a smile, "my title is executive assistant. Is that impressive enough?"

"It is, but I need someone with a different impressive title."

"Do you have an impressive title?"

I showed her my newly-minted PI license. "You tell me."

"That could be interesting." She sighed and swept the room with her eyes. "It's probably more exciting than anything else around here, you know?"

"I'm sure it is. I'd like to talk to whomever would supervise Paul Fisher."

"What's wrong with Paul?"

"Nothing, I hope." I leaned closer and lowered my voice. "I'd appreciate you not mentioning anything about this little visit to Paul."

She nodded. "No problem," she said in a whisper. "I don't even like him."

"Very good. Now, whom can I talk to?"

"I'll see if Mr. O'Neill is in."

"Thank you."

She picked up the phone and dialed a few numbers. For the first time, I noticed the nameplate on her desk. In my defense, the phone did a good job of hiding it. Still, now that I worked as an alleged professional sleuth, I would need to sharpen my powers of observation. They had to be used for more than just looking at the cleavage of women like Sally Willis (not a bad use, of course). Sally talked to someone for a few seconds, then hung up. "Mr. O'Neill is in, and he'll see you," she said.

"Great. How do I get to his office?"

"I'll have one of our security guys take you up." She spoke into her handset once more, then replaced it. "He'll be right over." Sally smiled at me again.

"Great, thank you." I took a business card out of my case and put it on the near edge of her desk. "I'll leave this. Call me if you think of anything important about the person you don't like."

She smiled. "I will."

* * *

THE SECURITY GUY who took me up didn't say anything other than a semi-polite "hi" when we first met. I didn't really see the need for him to accompany me at all. Was I going to slip a copier inside my coat and dash for the door? I hadn't come here for technology, and I had no interest in office machines, anyway. We made the elevator ride in silence. Then the security fellow—who didn't wear a name tag—escorted me to David O'Neill's office.

I knocked on the door. O'Neill was on the phone but waved me in. I walked in and waited for his conversation to end. His office looked to be about the size of mine at home, though O'Neill had a larger desk. It probably made him feel important. Two diplomas hung on the wall, along with a couple of cheesy motivational posters and a very nice shot of a sunset at the beach. I couldn't see much of the desk because of the massive clutter. The litter of dead trees was broken by every office machine O'Neill could possibly need and a couple I'm sure he didn't. So much for the paperless office.

O'Neill hung up the phone and turned his chair toward me. "Hello," he said and stood. "David O'Neill, Vice President of Commercial Sales." He extended his hand, and I shook it.

"C.T. Ferguson. I'm a private investigator." This marked the first time I introduced myself with a title. I didn't care for the sound of it.

"What is it you're looking into?" O'Neill gestured to a task chair on the outside of his desk. I looked at it and frowned but sat anyway.

"First, I have to say this conversation needs to be kept in confidence."

"An insurance company sent you?" O'Neill narrowed his eyes.

"No, I'm here—"

"Was it a supplier? They could just tour the damn place if they wanted."

"No, I was—"

"Insurance," he said. "Gotta be insurance. Can't imagine why, though."

"Do they send VPs for training in cutting people off?" I said.

O'Neill frowned. "Guess I've gotten used to it."

"Guess so. Now, like I said, what we discuss today needs to be kept in confidence. My client is an individual, not a business."

O'Neill looked at me for a few seconds. I couldn't read his expression. Then he nodded. "OK, sure."

"I want to talk to you about Paul Fisher. Have—"

"Paul? What did he do?"

I glared at O'Neill. "What did I just say about cutting me off?"

"Oh, right." He frowned. His backbone got more malleable when he saw he couldn't push someone around with his fancy title. Typical. "Sorry."

"Anyway, Paul Fisher. Does he socialize a lot at the office?"

"I don't think so. No more than anyone else, really."

"I hear he's been working late recently."

O'Neill nodded. "A couple months now."

"What does he do after hours?" I said.

"The same thing he does during hours, I suppose."

"What's that? What does an account manager do?"

"He's responsible for several of our corporate clients. He follows up with them, schedules service, maintains their contracts, and recruits new clients."

"So he's a glorified salesman?" I said.

"I don't like that term," O'Neill said, frowning again.

I ignored his objection. "Is there anyone here Paul is really friendly with? Especially a woman?"

"Do you think he's having an affair?"

I just looked at O'Neill. He met my gaze for a few seconds, then looked away and took a deep breath. "I don't think Paul's the cheating type."

"I'm glad you think so," I said, "but it's not what I asked."

"Oh. Um . . . he talks to several of the girls here. We're all pretty friendly."

"I have it on good authority Paul isn't reachable at his desk after hours."

"So?"

"So I asked you what he did after hours, and you said the same thing he did normally. If he did, wouldn't he be at his desk?"

"Well . . . I suppose it would, yes."

"Do you know what he does after hours?" I said.

O'Neill fidgeted. I guessed he didn't like being on this end of a conversation. "Not really, no."

"But he's here," I said.

"Far as I know," he said.

"Is his office on this floor?"

"Yes, it's right down the hall, just past the elevator."

"All right. I have what I need for now. Thanks for your time." I stood and started toward the door.

"Oh, of course," O'Neill said as I was on my way out of his office. I walked along the hall and past the elevator. Paul Fisher's office was the second on the left. He had a window offering a spectacular view of the company parking lot and the industrial complex across the street. At least he had a window. I made a mental note of the landmarks outside so I could find Paul's window when his shift ended. I didn't know where he went or what he did—neither did O'Neill—but I wanted to be sure he left his office.

\* \* \*

I HAD no intention of waiting around for Paul to leave his office. After I left Digital Sales, I lunched at a Japanese restaurant, then went back home. What could Alice be hiding? She lied to me. A thought came to me: if she had a habit of lying, maybe she was the one sleeping around or with something similar to hide. Why she would then hire a detective to look into her husband confounded me. People were confounding creatures on both sides of the ocean.

Looking into Alice Fisher might get me closer to the answer. I ran a background check and discovered Alice Fisher (nee Chester) was born in Garrett County to Dean and Donna, went to college at Towson, and moved to the Baltimore area after graduation. She married Paul two years later. Alice had no criminal record, a few old speeding tickets, and worsening credit. Her three credit cards were all maxed out. Being underwater wasn't the problem; the Fishers—or at least Alice—were getting killed in interest charges.

Alice worked as a patient coordinator, whatever that was, at Upper Chesapeake Hospital in Bel Air. I drove up there to talk to her boss. Finding where to go in the hospital directory felt like navigating a maze. Eventually I found I needed to visit the fourth floor, so I got a pass from a security guard who looked like he wanted to be anywhere but Upper Chesapeake Hospital and took the elevator to level four.

Once off the elevator, I wandered around the labyrinth of glass and steel until I came to some administrative offices. I didn't see a receptionist—nor did I see Alice Fisher, which would have been awkward—so I knocked on the half-open door of Erica Sousa. When given a choice of doors to rap on, always choose the one belonging to the pretty girl. "Excuse me," I said. "I'm trying to find someone."

Erica Sousa looked up from whatever she was working on and flashed a brief smile. "Aren't we all? Who are you looking for?"

"I don't know his or her name, unfortunately. Whoever is in charge of the patient coordinators."

"Do you have a problem?"

"No, just some questions. Can you direct me?"

She looked at me and thought about it, then said, "Sure. You're looking for Corey Dunn. If he's in, he's down the hall to the left."

"Thanks." I walked the hall again and looked for Corey Dunn's office. I also kept an eye out for Alice but didn't see her. She must have been off coordinating some patients, or maybe helping them with their coordination. I found Dunn's office. The door was open, and I saw someone sitting at the desk inside. I knocked.

"Come in," he said without looking to see whom he just beckoned.

I walked in and sat in a guest chair on the other side of his desk. It had a few papers and a keyboard atop it but was otherwise bare. No family pictures. No degrees on the wall. Just Dunn, who looked to be about fifty and in desperate need of directions to a jogging track. He finally looked up and did a double take. "Who the hell are you?"

"My name is C.T. Ferguson," I said, showing him my ID. "I'm a private investigator."

"Did some insurance company send you?"

"Why does everyone think that? I work for an individual."

Dunn nodded. "All right. What do you need?"

"First, to tell you this conversation has to remain confidential. Privacy laws and such." Not the real reason—I just didn't want him blabbing to Alice Fisher. Because the healthcare industry is awash in privacy laws, I figured he would buy it as a legitimate excuse.

"Sure, sure."

"What can you tell me about Alice Fisher?"

"Alice?" He frowned. "Good worker. Comes in and works hard. The patients like her, and so does everyone here, as far as I know."

"Anyone like her a little more than they should?" I said.

"You mean is she having an affair?" said Dunn.

"Yes."

"No."

"She ever talk about money?"

Dunn shook his head. "Why do you need to know all of this about Alice? Who hired you?"

"I'm afraid I can't tell you. Confidentiality laws. You understand."

"I understand I don't want to deal with anymore of your questions."

"Too bad, because I'm going to sit here and keep asking them."

"We'll see about that." Dunn picked up the phone. "Can you send security to my office?" he said into the receiver. "Thanks." He hung up and gave me a smug smile. "You should leave now."

"I think I'll stay," I said. "Wouldn't want to miss any of the scene you're causing."

"I'm not causing a scene!"

"Sure you are. Two people have turned to look at what's going on in here." I inclined my head toward the hallway, and he looked to be sure.

After I spoke, a burly man in a pale blue shirt and dark

pants strode into the office. He wore a baseball cap, black athletic shoes, and a nightstick on his belt. His cheap-looking badge read "Security," and he had a name tag on a lanyard around his neck.

"Problem, Mr. Dunn?" he said.

"Yes," Dunn said. "This man is harassing me and won't leave."

"Sir, you'll need to come with me," the guard said.

"No, I won't." I showed him my ID. "I'm merely asking your boss some questions."

"You'll need to come with me."

"There's no harassment going on."

The guard sighed and stepped into the room. He looked to be about six-four and close to 300 pounds, giving him two inches and over 100 pounds on me. His tattooed arms showed muscles but also a decent amount of fat. I knew he could shame me on the bench press, but I also knew guys like him were used to fights lasting one punch. He wasn't fast enough to do much in a longer fight, if it came down to it. He glared at me. "Last warning."

I needed to think. On the one hand, I didn't enjoy being stonewalled and didn't want to leave. On the other hand, I didn't know if Corey Dunn would have much to tell me even if he were cooperative. Regardless of his attitude, nothing compelled him to talk to me. I needed to remember it, now and in the future. Picking a fight wouldn't benefit anyone, and word could get back to Alice about what I had done. I wanted to avoid this coming back on me.

I stood. "Fine. I'll go."

"I thought you might," Dunn said with a smug smile. Prick.

"I'll walk you out," the guard said.

"I can find my own way," I said.

"I'm sure you can, but you'll find it faster if I'm with you."

I didn't doubt his words. A few people, including Erica Sousa, watched what happened in Dunn's office. I needed to get out of here without making a further ruckus. Office gossip about the handsome PI arguing with Dunn couldn't reach Alice Fisher. "Fine," I said and started toward the door. "Let's go." The guard opened it for me. I readied myself for some macho display from him, but he simply held the door as I walked through it. I smiled to the crowd of four people watching in the hallway and walked back to the elevator with the guard in tow.

* * *

I SAT in the parking lot at Digital Sales. Alice Fisher wasn't cheating on her husband, if her coworkers and jackass boss could be believed. I also hadn't learned anything about why Alice lied about their mortgage situation. For all I knew, they could have been underwater at one point. The housing market had been interesting, in the ancient Chinese curse sort of way, for almost a decade now.

Each time I pondered a question in this case, it spiraled into more questions. When it started, I thought I might solve a simple case of infidelity. So far, it proved anything but. I didn't have the foggiest idea if any infidelity even took place. Here I waited on the dingy asphalt of a business I would never patronize trying to see if I could gain any insight into the Fishers' situation. Perhaps Paul would grope a coworker in the doorway and settle everything.

I told my father "hackers are the new detectives," but I didn't feel like much of a new detective now. Maybe on the way home, I could get fitted for a grimy trench coat and fedora. They couldn't serve me worse than database exploits right now.

I watched a bunch of people leave Digital Sales from my

vantage point near the back of their lot. Paul Fisher's office light remained on for a good fifteen minutes after the mass exodus. Then it went out. I followed the lights on the elevator down to the first floor. A few seconds later, the light at the far left end of the building went on. Whatever Paul Fisher was doing, he did it at work, though not in his own office. That would explain why Alice couldn't reach him. What happened on the first floor? If he needed overtime, why not put in more hours as an account manager? Maybe there was only so much managing of accounts a body could do in a week before realizing his job didn't really mean anything.

In the future, I would need to contact Digital Sales and find out what happened on the first floor, west end of the building. Now, though, I had a dinner planned with Jessica Webber. She roped me into taking her to Le Petit Louis. French didn't top my list of places to go, but if dinner and dessert (and, I hoped, a nightcap) with the lovely Miss Webber kept the more salacious details of my life out of the paper, I would pay the price.

The Fishers' situation bugged me the entire drive home. I knew I would be distracted over dinner, and I hoped Jessica wouldn't notice.

CHAPTER 4

JESSICA WEBBER WORE AN OUTFIT MADE FOR PRIME-TIME news, and it showed off a body made for late-night cable. We sat at the bar at Le Petit Louis while waiting for our table. I sipped a glass of French red wine while Jessica drank a Toblerone. I had never heard of it, and neither had the bartender, but he and Jessica (mostly Jessica) figured out the ingredients on the fly. It looked like chocolate milk that yearned for more chocolate syrup. Jessica smiled when she drank it and said it tasted good.

I sat at the bar and watched the other patrons. About half the barstools were occupied, and a couple of stragglers stood around—men trying to pick up the girls who sat by themselves. I watched the girls for their reactions. The subtle eye roll, the smirk I could see in the mirror but the guy standing next to her couldn't, keeping her hands and arms close to her body. Those guys weren't getting anywhere. I looked over at Jessica, who studied me with an amused smile.

"People watching?" she said.

"I'm a detective," I said, "I need to keep the keen edge on my powers of observation."

"Of course."

"Besides, watching guys strike out with girls is always funny."

"You've never struck out?" Her eyes shined as she sipped her drink through the straw.

"Everyone strikes out; I'm no exception. But I keep swinging, and I think my batting average is solid."

"I don't doubt it."

"Oh, really?" I checked for a reaction.

Color Jessica's makeup couldn't hide came to her cheeks. "Yes, really." She twirled a lock of her blond hair around her left index finger. The hair on the other side of her face hung down past her shoulders, settling nicely around her top, which had a low and open neckline.

"Most people are afraid of striking out," she said, "so they don't bother getting in there and swinging the bat."

"Never let the fear of striking out keep you from playing the game," I said. "Something I read on a motivational poster somewhere."

The maitre d' came and led us to our table. Le Petit Louis is aptly named: it's a small restaurant. I don't know if anyone named Louis has ever been involved with the place, but the restaurant bearing his name certainly favored the petit. We had a table for two, sized exactly for two average people. I took the seat against the wall, which also put me close to a post on my right side. Jessica sat on the aisle, which was barely wide enough for one person to walk up and down. The waiter came, took our drink and appetizer orders, and left.

"Have you been here before?" Jessica said.

"A few times during high school and college," I said. "My parents live pretty close, and they always liked the place."

"What about you?"

I shrugged. "It's pretty good. French isn't my favorite. I'm more of an Asian guy."

"With a name like Ferguson, I figured you for English."

I smiled in spite of myself. "Guilty as charged."

The waiter brought our drinks and appetizer. We put in our dinner orders: Truite Almondine for Jessica and steak Bordelaise for me. We noshed on the aubergines croquantes and downed some of our drinks in silence.

"So how's the business?" Jessica said.

"It's OK, I guess," I said. "I have a case."

"You do?" She leaned forward in her seat. "Tell me about it."

"It's not very exciting, but it's confusing. A woman suspects her husband of infidelity." I told her the details, including Alice Fisher lying, but left out the names.

"Sounds like it might get interesting," she said.

"Maybe. Right now, it's convinced me I don't want to handle any more adultery cases. Who people sleep with isn't any of my business. Unless they're sleeping with me, of course."

"Of course." I saw the color fade back into Jessica's cheeks.

The narrow walkway barely allowed our waiter to carry a tray full of food and not whack anyone in the head. I figured his circus act should earn him another five percent on the tip. He set the tray in a space barely large enough for it, served us our food, promised to bring more drinks, and did the dexterity dance back up the walkway.

Jessica looked at her food and inhaled a deep breath of it. "It smells really good," she said. She picked up her silverware and cut. I did the same. Conversations came and went. I couldn't focus on any particular one because of all the ambient noise. Instead, I settled for people watching as I ate. The wait staff moved carefully around the room, but they only slowed if a collision was imminent. When Jessica looked away from her food to engage in some people watching of her own, I took in her outfit. How did this woman not have her own TV news show? She simply needed a wardrobe full of plunging necklines to ace the ratings.

"Let's talk about your past," Jessica said when we had both eaten most of our respective dinners.

"What about it?" I said. "I think I told you the juicy bits already."

"I meant what it will take me to keep those bits out of the story."

"I thought dinner and dessert were enough."

"Maybe I want a little more."

"Like what?" I said.

"You're a private investigator running a free business," Jessica said. "I'm curious how this case is going to turn out. I'm sure the people would be, too."

I said, "So in order to forget about printing my past, you want a peek into the present and near future."

"That sounds about right."

"Well, Miss Webber, since you have me over the coals here, I suppose I have to go along."

"I was hoping you'd agree, Mr. Ferguson."

"Then we'll start tomorrow . . . after breakfast."

Jessica regarded me with a spark in her eyes. "After breakfast?"

"It wouldn't make much sense to start before breakfast, would it?"

The waiter came back to collect our silverware and ask about dessert. Jessica looked at me. "I have dessert taken care of," I said.

"I'm sure you do," Jessica said.

* * *

AND I DID. Fresh strawberries (with the ends already sliced off), whipped cream, and a light and fruity wine. I got everything out of the refrigerator (including the wine, always better chilled) and set it on the small island in my kitchen while Jessica freshened up in the bathroom. I popped the cork, fetched two wine glasses from my cabinet, and filled each glass. Jessica came out, walked into the kitchen, and smiled when she saw the dessert spread. "You weren't kidding, were you?" she said, approaching the island and standing beside me.

"Dessert is serious business," I said. I took a strawberry from the basket and held it toward Jessica. She ate it off my fingertips.

"You don't seem like the type to be too serious about things," she said.

"I'm probably not."

"Wouldn't that hurt you as a detective?" She grabbed a strawberry, added a bit of whipped cream, and fed it to me.

"I don't know yet," I said. "It hasn't been an issue so far. I'm tenacious, though. Once I start something, I finish it."

"Cheating husbands of the world, beware." Jessica took a drink of her wine.

"This is my last infidelity case." I fed Jessica another strawberry, this time with a small dollop of whipped cream atop.

"Tell me something," she said.

"I've told you a lot already."

"Something specific this time. Why be a detective? You're a smart guy. You have skills. You have a masters in computer science. How does all of that lead you to becoming a detective?"

Before I could answer, Jessica offered me another strawberry, which I ate. "Off the record?" I said. She nodded. I thought about the best way to sanitize my story before I answered. "I tried to help people overseas, mostly keeping the

Chinese government off their heels. When I got back from Hong Kong, my parents insisted I get a job helping people. I had gone through most of my own money living abroad, and they knew it, so they threatened to cut me off from the family money unless I did what they said."

"So you go from hacker and pirate to crusading detective?"

"I don't know about the crusading part."

"But you're in this for the long haul."

"At least for a while," I said.

Jessica grabbed a strawberry and fed it to me, then ate one herself. "I think you'll do well at it," she said. "I've noticed you looking around at a lot of things."

I downed the rest of the wine in my glass. "I do try to be observant."

"You've definitely observed my chest at several points this evening." She smiled and picked up her glass, taking a sip of the wine.

"Guilty as charged again."

Jessica drained the rest of the glass in one swig. She reached up and undid one of the buttons on her shirt. "You've been looking at these all night," she said. The overhead light reflected and danced in her eyes. She undid another. I didn't blink. With her shirt two-thirds undone, Jessica stopped, ate a strawberry, dipped another in whipped cream, and gave it to me. She undid another button, another, then the last. Jessica pulled her shirt back. Her low-cut bra matched her shirt almost exactly in color, and the breasts it half-hid did not disappoint. They combined with her toned stomach to make me want to rip off the rest of Jessica's clothes right here in the kitchen.

She walked up to me, stopping inches short. I felt her breath on my face and neck. Her eyes bored into mine. "If you want to see anymore, you'll have to take me to your bedroom," she said.

I held out my hand. We went to my bedroom.

* * *

THE NEXT MORNING, I worked in the kitchen while Jessica remained asleep. We left the strawberries and whipped cream on the island overnight so I threw them away. I had a container of blueberries in the refrigerator ready to go in case I needed to cook breakfast for a lovely young woman. I also had the usual pancake ingredients and started making blueberry pancakes. While I whisked the batter, I heard Jessica walking down the hall.

She padded into the kitchen wearing my bathrobe and looking much the same as she had before undressing in this very room last night. Jessica rubbed at her right eye, walked up to me, put her hand on my chest, and planted a big minty kiss right on my lips. "I love the taste of mouthwash in the morning," I said.

"Me, too," she said, looking at the mixing bowl. "Blueberry pancakes?"

"Your reporter's eye is keen."

"Years of practice as a journalist. I didn't peg you as the type who knew your way around a kitchen."

"I went to college. No one else I lived with knew how to cook worth a damn." I added a handful of blueberries, then a few more, and gently whisked the mixture. "I'm not a gourmet or anything, but I do pretty well."

"A pro bono PI, and he makes breakfast the morning after." Jessica smiled. "Don't put that in your next ad." She opened the refrigerator and looked for something to drink, settling on orange juice.

"I don't plan to," I said.

I had the skillet already heated. It fit two pancakes at a

time. As always, I cooked them a little too long on one side but I never thought it affected the taste. While the pancakes cooked, I got butter and maple syrup out of the refrigerator and set them on the table. Jessica sat at the table with her glass of orange juice. "Real maple syrup," she said. "And you say you're not a gourmet."

"Corn syrup is for philistines," I said. I put two pancakes onto a plate and poured the batter for two more on the skillet.

"Now you're just showing off your education."

A kettle of hot water heated for tea, and it whistled as I flipped the pancakes (again, a few seconds too late—this would serve as my culinary trademark). Jessica got up and walked to the stove, putting the kettle on another burner and turning the hot one off. "Where are the mugs and tea?" she said. I told her, and she pulled two mugs down and looked at my vast tea collection. I never kept fewer than five varieties in the house at a time. Some things are important.

Jessica kept considering teas while I worked on more pancakes. "I'll surprise you," she said, taking two teabags down. I couldn't see what flavor they were.

"You surprised me last night," I said. "I don't know if I can handle any more."

I watched the color rush back into Jessica's cheeks. "I think you'll manage," she said as she added teabags to the mugs and filled each with hot water. She carried them to the table and sat again. "Now I'll wait for your pancakes to surprise me."

A few minutes later, after slathering her pancakes in butter and adding a dash of maple syrup, Jessica admitted they were good. She didn't even comment about one side of each being browner than the other. I put the darker sides down out of habit. "Can I run something by you?" I said as we ate.

"Is it about your case?" she said.

"Yes. Something bugs me about it, and I want another perspective."

"Go ahead."

I told her (still omitting names) about Alice Fisher hiring me to look into her husband's suspected infidelity, her general shiftiness, the lie about the mortgage, and what I learned at each of their workplaces—which I had to admit wasn't much. Jessica pondered these new facts over a few bites of pancakes.

"You're wondering why the wife lied," she said.

"It bothers me. Would it bother you?"

"Inconsistencies always bother people in my line of work. In yours, too. But I don't think that means you look into her."

"Why not?"

"Because you shouldn't investigate your client. Besides, it may not be important. Maybe there's something she doesn't want you to find. That doesn't make her wicked."

"Why lie about it, then?" I said.

"I don't know." Jessica ate another bite of her pancakes and pursed her lips. I noticed how cute she looked when she got contemplative. "She's using the lie about the mortgage to cover up something she doesn't want you to know."

"What would it be?"

"Is her credit bad?" I nodded. "Probably something related to money."

"She doesn't want me to know." I took another forkful of pancakes and stopped in mid-chew. "She doesn't want *me* to know." I finished my mouthful of food and swallowed. "I wonder if it means she doesn't want her husband to know, too."

"It could," Jessica said with a nod.

"It would have to be something pretty bad if it's money-related, and she's hiding it from him."

"I think it would." Jessica nudged away her empty plate. "What are you going to do now?" she said.

"There's someone else I want to ask about this. Then I think I need to see the Fishers together."

"I think that's a bad idea," said Jessica.

"The whole thing about not investigating my client?" I said.

She nodded. "Yes, and you might reveal whatever she's keeping from her husband."

She made sense. "OK, fair enough. I won't investigate her . . . for now. I'll see where else the rabbit hole goes."

"I think that's a good idea." Jessica sipped some tea. "It all may lead back to the wife anyway, but I think you have to branch out first."

"Good thing I went to college," I said.

WHEN I GOT to the restaurant, Joey Trovato was already there. I remembered he liked this place, and I liked it enough to eat there with him. "Jesus Christ, look at you," he said as I approached the table. Joey stood and gave me a bear hug. I embraced him and pounded his back, both as a sign of friendship and to try and get him to let go before I suffocated.

Joey was a black Sicilian with a light mocha skin tone and wavy black hair. For his whole life, he fought the battle of the bulge but could never be counted among the victors. Joey stood six feet tall on the dot, two inches shorter than I am but outweighed me by at least 100 pounds. He was fat, to be sure, but his girth belied a surprising amount of strength and athleticism. I could outrun Joey, but I knew a bunch of people who couldn't. Especially if they carried food as he pursued them.

"How are you, Joey?" I said. I slid onto the chair opposite him. "When's the due date?"

"You're hilarious," Joey said. "I'm a growing boy. I gotta eat. Ah, I've been good. Business hit a slow spot for a while, but it's picked up again. I'm regional now. People coming from all over the state, DC, hell even some from northern Virginia and southern Pennsylvania." After we finished four years of college, Joey learned the science and art of setting people up with new identities.

"Good, especially since you can't exactly hand out business cards."

"Ain't that the truth?" A waiter came, handed us menus, and introduced himself. We placed our drink orders, and he walked away. "So what the hell happened to you? You went overseas, and all I got was a bunch of emails, then some phone calls asking for help."

"I tried calling you a few other times. And I told my parents to check on you at the holidays, make sure you had a place to go."

"They did. They did." Joey smiled wistfully. "Your parents are good people. What happened to you overseas? Why'd you come back all of a sudden?"

I told him, in a lowered voice, about the hacking and piracy ring, our arrests, the edited version of my 19 days as a guest of the Hong Kong penal system, and everything since. Joey shook his head. "Jesus Christ," he said. "What a fucking story."

"Yeah. You know the rest. My parents are shoving their altruism on me. Thanks for helping me with the background, by the way. There's no way I would have sniffed being a PI without it."

"I still can't believe you're a private eye," he said. Joey looked at me and shook his head.

"We all have our crosses to bear."

"Looks like we both ended up with jobs helping people, in our own ways." The waiter brought our drinks. We placed our orders. Joey asked for two appetizers and an entrée with an extra side. I wanted only pasta with a side salad. Joey raised his glass of soda. "To us . . . helping folks," he said. "What a fucking pair we make."

"Hear, hear." I knocked my glass into his.

We exchanged war stories until the appetizers showed up. Joey ordered both mozzarella sticks and fried calamari. I don't think I could have eaten both of those, and he still had a heaping plate of food coming later. Joey picked up a mozzarella stick, dunked it into the marinara sauce like an angry LeBron, and shoved the entire thing into his mouth. I looked away and admired the fake Donatello on the wall. When Joey took a large piece of calamari, I grabbed a mozzarella stick. He said something around his mouthful of food sounding like, "Hey!"

"You'll thank me later," I said. "I'm pushing back your stroke by a half-hour."

"And speeding up your own."

"Unlike you, I'll burn off the calories later." I dipped the mozzarella stick in the marinara and bit off half of it.

Joey smiled, dunked the calamari in its vat of marinara sauce with a force suggesting a deep-seated hatred of squids, and ate it. "How do you know I didn't get sensitive about my weight while you were gallivanting all over the globe?"

"Because it's you."

"Fair point."

"It's good to catch up."

"But. . . ." Joey eyed me as suspiciously as someone cramming a whole mozzarella stick into his mouth can eye someone.

"I also asked you here for your professional opinion."

"You don't need a new identity."

"Nor do I want one." I lowered my voice again and went over the whole situation with the Fishers. Joey listened while gorging himself on his appetizers. I paused while the waiter freshened our drinks, then picked up again when he left. "It bothers me," I said when I'd finished, "her lying about her finances."

"How the hell can I help?"

"You relocate people. You see them at their worst. They come to you with money, desperation, and a bad beat story. You've probably heard worse than a husband who might be diddling someone at work and a wife lying about money."

"I have." Joey finished off the mozzarella sticks. I used his momentary distraction to snag a piece of calamari. He chuckled at me before continuing. "She's hiding something. It's gotta be related to money. She wants the husband to think they're poorer than they really are because she's blowing cash on something."

"Drugs?"

Joey shrugged. "Usually. She look like a druggie to you?"

"No, but I'll admit I wasn't looking for the signs."

"She's your client, you know," said Joey. "You're not supposed to investigate her."

"And she's not supposed to lie to me," I said.

"People lie. You lie. Get over it."

I shrugged. "I don't think the husband is cheating. Her lie is something I can pick at."

"What are you going to do next?"

"It's bad form to look into my client, so I guess I'll investigate the cheating angle."

"Even though you don't think he's a cheater."

"Even though," I said.

"What if he is?" Joey said.

"Then I guess I need to buy a fish-eye lens and practice hanging out of trees."

"Good luck with that."

"If there's nothing there, though, I'm coming back to Alice."

"You're awfully worked up over her telling a lie."

I sipped some iced tea. "I guess I am," I said. "Am I making too much of it?"

Joey shrugged. "Maybe. She could be a cokehead for all you know. Or it could be nothing."

"I wish I knew which was more likely," I said.

CHAPTER 5

JESSICA AND JOEY HAD CONVINCED ME TO BACK OFF ALICE
Fisher. I would comply, for now, but if my instincts were right,
and Paul wasn't diddling someone at the office, then I'd come
back to Alice. In the meantime, I looked into Paul's coworkers
at Digital Sales. Their website, with a little prodding, was
helpful enough to give me an organization chart. I looked into
all of the women of Digital Sales. They had helped me out by
having a heavily male workforce.

Digital Sales was a company of sixty employees. Of those,
only eleven were women, and only one of the women appeared
at the top of a division on the org chart. She would be Mary
Dietz, whose social media pages revealed a marriage full of
children and hugs. I knew wedded people could cheat, especially with other married folks, but I decided to rule out those
whose marriages looked happy. At least on my first pass. On the
second pass, I could plumb the depths of matrimonial misery.

It turned out all of the women of Digital Sales were hitched
save for executive assistant Sally Willis. Her Facebook and
Instagram pages overflowed with pictures. Many of them
showed Sally out on the town, in the company of a succession
of men. I spied wedding rings on the fingers of a couple of the

men. Nothing said Sally and these men were anything beyond friends. Other than Sally, I could infer unhappiness in the marriage of only one woman. I didn't have much to go on.

Paul Fisher had a boring social media presence. He lacked Instagram or Snapchat, his LinkedIn contacts were almost all coworkers, and his Facebook yearned for an update. He and Sally were contacts on LinkedIn, but the overlap stopped there. Sally told me she didn't like Paul Fisher. It may have been true. I couldn't find anything online to disprove it, at least not yet.

The woman whose marriage didn't consist of sunshine and puppies was Debbie Wilder. Like Paul Fisher, her social media presence consisted of LinkedIn and Facebook. Her Facebook featured many pictures with men not her husband and also not Paul Fisher. I felt it likely this meant nothing—only a foolish cheater would be so brazen about it, after all—but it was more than I found elsewhere.

Still, none of it gave me anything concrete. I had no smoking gun, or even a sparking and smoldering one. I did some mining in the rabbit hole of this case, and I figured to do more later. For now, however, the burrow led to Alice. I went after the Fishers' financials and found them within a few minutes.

Other than one bounced check six months prior, the Fishers had no red flags in their account. Their balance often skirted zero, especially following the crush of bills the first week of the month. Alice transferred funds to another account at least once a month, always a few hundred dollars. She also took out a personal loan of $5000. What was she doing with the money? It could be enough to support a drug habit. I got the account number from the transactions and accessed it. It was a personal checking account with a debit card. Alice withdrew money from ATMs often, usually two hundred or three hundred at a time. Possibly to finance a drug habit. Combined with her solitary loan, it didn't paint a good picture.

I could go back to Upper Chesapeake and ask if Alice showed signs of drug abuse, but I got the feeling I was *persona non grata* there. Alice's boss probably wouldn't talk to me again. Then I remembered Erica Souza. She had the most contact with me of anyone there, so her opinion may not have been tainted by the security guard getting called to show me to the elevators.

I did some clever Googling to find Upper Chesapeake's employee directory. Once I found Erica's number, I called her. She answered on the third ring."Upper Chesapeake, this is Erica."

"Erica, this is C.T. Ferguson."

"How may I direct your call, Mr. Ferguson?"

"You can keep it right where it is. I'm the detective who talked to you yesterday."

She was silent for a few seconds. "And the one who badgered Mr. Dunn."

"Would you believe me if I said he had it coming?" I said.

"Did he?" Erica said.

"You and I both know he did. I have a couple of questions I'd like to ask you, if you don't mind. They're confidential. I can meet you somewhere."

I heard her sigh into the phone. "I haven't had lunch yet. The café isn't very crowded this time of day. Buy me lunch, and we can talk."

"Give me a half-hour," I said.

THIRTY-SIX MINUTES LATER, I walked into the café. I got to Upper Chesapeake ten minutes before, but it took that long to find a parking place, eventually settling on one only requiring me to walk about a mile to the hospital. If I arrived with a leg injury, I would have needed an amputation by the time I reached the door. Erica sat at a table near the back, one leg crossed over the other and her arms folded under her chest.

"I know I'm late," I said, approaching her with my hands spread. "In my defense, I had to park in Abingdon."

A smile slowly spread over Erica's lips. It didn't stack up to Jessica Webber's or even Sally Willis', but a man could get used to it. "Parking here is terrible," she said. "If we didn't have a staff lot, I don't know what I'd do."

"Probably have very toned calves."

She blushed. "Are you hungry?"

"Not really, but I'll stand in line with you and keep horny doctors at bay."

"My knight," she said with a smirk.

We got in line at the front of the café. There were only two people ahead of us, and not many more sitting and eating. I ordered an iced tea. Erica got a turkey sandwich, a salad, chocolate pudding, and a soda. The chocolate pudding had turned into concrete in the cup. I wondered how many spoons Erica would break trying to eat it, to say nothing of her teeth.

Back at the table, Erica nibbled on her salad. "Thanks for lunch," she said.

"Thanks for seeing me after the events of yesterday," I said. "I figure I'm probably not too welcome in your department right now."

She smiled. "You could say that. Dunn wanted to press charges for harassment, I think. Someone talked him out of it."

I shrugged. "At some point, I'm sure someone will try to say I harassed them. One day, it might even be true."

"It just might." She nibbled on her salad some more and took a bite of the turkey sandwich. She hadn't even looked at the pudding yet. "What did you want to talk about?"

"You know I'm looking into the Fishers." She nodded. "I

have reasons to . . . question some things in their finances. Have you seen anything from Alice to lead you to think they have money problems?"

She frowned over another bite of her sandwich. "Not that I know of," she said. "She may not mention something like that to me."

"Do you have any nursing training?" Erica shook her head as she ate. "Work with folks who do?" She nodded. "Any of them talk about Alice?"

"In what way?"

"Drugs," I said.

"Drugs?" She frowned again. "I haven't heard anything. I'm not a nurse, so I might not be in on all their gossip. If someone had a drug problem, I'm sure they would be gabbing about it."

"Any way you can ask? I know it might be hard to fit into a conversation, but you strike me as a resourceful girl."

She smiled over a drink of her soda. "I manage. I'll see what I can do."

"Good." I took out a business card and handed it to her. She looked at it and smiled. "What?" I said.

"Is that really your slogan?"

I rolled my eyes. "I knew it was awful."

* * *

I SPENT the rest of the day looking into a dojo where I could train and getting dinner. Once the clock hit seven-thirty, I set out for the Fishers' neighborhood. I still didn't have a plan for getting into their house, but I hoped inspiration would strike me on the drive. It didn't. I drove up and down the Fishers' street. Medium-sized single-family homes made from a cookie cutter stared back at me. Two houses were for sale, and one of them looked vacant. Inspiration struck.

There was plenty of street parking, so I left my Lexus near the Fishers' house and walked to it. I saw two Toyotas in their driveway. At least half the houses on the street had garages, including both of those for sale. I went to the door and rang the doorbell. If Alice answered, this could get awkward. Thankfully, Paul Fisher came to the door. He looked an inch taller than me, but thin, probably around 170 pounds. His brown hair showed a few wisps of gray at the temples and framed a face that sped past tired and now approached haggard. He opened the door wide enough to poke his head out. "Can I help you?"

"I hope so," I said. "I'm thinking about buying a house in this neighborhood, and I was hoping I could talk to you about it."

"Sure, come on in," Paul said with a smile. "I got home a few minutes ago, and my wife is still upstairs. Excuse the mess."

"Looks fine to me." I harbored no concern for how neat the place looked. I wanted to see signs of unexplained wealth, unexpected poverty, or obvious hiding places for drugs. The Fishers owned a very middle-class house. Their carpet screamed to be replaced, but the walls had been painted in the last year or so. Pictures of family hung there. There weren't any paintings or any elaborate throw rugs. The furniture in their living room looked straight out of a discount store. I didn't see anything to make me think they were awash in cash or suffered cash flow problems.

"You said you're looking in this neighborhood?" Paul Fisher said. I took a seat on the medium brown couch; he sat in a matching recliner snapped into a position too far forward. I didn't envy his spine.

"Yes. My family is still in Virginia. I'm moving up here for work, and I figured I would do a little advance scouting." When in doubt, try social engineering. It works.

"Good plan." He held out his hand. "I'm Paul."

I shook his hand. "Trent," I said. My middle name.

"What line of work are you in, Trent?"

"Finance." I heard footsteps coming down the stairs. "I'm starting with a new company soon."

The sounds moved into the kitchen. I looked to my left and saw Alice Fisher. She saw me and did a double take but recovered quickly. I didn't know whether Paul saw her reaction. Alice busied herself in the kitchen and tried not to pay attention to me. Paul didn't let her get away with it.

"Honey, this is Trent," he said. "He's looking to buy a house in the neighborhood and wants to know what we think about it."

"Oh, that's very nice," Alice said after a moment.

"Trent, do you want anything to drink?"

"I'm OK, thanks."

"Alice, did you get the juice?"

Alice froze. Her shifty gaze became furtive. "What?" She tried to look busy again, but she merely looked spooked.

"The orange juice . . . did you pick it up on your way home?"

"Oh." Alice's shoulders relaxed, and she let out a deep breath. "No, I guess I forgot."

"No big deal. Why don't you come and join us?"

"I don't mean to keep you if you need to make dinner or do something else," I said.

Paul waved me off. "Don't worry about it. We don't normally make anything too complicated. Right, honey?"

"Right," Alice said. She still looked like she'd witnessed a poltergeist invasion, but tension left her face, and she could look at me for two seconds before her gaze flittered away. Alice sat on the couch. Paul put his arm around her, but she didn't sit right next to him. The whole thing felt awkward. I wanted to observe the Fishers in their natural habitat to see if I could pick up a clue suggesting Paul had been unfaithful to his wife. All I saw so far was Alice freaking out over a simple question.

"You're looking at a house on this street?" Paul said. If he noticed the few inches of distance between himself and his wife, he didn't say anything.

"Among other locations," I said.

"Any kids?"

This is why I wanted to leave: avoiding questions like these. I tried to excuse myself earlier, only to be shut down by Paul. Now I was stuck for a while until the natives let me out of their sugary trap. "Just one," I said.

"In school yet?" said Paul.

"Getting closer every day."

"This is a good neighborhood." Paul gestured toward the front of the house as he spoke. "It's usually quiet around here. Good amount of kids around. The local schools are rated well, too. I think you'd like it here."

"I probably would. How do the houses hold their value?" I glanced at Alice when I said it. She looked down, apparently finding something on her lap fascinating.

Paul shrugged. "Every area took something of a hit when the bubble burst. This one's coming up, though. We've done better than average, I would say. Right, honey?"

"Right," Alice said, looking up briefly. She couldn't even meet my eyes before she looked down again.

"Listen, you've been very helpful. I think I've taken up too much of your time already."

"You sure?" Paul said. "We could talk about this neighborhood for a while."

Alice's head dropped at his words. Paul remained oblivious to it. "I'm sure. Thanks for your time." Paul got up and walked me out. I glanced back at Alice, who remained semi-catatonic on the couch. Now I had no idea how to proceed with the case. It was likely Alice would fire me—if one could fire someone who works for free—for intruding on her thin veneer of domestic bliss. Now seeing the house of cards for myself, I didn't doubt something was wrong with their marriage, but I doubted Paul's role in it.

* * *

"Did you get the juice?"

Alice's reaction to the question intrigued me. Spouses asked one another similar questions all across the country. Almost all the time, it got a simple yes or no answer. In the case of the Fishers, Alice freaked out as if a squad of zombies nipped at her heels. She obviously knew a different definition of juice than her husband.

Juice, in addition to being a delicious beverage, is also a gambling term. It refers to the bookie's take of the wager and is also an amount sought after to pay off loans or gambling debts. Jessica and Joey suggested Alice's lying and her evasive demeanor—not to mention the withdrawals from the joint checking account—indicated a drug problem. In fact, they indicated a gambling problem.

I didn't even know where someone would go to place a wager. Alice could have done her wagering online, but the online arena found itself hampered by legislation and didn't use terms like "juice" anyway. No, I had a strong feeling Alice used a real live bookie to place her bets. Now I needed to figure out who it was.

To do so, I wanted her phone records. She had given me her cell phone number, and from there, a simple search told me which provider she used, which was the easy part. Hacking into the carrier to get her calling records would take more time.

Over the years, telecom companies have implemented more rigid security. They're responsible for a lot of information requiring serious protection, so they dedicate resources to keep the bad hackers out. Well-meaning morally ambiguous fellows like me get caught in the same net.

It took me about twenty minutes altogether, but I got into the customer phone records. From there, I ran a simple query for Alice Fisher. I exported the results to a file and perused it. Alice called Paul a lot, both at home and on his cell. She also phoned her work, various little shops, and other people I presumed were her friends. One name jumped out at me, though: SERRANO, VINCENT

I stared at the screen. He was still at it and should have been my first thought. Vinnie Serrano and I went to school together. He setup a gambling ring even back then, and it cost him his college enrollment. It sounded like he expanded his little empire over the years, and Alice had fallen victim to him.

Now I wondered if I could get her out, and more importantly, if it was my job to try.

CHAPTER 6

I DECIDED TO SLEEP ON THE PROBLEM. ALICE GOT HERSELF into this mess. She hired me to look into her suspicions about her husband philandering. I saw nothing suggesting it to be true. Now knowing what I knew, I couldn't blame him if he went and diddled someone he worked with. Especially the receptionist. If I told Alice her husband wasn't cheating on her, she would probably want to end our arrangement. In which case, she would be fending for herself against Vinnie Serrano. I knew Vinnie. Alice was in over her head.

She thought she needed my help finding out if her husband cheated on her. I could offer assistance dealing with Vinnie. She didn't have to take it, and if she didn't want it, who was I to insist? Offering to help her felt like the right thing to do. I hadn't gotten used to doing the right thing over the last three and a half years, so I wanted to sleep on it and see if my sudden attack of conscience passed.

When I woke up, it hadn't. I still wanted to help Alice. It would be against my better judgment, and wasn't what I signed up for, but such is the way sudden attacks of scruples go. My parents would be happy. I decided not to tell them. My conscience creeping up on me felt bad enough; I didn't need them beaming about it on top of everything.

After breakfast, I called Alice on her cell phone. It went to voicemail, so I tried her at work. "Hello?" she said.

"Alice, it's C.T. Ferguson."

"Why were you at my house last night?" she said, as soon as I finished my salutation. I wondered if she had been practicing this conversation in her head all morning.

"I wanted to observe you and Paul at home. It's important in cases of possible infidelity."

"Oh." She took a breath, and the accusatory tone vanished. "What did you find out?"

"I don't think he's cheating on you."

"But the hours he works . . . how evasive he is about every-thing . . . he has to be."

"I really don't think he is. There's something else I found, potentially concerning. I'd rather not discuss it with you on your company phone."

Alice sighed into the receiver. "Can we meet for lunch?"

"Sure. You tell me where."

"Do you know the Sakura Steakhouse in Bel Air?"

"I'll find it. What time?"

"Twelve-thirty?"

"See you then."

* * *

I GOT to the restaurant four minutes late. Alice had already found a table. I walked in and sat down. The waitress arrived so quickly I thought she materialized. I ordered an iced tea and said I would look at the menu for my lunch selection.

After the waitress returned with my drink and I ordered a

sushi assortment, Alice got right down to business. "What's so delicate that you couldn't tell me on the phone?" she said.

"First, I want to reiterate I don't think Paul is cheating on you," I said as I added raw sugar to my tea.

"Why not?"

"From watching the two of you last night, I don't think he's capable of it. You were more distant than he was."

"I was . . . I just had a bad night." She avoided my eyes. Her gaze had never been steady, but she avoided looking at me now like I had a huge zit on my face.

"We all do."

"That's it?" she said. "He acts nice one night, and he's not a cheater?"

"He goes to work in a different part of the building when his shift ends, is why you can't reach him in his office."

"What's he doing? Who's he working with?"

"Maybe you should ask him," I said.

She nodded. "I guess I have to." The waitress came with our food. Alice ordered a boring chicken and rice dish. My sushi plate, packed with a rainbow roll and other varieties of fish, looked vibrant by comparison. I poured soy sauce into the side dish and added wasabi. I mixed them and added more wasabi until I got the color looking exactly right—kind of a mottled brown with bits of green. Alice ate her lunch. I broke apart my chopsticks and devoured my sushi.

When we had both eaten most of our lunches, Alice looked at me again. She did a good job keeping her eyes on me most of the time. "Does this mean our arrangement is over?" she said.

"Up to you," I said. "I still haven't told you what I wanted to tell you."

Alice took a few more bites, leaving only a few stray grains of rice on her plate, and put her fork down. "OK, I'm ready."

"It's a question, really. How much do you owe Vinnie Serrano?"

Alice didn't know how to react. Her eyes went wide. Then she frowned. Then she looked around like she had no control of her eye muscles. "I . . . I'm not sure who that is," she said after taking a drink of water.

"You seem to call him a lot."

"You saw my phone records?" A couple of nearby patrons took an interest in the conversation at this point. I glared at them until they looked away.

"Of course I did," I said.

"Isn't that illegal?"

"I'm a licensed investigator, Alice. I can see a great deal of things."

"What makes you think I owe this person any money?"

"Because I went to school with Vinnie. Because he's always had a numbers racket and some other schemes going. Because you make unexplained withdrawals from your joint checking account. And because you acted like two assassins were in your house when Paul asked you if you got the juice."

She swallowed hard. "I hope he didn't notice that."

"I don't think he did. He seems very devoted to you. Maybe more than he should be."

"What's that supposed to mean?" said Alice.

"You lie about being underwater to cover your gambling problem, you hire me to spy on your husband because you somehow think he's cheating on you, and all I see is a man who loves you. Honestly, I think it's more than you deserve."

Alice looked down. "Maybe it is." She took another deep breath. "Now what?"

"I don't know," I said. "I'm pretty sure your husband isn't cheating on you, which means the case you hired me to work is over. But you're in worse trouble than you would be if your husband were sleeping with every pretty girl in his office, aren't you?"

She nodded so slightly I could hardly tell. "I am." I had trouble hearing her breathy whisper over the ambient conversations.

"Maybe you need help getting out of this hole."

"Why do you want to help me?" she said.

"Why do you care?"

Alice looked at me, and for the first time, managed to hold my gaze. Maybe now with the lies exposed, she could have an honest conversation. "You said my husband's devotion might be more than I deserve. You may be right. I'm a mess, and I'm in over my head. But our arrangement is done. You don't need to help me anymore, but you still want to. I wonder why."

I ate my last piece of sushi and took a long drink of my tea, wishing it were the Long Island variety. "Because," I said, "despite my best efforts to suppress it, I've been cursed with a conscience. I know you're in over your head. I know Vinnie probably got a lot bigger since the last time I saw him. Alone, you're going to drown, and probably take Paul down with you. With me, you have a chance to make it back to shore."

Alice didn't say anything for a few seconds. She grabbed my hand and squeezed it. "Thank you," she said. Her eyes glistened. "You just might be able to pull me up from rock bottom."

I didn't draw my hand back. She gave it another squeeze and then let go. "Now since I'm helping you, you need to answer my initial question. How much do you owe Vinnie Serrano?"

"Thirty thousand," Alice said in a whisper.

I bit my tongue to keep from shouting the number back at her. "Holy shit," I said. "He must have the hooks deep in you."

"He does." Alice used her napkin to wipe a stray tear sliding down her right cheek. "I can get some overtime at work, but it's hard to keep up with the juice."

"How do you plan to pay him?"

"I figured a big Super Bowl bet would get me even."

I rolled my eyes. "Or put you twice as deep in the hole. Alice, you can't bet money you don't have. Gambling doesn't pay itself off."

"What should I do?"

"Stop placing bets," I said. "Right now. Quit cold turkey. Get help if you have to but stop. You can't go any further in debt." The waitress took our plates away. When we declined to order anything else, she returned a minute later with the check. Alice grabbed her purse, but I waved her off. "I got it. You save as much money as you can. We can figure out a more detailed plan later."

"What are you going to do?"

"I haven't seen Vinnie in years. Time to pay him a visit."

* * *

VINNIE SERRANO and I went to high school together at Gilman. If you think that sounds like a fancy prep school in a ritzy neighborhood, it is. Gilman is in the Roland Park area of Baltimore, where it shares a ZIP code with my parents and other people who are pleased to write those five digits on their envelopes. Vinnie and I both played sports—we were on the lacrosse team, and I also ran track. We had been friends, though I don't think we could have been called great friends. Even back then, Vinnie organized pools for pretty much every major sporting event and took bets from the kids at school. He kept a record of everything in the back of his history notebook. By the end of the school year, he had amassed more gambling notes than history notes.

After graduation, Vinnie and I both ended up at Loyola College. I lived on campus for the experience (and to be away from my parents); Vinnie commuted. Gilman was a lot smaller and much more insular. On the college campus, Vinnie organizing pools and running a sports book got a few people talking and drew too much attention. He got expelled during the first semester of our sophomore year. I saw him a few times afterward, including a party about a week before I went overseas. He had refined his sports book to a more professional gambling business and sounded ambitious about branching out into other areas. Never underestimate bored, curious rich kids who have too much free time and too little supervision.

I wondered if time and a taste of the finer things changed Vinnie's preferences. Before I went overseas, I knew he regularly took a late lunch at Donna's in Cross Keys. Vinnie would sit in a booth with his notebook, taking bets on his cell phone. He probably hired people to handle legwork for him now. I drove to Donna's to see if he would still be there. When I walked in, I saw Vinnie in a booth at the back. The restaurant wasn't very crowded. A man in a cheap suit at the bar watched me over the rim of his glass.

As I got closer to Vinnie's booth, a short, burly Asian man got up and stared at me. He stood five-three only because his shoes helped him with the last two inches. He appeared Chinese, and tried to grow a Fu Manchu mustache that ended up looking like a rough goatee. He glared at me through narrowed eyes and blocked my path to the table. This marked the closest I had come to a Chinese person since getting out of their prison. I took a deep breath.

"Sorry," I said, holding my hand a couple inches above his head, "but you have to be this tall to try and fight me."

The Chinese fellow glowered at me and started to say something when Vinnie spoke. "I know that voice." He looked up and smiled. "Hot damn. Haven't seen you for years, C.T. It's OK, Sam, he's an old friend."

Sam kept glaring at me, but I simply smiled and stepped around him. I hoped I had masked my nerves. Chinese men still made me anxious. I slid into the booth opposite Vinnie. Sam went back to his table. "When did you start hiring midgets?" I said.

Vinnie shook his head. "Sam does good work."

"I'm sure his name isn't Sam."

"I don't know his fucking name. I just call him Sam, for Small Asian Man."

"Ah, Vinnie," I said, "sensitivity was always your best trait."

"Like hell it was," Vinnie said with a slight laugh. "What brings you by? I heard you were overseas living the high life."

"I was overseas. I don't know about the high life part."

"Hong Kong, wasn't it?"

"It was." I told him most of the details of my excursion there.

"So now you're back here," he said. "Living with the folks?"

I said, "No, I have an apartment."

"Money must be getting tight for you. First time in your life you've had to think about cash, I'm sure."

"I'm working on something."

"Ain't we all?"

A waiter brought Vinnie's lunch, a barbecued chicken pizza. He asked what I wanted, and I ordered only an iced tea. Vinnie's cell phone, sitting atop his notebook, vibrated when the waiter walked away. Vinnie looked at the number and ignored it. "I'm always working on something," he said.

"You always were."

"I was small-time then. Just some numbers, really. It gave me a taste. I still do the numbers . . . have a girl who takes a lot of my bets for me. A few longtime clients call me directly. When I have problems, I use Sam and a couple other guys."

"I heard you were getting bigger."

"I am," Vinnie said a little too quickly, as if my role in the conversation had become superfluous. I felt like a test screener for a commercial too poor to ever air. "The numbers game still makes bread, but I'm getting started in the loan business. Interest is higher, and I get to keep another guy or two gainfully employed." Vinnie's voice, already low, dropped to a whisper. "I got offered a role in the drug business, but I'm leaving that shit alone. I don't need any crazy Mexicans chasing me with burning tires and machetes."

"I don't think they light the tires until they've thrown a few around you."

"You know what I mean, though."

I nodded. "I do." Vinnie was wise to stay out of the drug business. His budding loan shark career, though, had me worried. Loan sharks hired legbreakers to collect debts. Sam didn't look the part, but anyone with a suit, menacing stare, and tire iron could fake it. I had an idea who offered Vinnie this chance to branch out, but I felt sure he wouldn't confirm it for me.

"What are you into now?" Vinnie said. He ate his pizza as we talked but remembered enough of his Roland Park manners to chew with his mouth closed.

"My parents made me get a job helping people," I said.

Vinnie laughed, then took a drink of his soda. He laughed some more. "Man, funny shit. What the fuck do you know about helping people?"

"More than you might think."

"So what goody-goody job are you doing?"

"I'm a private investigator."

Vinnie stopped eating and stared at me. "A PI? You?"

"I was almost as surprised as you."

Vinnie looked at me for a few more seconds, then scarfed down another bite of pizza. The smell of the barbecued chicken stirred my hunger again. Sushi never filled me. "What do you want, C.T.?"

"Alice Fisher owes you a lot of money."

"You think I know who she is?"

"Come off it, Vinnie. I've known you long enough to know you don't forget names, especially when they're on the wrong side of your balance sheet. Alice Fisher."

"OK, so I know her. She owes me money. You gonna pay off her debt?"

"No," I said. "She's working on it. I came to ask you to give her a break. She's trying to give up gambling, so she can focus on paying you off. She'll never be able to manage more than the juice if she keeps making and losing bets."

"She don't lose all her bets." Just like the Vinnie of old, his private school education ran and hid when he was in a mood about something.

"But she loses enough of them."

"I'm glad she wants to pay me but why would I want her to quit?" Vinnie said. "The longer she has to pay me just the juice, the longer she pays me, period. Why the fuck would I want her to stop? Not good business."

"Can you go easy on her?" I said. "A favor for an old friend?"

Vinnie chuckled and shook his head. "We weren't that tight."

"Think about it, at least."

"I did. Answer's no."

I shrugged. "All right." I got up from the booth.

"You gonna fight me over this?" he said.

"Don't you mean fight your midget?" I said.

"You know what I mean. I might like you, but I don't like problems."

"I'm not looking for trouble, Vinnie."

"It's Vincent now."

"Of course it is," I said.

* * *

How was I going to deal with Vinnie? So far, he hadn't sent the big guns after Alice Fisher. Maybe she paid enough to keep them at bay. Perhaps Vinnie didn't like the idea of sending a legbreaker to menace a woman. I wondered if Alice used makeup to hide a black eye from her husband, friends, and coworkers. Vinnie wanted Alice to pay him, including taking new bets. Hell, in his place, I would want her money, too. I was sure any reservations he harbored about sending legbreakers after women didn't apply to nosy detectives.

Vinnie ran a numbers racket, and said he branched out into loan sharking. It meant he had to be operating with the blessing of Tony Rizzo, if not his protection. Tony ran what passed for organized crime in Baltimore. He owned an Italian restaurant in Little Italy called *Il Buon Cibo*, and it earned its name. Tony had been friends with my parents for years, which meant my mother didn't know he was a gangster. She would have disowned him after a fierce bout of sniffing and tsking if she had.

I would talk to Tony if I had to. In the meantime, I decided to call Joey. "Can't get enough of me?" he said when he picked up.

"People your size don't come in small doses," I said.

"You're hilarious. What do you need?"

"Remember Vinnie?"

"Serrano? What about him?"

"I hear his bookie business has taken off since college. He has someone take a lot of his bets for him now. You have any idea who it is?"

"Do you think I'm the type to place a wager with a bookie? Gambling is illegal."

"Forgive me for offending your upstanding tendencies," I said.

"He has a girl take bets, I think. Don't know her name. Why?"

"Our suspicion about drugs turned out to be gambling, and the bookie turned out to be Vinnie. He's squeezing her dry."

"She been beat up yet?" Joey said.

"She hasn't said so. If Vinnie's giving her time to avoid a beating, he won't wait forever." I remembered Alice telling me about Paul's black eye. Vinnie or one of his goons struck me as the likely source.

"Sounds like you need to poke around Mr. Serrano's gambling empire some more."

"I think I do."

"Be careful, C.T.," said Joey. "Vinnie's changed since you left. He's more ruthless than he used to be."

"He killed anyone?"

"No one's ever proven anything."

"Right," I said. "I'll be careful."

* * *

VINNIE'S PHONE records were as easy to get as Alice Fisher's. I exported my findings and sorted by the frequency of calls. Vinnie only talked to one woman every day: Margaret Madison. I jotted her information down and did a background check on her. The lovely Ms. Madison had been arrested twice, both times for assault and battery. She had a history of fights in school and had been expelled from two colleges: one for fighting and one for being a degenerate gambler. Vinnie found a girl who could take care of herself.

To get to Vinnie, I needed to find out more about Margaret Madison. Maybe I would even place a wager. If Vinnie used her to handle betting, she had to be smart and capable. The fighting arrest and expulsion meant she liked to fight; she didn't have to be any good at it. I would have to follow her around and see how she handled herself. Maybe I should have invested in a trenchcoat and fedora after all. For all my talk to my father about how hackers were the new detectives, I had used a lot of old-school detective work so far, and I felt sure the trend would continue.

Somewhere, my parents had to be smiling.

Margaret Madison's MVA records said she drove a late-model Acura SUV and lived in Canton Square. I sat in my Lexus in a parking lot across from her house. A quick check of the alley behind the rowhouses showed her Acura sat on her parking pad. She could have been out—many places were an easy walk from Canton Square—but I saw two lights on inside her house. I played with the apps on my smartphone while I waited for something to happen. How did detectives do this in the days before smartphones? I couldn't imagine sitting in a car, drinking stale coffee, and doing a crossword puzzle or even worse, a word search.

When I considered downloading an app to help me gouge my eyes out, one of the lights in Margaret's house went off. A minute later, she walked through the front door. She had a jumpsuit on and a light jacket zipped halfway up overtop it. From my perch across the street, I thought I could see the bulge of a gun under her coat. Margaret headed up the street. I gave her a head start, then got out of my car and followed her on foot.

Three blocks later, she met a man in an empty parking lot. I stood behind a parked van. Margaret and the man talked for a minute. Then he became dissatisfied with the progress of the conversation. He took a swing at her, which she sidestepped. A punch, a kick, an elbow, and a knee later, Margaret had taken the man to the ground. She stood over him with her foot on his throat. I couldn't hear what either of them said, but he nodded a few times. She removed her foot and kept walking. I let her go about 50 feet farther before I stepped out from behind the van.

As soon as I did, someone shoved something into my back. It felt like a gun barrel. "What do you think you're doing?" the voice said.

## CHAPTER 7

THE THING PRESSED INTO MY BACK FELT LIKE A GUN through my coat, but my dearth of experience at having artillery shoved into my back meant I lacked the means for a comparison. I felt my heart start to thump in my chest. This reminded me I needed to pick up the guns I purchased and had to wait for. Not as if having one of them on me would make a difference right now. Sudden movements were not my friend.

"You deaf?" the voice said. It was rough and unfriendly.

"If I were, asking me wouldn't be very effective," I said. I raised my hands so they were about even with my shoulders. I cursed this blasted case to myself. There had to be a better career choice than private investigator for someone with my skill set, antipathy toward work, and general lack of interest in my fellow man.

"Ah, a wiseguy. Well, Mr. Comedian, what were you doing following that lady?"

"I just stopped to see the fight. It's not every day you see a girl beat up some guy in parking lot."

"Uh-huh. So that's the reason you got out of your car a minute after she left her house?"

"Coincidence."

"Why don't I believe you?" The voice sounded vaguely Italian, like an accent lurked below the surface, beaten down by years of disuse. "Now, you gonna tell me what you're doing here?"

Vinnie had to have some backing or at least a blessing from Tony Rizzo if he loan-sharked in Baltimore. I was already in a bad spot here, so I took a chance. "Tony sent me."

"Tony?"

"Yeah. Maybe you're the deaf one. I said Tony sent me."

The muzzle or whatever had been pressed into my back, fell away, and gave me an opening. I spun around, slamming my left fist into my assailant's hand. The gun clattered to the pavement. My right fist hit him smack in the left ear. He grunted in pain and put his head against his shoulder. While he was stunned, I gave him a solid kick in the solar plexus, and when he bent over from it, I booted him hard in the face.

He fell to the sidewalk. I kicked the gun away from him. So far, we hadn't drawn any attention, but the situation could change quickly. Of course, people in Baltimore might have been so used to seeing violence on their streets to simply shrug and keep going. I looked down at my assailant. He held his hands to his mouth to stem the bleeding. He was bald, a little shorter than I, but wider. I spared a quick glance over my shoulder. Margaret Madison was gone.

"Who hired you?" I said.

He mumbled something I couldn't hear past the hands covering his face.

"Who hired you?"

"Go to hell," he said. I kicked him in the groin. The goon took his hands from his face and covered his family jewels. Watching him fold in half on the ground felt satisfying. "Does someone always watch the girl?"

He grunted a few times. "Go to hell," he said again.

This wasn't going anywhere. I wouldn't shoot him for the information, nor would I torture him for it. "Yes or no. I won't care who sent you if you answer my question." Before he could wish me a fourth extra crispy afterlife, I gave him a sharp kick in the gut. "You're running out of hands to cover all these injuries."

The goon gasped for a few breaths before he nodded. "Sometimes . . . depends what . . . she's doing," he said.

"Thanks," I said. I put a glove on, picked up the gun, and dropped it down a nearby sewer grate. I left my assailant to gasp and writhe on the ground while I walked up the street a few blocks. After about ten minutes, I gave up. Margaret Madison had disappeared somewhere. Maybe she saw her protector accost me and went into hiding. Or she picked another parking lot to part some poor sap from a few of his twenties and a few of his teeth. Regardless, I didn't see her anywhere, so I turned around.

When I got back near the spot of my assault, the goon had left.

* * *

Had I been more of a traditional detective, I would have known what to do next. Instead, I had no idea. Alice Fisher got in over her head with Vinnie, who didn't want to give her a chance to breathe. Paul Fisher worked overtime at his job for reasons unknown and was not cheating on his wife so far as I could tell. From the glimpse of them in their home, they looked like a happy couple.

Why, then, did Paul work so much overtime?

What if the happiness proved to be a façade? If so, it had been a damn convincing one. Alice seemed spooked, both by my unexpected arrival and Paul asking her about juice, so her weird behavior could be explained. Paul, however, struck me as a devoted husband. Maybe he didn't know his wife behaved strangely, but I felt it more likely he did know and chose to ignore it, especially with a guest in the house.

I drove back to Digital Sales. Talking to Paul may not have been the best of ideas. After all, it wasn't my place to tell him his wife was a compulsive gambler who owed the bulk of her annual salary to a bookie who—oh, by the way—happened to dabble in loan sharking and employed some legbreakers. This information might stretch the limits of his devotion.

When I walked into Digital Sales, Sally Willis smiled at me again. She wore the same kind of top as the last time I saw her. "Not going to ask if I'm carrying a gun?" I said as I stopped at her desk.

"I can tell you aren't," she said, flashing a grin. "What brings you by?"

"What goes on at the far end of the building on the first floor?"

"Is this related to your case?"

"I think so."

"That's the repair lab. We have full and part-time technicians there who fix copiers and office machines."

I frowned. "I would imagine a technician gets paid significantly less than an account manager."

"I'm sure they do." Now Sally frowned. "Is this about Paul Fisher?"

"How come you don't like him?" I said.

"Is it relevant to your case, too?"

"At this point, anything I can learn is relevant to my case."

Sally sighed. "I don't know. He just . . . rubs me the wrong way. Like, he makes himself out to be a loving husband, and he flirts with everyone here."

"He flirts with you?"

"He tried to," Sally said. "I put a stop to that."

"Maybe he's simply friendly."

"Maybe he's a creeper."

"Do you flirt, Sally?"

"Not here. I don't think it's professional in the workplace."

"Do a lot of the men here try to flirt with you?"

"They pretty much all stop and talk to me." She blushed and pushed her glasses farther up on her nose. "I don't know why, really."

"Maybe you're simply friendly," I said.

Sally started to say something and paused. "I am friendly," she said after a second.

"Maybe Paul is, too."

She shook her head. "I don't know."

"And maybe the men here stop and talk to you because you wear your shirt buttoned as low as possible without them being able to read your cup size." She looked up at me and frowned. "Which I would guess at 36C, for the record."

Sally buttoned a button. "That's just how I dress."

"You work in a building I'm guessing is predominately male?" She nodded. "You're an attractive girl, Sally, and you seem very outgoing. Your boss probably hasn't said anything about the way you dress because he likes the view when you lean down."

Sally blushed again. "You're wrong, you know," she said.

"About what?"

"I'm a 34C."

"Closer inspection might have enabled me to be more accurate," I said.

"I'm sure it would have."

I couldn't read her expression, so I moved on. "Do you know how late Paul works when he's in the repair lab?"

"It's after I leave. His timesheet usually says seven-thirty or eight."

"All right," I said, "I'll come back then. Thanks."

\* \* \*

I SAT in the parking lot at Digital Sales at 7:25. There were a few cars near the main entrance, right under a light stanchion, so I parked close to them. A couple guys who looked to be fresh out of college came out at 7:35. Paul Fisher left at 7:45. I got out of my car and walked to his. He did a double-take when he saw me. "Trent, isn't it?" he said. "What on earth are you doing here?"

"Trent isn't my name," I said. "Well, it's my middle name, but it's not what I go by." I took out my wallet and showed him my ID. "We should talk."

Paul frowned and crossed his arms under his chest. "Why did you come to our house the other night?"

"I really can't say. I need to ask you a question."

"So you're going to ask me a question and not answer mine?"

"Nature of the business. Why do you work all this overtime? You have a good job, Alice works, you're not underwater on your house . . . why all the late nights?"

"I have my reasons." Paul said. His gaze flittered away from me. "We have some bills we need to pay."

"I'm sure you do. Anything you can tell me about them?"

"Who hired you?"

"Who hired me is one of those things I can't tell you. I'd appreciate it, though, if you kept this little chat between us."

"You don't want me to tell Alice?" he said.

"I work in a pretty confidential business," I said. "I'm sorry I had to mislead you the other night." I wasn't the least bit sorry, but I hoped a calculated apology might get me past Paul's guard.

"We all do what we have to do," he said, "including working overtime."

I gave him a business card. "In case you find out overtime isn't enough for these bills you have to pay, give me a call. I might be able to help."

Paul put the business card in his wallet. "OK, I will."

"Good luck."

"I hope I don't need it," Paul said.

I had a feeling he would.

CHAPTER 8

PAUL FISHER HAD BEEN EVASIVE IN THE PARKING LOT. HE must have learned it from his wife. He even had that same shifty-eyed look, albeit only for a few seconds. I ruminated on this as I ate breakfast the following morning. Paul worked overtime doing a job he was overqualified to do. I thought back to my look at the Fishers' financials. Paul's paychecks went in via direct deposit, and the amount being constant. Where did the extra money go, then?

After I finished breakfast, I went back into my office and accessed their financials again. Sure enough, Paul's checks from Digital Sales were deposited every two weeks, and the amount didn't change going back three months. I knew he wasn't volunteering his overtime, so the money went somewhere, like another bank account. In case Paul hadn't planned the whole thing too well, I searched the bank using his SSN (helpfully found on the joint account—no wonder identity theft is so rampant) and found only their joint account.

From there, I broke into local banks until I found a match for Paul's SSN on a savings account at First Mariner. As with the joint account, this one saw regular deposits every two weeks, though for a less significant amount. The deposits were usually around $300. Twice a month since the account opened, I saw a $250 withdrawal. I could have tracked a transfer, but this was a good old-fashioned withdrawal from a real live teller. How quaint.

What was Paul doing with the money? I didn't think he would tell me, and I also didn't think Alice knew about Paul's separate account. Paul wasn't cheating on his wife, but a secret bank account and regular withdrawals didn't look good. He never came across as a druggie of any kind. Half a grand a month didn't make for an expensive habit, though, so he could have been a light user of whatever he took.

While I pondered the drugs someone could buy with five hundred dollars a month, and how bad they would be, my cell phone rang. Caller ID pegged it as my mother. I thought about not answering it but did anyway. "Hello?"

"Coningsby, you made the paper," she said.

"I did?"

"Yes, dear. Some lady named Jessica wrote a lovely piece about you. It's quite flattering."

"Well," I said, "it certainly should be."

"What?"

"Nothing. Great, Mom. I'm sure it will help the business." It probably would. Any publicity would be good publicity, but actual good publicity was twice as nice. Of course, it meant more clients, more sob stories, more work, and more people who thought their spouses were dipping their quills in the company ink. No, no more adultery cases. This would be my line in the sand.

"Of course it will, dear. Speaking of the business, how is your first case going?"

I groaned. "It's become a lot more complicated than it seemed at first glance." I told my mother a few of the details. She didn't need to know everything.

"That does sound troubling."

"I think this might be the last domestic case I work."

"Coningsby, you can't simply pick and choose."

"Of course I can. I'm providing a free service. I need to prioritize who benefits from it. The ambulance chasers of the PI world can break out their fish-eye lenses and investigate possible adultery as much as they want."

"You shouldn't be turning away people who need your help."

"Like I said, it's a matter of priorities."

"How did you prioritize tonight?"

Uh-oh. "What about it?" I said.

"Our friend has the exhibit opening at the Walters. We bought a ticket for you, remember?"

"Her thing is tonight? Shit, I forgot."

"Coningsby, watch your language!"

Arguing would have been pointless. "I will."

"All right. Come by the house tonight at six-thirty. Dinner and drinks start at seven, and I don't want to miss anything."

"I'll be there," I said.

* * *

I FORGOT all about the exhibit opening at the Walters. My parents had foisted it upon me shortly after I got back from Hong Kong. Something about doing things with the foundation I pseudo-worked for. Because I was still living at their house at the time and because it seemed important to my mother, I figured I should go. There were plenty of other ways I would rather spend a Friday night. I had a few ideas in mind for tonight, in fact, all of which I would have to scuttle for the Walters.

Until then, I had to get some things done. I picked up the

guns I ordered. Now I could feel like a real detective. I got a .45, a 9MM, a .38, and a .32. A .45 couldn't be worn under every coat, after all. With my carrying permits in tow and a bag of ammo, I left the gun store, went back home, and put the guns away. If I needed one at the Walters, Baltimore had really changed during my absence. I also purchased some nice lock-blade knives—I learned I should always carry one from *NCIS*.

Until tonight, I needed to figure out how to proceed with the case. My instincts told me there had to be something I could hack into and learn something new. I had done enough traditional detective work for one case. As I pondered investing in a fedora, my cell phone rang. I didn't recognize the number—something I would have to get used to in this line of work—but I answered it anyway. "Hello?"

"You dented one of my boys," said a familiar voice.

"Vinnie. I dented one of your boys? What a shame."

"In Canton Square," he said. "Margaret uses him . . . but still. What'd you go and do that for?"

"Well, he tried to dent me first. I ended up being the better denter as it turned out."

"Look, C.T., I'm willing to look past a few things since we were friends, but I can't have you messing around my operation. What were you doing in Canton Square, anyway?"

I was sure he already knew. "Just walking around," I said. "Then someone stuck a gun in my back, and the rest is history."

"I hope you don't go messing in my business."

"I'm not trying to, Vinnie. Did you give any thought to what I asked you about Alice Fisher?"

He was silent for a few seconds. "I've been patient with Alice. I work with her. I don't want to send anyone out to beat up a woman, you know?"

"And they say chivalry is dead," I said.

"Hey, I've always had principles. You know I did."

"And they've always been very much yours."

"We're not gonna have a problem, are we?" said Vinnie.

"I'm not trying to create one."

"Good. Let's not change it."

I said, "OK," but Vinnie had already hung up. Now I knew the goon had been one of his boys. I figured it already, but confirmation was always nice. If Vinnie kept a few regular legbreakers on the payroll, his business had to be doing well. Or he borrowed them from someone like Tony Rizzo, and at the rates Tony probably charged, Vinnie's business had to be booming.

But how well? I logged into the computer and launched an anonymized browser. This allowed me to hide my electronic footprints. My hacker friends and I first setup an anonymizer in Hong Kong. When I got home, I created one on this side of the ocean. Never trust one run by someone else. With my traffic masked from the world, I looked for Vinnie's bank records. I also ran a separate search for any businesses he had established in the name of banking his money legitimately. If he dumped it all into a personal account, it became too easy to find and audit.

The second search finished first. Vincent Renaldo Serrano setup a business shortly after he got the boot from college. He established VRS Consulting, which became Serrano Enterprises LLC. What consulting services someone like Vinnie provided was certainly a matter of debate. I didn't think Vegas odds, juice, and the ethics of legbreaking counted as consulting, but maybe those definitions changed during my time abroad. I amended my bank searches to include Serrano Enterprises and let the searches run while I made lunch.

When I finished, I had results waiting for me. Vinnie's personal savings and checking accounts looked normal, with each having a couple thousand dollars in it. Serrano Enterprises maintained a higher balance, always over ten thousand, though rarely over twenty. I saw plenty of deposits from individuals, a few from businesses, and regular withdrawals. The withdrawals went to a payroll service. Not only did Vinnie have his own guys, he hired a payroll service, probably for the appearance of added legitimacy.

Since I now knew a little more about how Vinnie operated, how much did the knowledge help me? More importantly, how much did it help Alice Fisher? Vinnie basically told me he had cut her a break because he didn't like to strong-arm women. How long would his spirit of generosity last? At some point, it always came down to money, and if Alice didn't pay enough of it in time, then one of Vinnie's guys would end up darkening her door. Short of writing her a check for thirty grand, which I was in no position to do, I didn't see an easy way to get her out of this anytime soon.

Maybe inspiration would strike me tonight. I didn't get any ideas sitting at my computer. I did a few more searches for Vinnie and his business, including seeing if they made the news. They didn't. I had hoped for a story about the business to make Vinnie squirm to explain what he really did. A story about the business. It gave me an idea I might be able to use later. For now, I needed to get a run in, check my wardrobe for tonight, and maybe buy some new clothes.

* * *

AFTER INVENTORYING MY CLOTHES, I decided to wear my tuxedo. Maybe it would make me overdressed, but I'd rather look boss than be underdressed, and it would make my parents happy. It ensured they would leave me alone for the night. I hadn't worn the tux since before I left for Hong Kong, but I've been the same weight for the seven years following my junior year of college. It needed a dry cleaning, however, and I paid extra for the rush job. When I picked up the tux, I had about an hour to shower and get ready.

Two minutes after the appointed time—which is quite prompt for me—I pulled into my parents' driveway. Their private road always felt four miles long, especially when I ran late. Another two minutes after I hit the driveway, I walked through the front door. I entered the living room, and my mother came in from the opposite end a second later. She wore a black ball gown, with white gloves and a necklace depriving a colony of oysters of their pearls. "Coningsby, you're almost on time," she said, "and you look very nice. Thank you for dressing up, dear."

"This old thing?" I said.

"Your father is wearing a tux, also. Here he comes now." I heard his footsteps come down the stairs. He walked into the living room sporting a tux a lot like mine. My jacket had different highlights, and he opted for the blue bowtie and vest, so we didn't look exactly alike. If we did, my mother might have fainted.

When we got to the Walters, a good crowd had already assembled. Most people wore suits or nice dresses; I saw few tuxedoes and even fewer ball gowns. The new exhibit was still under covers until the official unveiling. My mother talked to the artist and waved me to them to meet her. Karen was pleasant but showed a space cadet look in her eyes common to artists. I suspected the exhibit would be full of things people would talk about, nod at, and pretend to appreciate without understanding. Doing the same got me through an art class in college. Besides, being here gave me a night away from my case.

I made sure to have a drink when the curtains came down and the new exhibit was officially unveiled. Unfortunately, my drink was mediocre champagne. It tasted American, not French. I wondered what became of the Walters while I had been overseas. Because my mother's friend's art had been revealed to the public, I figured I should at least look at it. My mother might decide to ask me about it later.

What I saw was difficult to describe. I had a master's degree from a good school and even took a couple of art and humanities classes along the way. The exhibit I saw didn't fit into any of the styles I learned about. I'm sure there were people who would say Karen's lack of conformity meant the artist was an innovator and risk-taker who refused to be shackled by convention. For all I knew, such an explanation may well have been true. To me, the whole thing looked like a mess.

I saw paintings trying to be surreal but ended up looking like someone censored all the genius out of Picasso. Small sculptures attempted to pay homage to the ancients while still displaying the trappings of modernity. I heard a lot of oohs and ahhs as I walked around. I wondered how many of them were polite, how many were legitimate, and how many were uttered in sheer confusion.

Once around the hall was enough for me. I made my way back to the refreshment stand. Even a glass of mediocre champagne sounded better than wandering around waiting for my brain to leak out of my ears. Then I saw her: the most captivating girl in the room. She wore a red ball gown I would swear had been custom-made for her. It hugged all the curves she wanted it to, and its plunging neckline showed two works of art far finer than any others I had seen this night. Her chestnut hair was pulled back into a bun. She scanned the room with slightly narrowed eyes. When she looked at me, they stopped, settled on me, and her expression softened.

Never one to refuse so clear an invitation, I approached and stood behind her in the champagne line. "You look bored," I said. "Or maybe annoyed at having to wear your hair up and look at God knows what."

She shook her head. "This is awful. I only came here because my parents wanted me to."

"I'm in the same boat."

"And this champagne tastes like it's from the poorest section of California."

Normally, I find snootiness annoying. I'm sure this tendency makes me several shades of hypocritical, but I do. In this girl, though, I found it strangely endearing. It was like she never knew anything else and read about middle-class people in scrolls delivered to the family mansion on the hill. "I had better champagne in Hong Kong," I said.

"You were in Hong Kong?"

"For three and a half years."

"Business or pleasure?" she said.

I said, "Some of both."

"Tell me about it, but take me somewhere else."

"How about the Red Maple?" When she wrinkled her nose, I added, "They have a few deserving wines."

"Let's go," she said.

* * *

THE RED MAPLE wasn't quite as upscale as it pretended to be, but I liked the place. She didn't want to walk, and the poor dear nearly fainted when I suggested we Uber the few blocks up the road, so I drove. We parked in a lot on the opposite side of Charles Street, and she dashed across it like someone chased her. We went in and got a table with surprising ease on a Friday night.

Between the walk out of the Walters and the drive to the Red Maple, I learned the girl in the scandalous red ball gown was Gloria Reading. She made sure to tell me she graduated from Brown with a degree in literature, and she seemed equally proud she never worked a day in her life. Her parents were Hugh and Susan Reading, and due to their money, her trust funds, rich aunts and uncles, and whatever money she had, Gloria wouldn't ever need to lift a finger. I envied her for it, but I didn't tell her. Her parents knew mine, though she and I never met before this evening.

Once we were inside, everyone in eyeshot turned to look at Gloria. She was definitely a beauty, though not the most beautiful girl in the world. Her height (she had to go five-nine without heels), the way she carried herself, the clothes she wore, how they fit, and how she wore them all mattered. She had a presence past the imperious look on her face, and sex appeal trailed in her wake. All of it more than made up for any tiny flaws in her appearance.

The Red Maple featured jazzy music and had enough decency to keep it to a volume to foster conversation. A sign near the front door advertised a DJ playing later tonight, but I hoped to be gone, with Gloria in tow, before having to suffer such a fate. The table had a card with suggested wines, so I asked the waiter for a full list. Gloria and I looked over it when he returned. She immediately went to the bottom where the pricier vintages resided. I saw a few I liked near the top, but I had a feeling Gloria would wrinkle her nose at something under $100 a bottle.

Gloria pointed at Opus One Bordeaux Red Blends. "I've heard of that," she said. "Let's get a bottle of that." A bottle cost $210.

I had heard of Opus One, too. Before I tried it, someone described it to me as a label-buyer's wine, and after sampling it, I had to agree. Its price tag far exceeded its taste. I could put up with it, though. "Sounds good," I said, and signaled for the waiter. He told us how good our choice was (what else would he say to a bottle the place sells for over two hundred?) and promised to return shortly.

"Do you come here often?" Gloria said.

"I think you stole my line" I said.

She smiled. I liked it. "I'm sure you've used better lines than that."

"Since I was in high school. And no, I don't come here often. I think I've been here once before. Mostly, I see the place when I drive past."

"So you're Robert and June's son," she said. "How come I've never met you until tonight?"

"You've merely been unlucky, I guess," I said.

The waiter came back with our wine and two glasses on a tray. He set the bottle on a cloth napkin, uncorked it, and let us both sample the bouquet. I've never known enough about wine to have any idea what I'm supposed to smell, so I gave a nod with the hope it satisfied all involved. It usually does, and it did this time, too. The waiter put both glasses on the table, poured a splash of wine into each, and let us sample it. Gloria reacted as if she drank pure ambrosia. I simply gave another nod. The waiter then filled our glasses and walked away.

"A toast," I said, raising my glass.

"To what?" Gloria said.

"To your luck changing for the better." She grinned, and we clinked our glasses, before each taking a sip of wine.

"Apart from bad luck, I really do wonder why I haven't met you before."

"I got back from Hong Kong about two months ago."

"That could explain it," said Gloria. "I was finishing college while you were going overseas. How did you like Hong Kong?"

"It was interesting. Old in a lot of ways, but modern and new in others. The food was fantastic. I managed to learn a lot while I was over there."

Gloria wrinkled her nose. "You went there to learn?"

"I went to see the world. I stopped in a couple other places first, but I really liked Hong Kong. While I was there, I made a few friends, and they convinced me to stay for a while. Basically, what happened is it turned into three and a half years." *I met some hackers; we both had skills, and I had money to keep everyone in business. It worked out well for both sides until the police kicked the door down.*

"Why did you leave?" Gloria said.

"The government wouldn't let me extend my stay any longer," I said.

"That's a shame."

"They're commies. They don't have a history of getting things right."

Gloria chuckled. "So now you're back in the States. Living on your own?"

"I have an apartment in Fells Point," I said.

"How do you pass the time during the day?"

"I started working a few days ago."

"Working?" Gloria wrinkled her nose like she caught a whiff of a decomposing body in the next chair. "Why would you do that?"

"It's something of a long story."

"Did your parents make you work?" she said.

"More or less."

She took a sip of her wine. I did the same, mostly to get rid of it. It wasn't bad, just very average. "What are you doing? Consulting? Finance?"

"I'm actually a detective," I said.

Gloria almost dropped her glass. "A detective? Why?"

"I said it was a long story, but we still have plenty of wine left, so I'll tell you." I told her about Hong Kong, trying to help Americans while there, the arrest, prison, coming back home, and being forced to get a job helping people. To her credit, Gloria managed not to faint during the narration of my travails. I left most of the details in because I didn't see the harm in telling her, though I skipped most of the prison story because I didn't want to think about it. Toward the end of my tale, I refilled both of our glasses.

"Wow," she said when I finished, "I'm not sure I like your parents anymore. That's an awful thing to do. Do you like being a detective?"

"I'm still pretty new at it, but I must confess I'm not a fan so far."

"How long will you do it?"

"Until I've made enough money from my parents so I don't have to work anymore. I hope no longer than a few years."

"I hope so, too," she said. "Do you work a lot? Do you still have free time?"

"I believe in working smart, not hard," I said. "Right now, I have one case. I don't think I want to juggle several at once."

"That makes sense."

"Enough about work," I said. "Tell me about you. What were you doing while I was gallivanting all over the globe?"

"Going to parties, openings, socializing," said Gloria. "I've learned the piano a lot better, and I'm taking tennis lessons now."

"Ah, the life of a socialite." I raised my glass toward Gloria. "Are you trying to become famous for being famous?"

She smiled. I noticed her flawless teeth, each as white as the pearls around her neck. Either she had remarkable genes with respect to dental matters, or she had some work done. Maybe both. "I don't really want to be famous," she said, "I just want to have a good time with fun people."

"Are you having a good time now?"

"Definitely." She smiled. "This is much more interesting than looking at art that I really don't care about."

I was about to agree when my cell phone rang. The caller ID indicated Rich. Why would he be calling me so late on a Friday night? I excused myself from the conversation with Gloria and decided to find out.

"It's after 10:30," I said. "You're keeping late hours."

"You should get down here," he said.

"Where is here, and why should I get there?"

"Herring Run Park. You know where it is?"

"Sure," I said. "Why am I going?"

"We got a dead guy," said Rich.

"I can't imagine what you need me—"

"He has your business card in his wallet."

I felt my lungs deflate as the air left them. I looked at Gloria, who frowned in concern. Rich filled the gap in the conversation. "C.T.? You still there?"

"Yeah," I said. "Yeah, I'm here. Is it Paul Fisher?"

"You got it."

I let out a long, slow breath. "How did he die?"

"Car accident," Rich said. "You need to get down here."

"I'm leaving now." I put my phone away. Gloria's brows were still pulled into a frown. "I have to go. Something . . . unpleasant has happened in my case. Now it's gone in a totally different direction." I flagged down the waiter and handed him my card.

She nodded. "OK. Wait a second before you go." Gloria took a pen from her dainty purse, wrote her phone number on a napkin, and handed it to me. "Call me later. We can continue our conversation and see where else it leads."

I considered giving her a business card, but didn't want her to laugh at my father's terrible tagline. What the heck? She seemed interested enough to this point. I gave her one anyway.

"My cell number is on there," I said. "Sorry to have to run out like this."

"I understand," Gloria said with a smile. I knew she didn't, but I appreciated the effort.

"You're OK to get back?" I said as I signed the check.

"My parents will send the driver to get me," Gloria said.

Of course they would.

I left the Red Maple, wondering what the hell had happened to Paul Fisher.

CHAPTER 9

WHEN I CAME UP BELAIR ROAD FROM DOWNTOWN, I SAW flashing lights from police cars and an ambulance on Chesterfield Avenue. Those streets form two borders of Herring Run Park, which ran all the way from Belair Road to Harford Road. It has a few baseball diamonds and also plays host to soccer and football games in season, but the bulk of it is covered by trees and two walking trails. Those pathways, usually dark at night, now had police cars and ambulances to brighten the way.

The lights covered my windshield as I drove down the road, bathing everything I saw in blue and red. How did I get into this? Alice Fisher hired me because she thought her husband guilty of playing grab-ass at his office. He hadn't. Now he was dead. Maybe it had been a legitimate car accident. Maybe not. The Fishers lived far enough away from Herring Run Park to make me wonder what Paul was doing there.

I parked on the street near all the commotion. Residents stood in their front yards, talking to one another and taking pictures and videos with their cell phones. A couple of uniforms maintained the perimeter of the accident scene on my side. I showed them my ID. They merely looked at me until Rich walked up in plain clothes rather than a uniform. "He's

OK," he said, and they waved me in. I lifted the yellow tape, and it hit me how I just walked into my first crime scene, or whatever they called this. The realization gave me pause. I had watched enough cop shows to know the things to do and not do at scene like this. None of them prepared me for actually being in one.

"Glad you could make it," Rich said.

"Yeah, thanks for calling me," I said. I still felt like I had walked in on some surreal movie. I would need to ask him about the suit later.

"Try not to touch anything," Rich said, smirking.

"I know what I'm supposed to do and not do."

"First accident scene, though, isn't it?"

I nodded. "Yeah." After a pause, I said, "isn't this a crime scene?"

"Where's the crime? A guy drove into a tree."

We walked along Chesterfield, deeper into the sea of police cars, officers, and paramedics. I looked at the yellow tape. "POLICE LINE—DO NOT CROSS," it told everyone. Nothing about a crime scene. I could see what happened as we approached. Paul Fisher's car went off the road, down a long hill, and crashed into a tree. The driver's side door was open. The body had already been bagged and put onto a gurney. Rich and I descended the hill toward the car. Once I got closer, I saw the windshield had been destroyed.

"Looks like he went through," Rich said.

"No seat belt, then," I said. "Interesting."

"Why is that interesting?"

"Paul Fisher is a . . . was a happily married man with a good job. He was devoted to his wife. Their house was plain and boring. He's not a risk-taker. He doesn't seem like the type to go around without a seat belt."

"People surprise us sometimes," said Rich.

"Not often," I said.

We walked to the car. Because this was my accident scene initiation, I wanted to pay attention and not miss anything. That sounded good for all crime scenes, but I knew the mockery from Rich would be worse if I missed something important at the first one. Paul Fisher's car hit the tree hard enough to crumple the front end. It struck to the right side of the center. The windshield looked like something heavy had gone flying through it. I wondered how fast a car had to go for a body to smash through. Should I know those details? The detritus Paul collected in his car had been thrown forward at impact, leaving a couple of coffee cups and other random trash scattered about on the grass. The driver's and passenger's seats were even with one another. The driver's door was open, but I didn't know if it had been found that way or if the police opened it to look around the car more.

"Was the door open when you found it?" I said.

"No," Rich said, "I did it so we could look around. The ME already looked at the body by then."

"Pictures taken?"

"Enough to fill a scrapbook."

"Body is beaten up?"

"Like it's been in a car accident."

I looked around some more. Nothing jumped out at me as suspicious. It certainly appeared as if Paul Fisher drove off the road, crashed into a tree, exited his car via the windshield, and died. I couldn't figure out why he'd been here in the first place. He and Alice lived a good half-hour away. Why had his car veered into a tree? I strolled around and looked at the tires; they were all intact, taking a blowout off the table. The matter of Paul Fisher going through the glass bothered me, too. I had painted an accurate picture of him: a family man with a good job who appeared normal and careful in his everyday life didn't drive around without seat belts.

"Something bothers you, doesn't it?" Rich said.

"A few things," I said. "No seat belt is one among them."

"We'll figure it out. The ME is going to do an autopsy, and we'll have several people going over the accident."

"Anyone tell his wife yet?"

"No, not yet," he said. "You want to go with me? You seem to know her. Maybe that'll make it a little easier."

"It won't," I said, "but I'll go."

* * *

IT WAS after eleven-thirty when we got to the Fishers' house. Rich and I got out of the Lexus and made our way up the sidewalk. "Ever have to talk to a sudden widow before?" I said.

"Unfortunately, yes," Rich said.

"Does it ever get easy?"

He shook his head. "No."

"What's with the plain clothes, anyway?"

"I'll tell you later." We got to the doorstep, and I knocked on the door. A light went on upstairs. Footsteps came down a few seconds later. Alice Fisher opened the door. The undone neck of her robe revealed a nightgown, and she wore a pair of pink slippers. She frowned when she saw me, then frowned more when she saw Rich's badge. "Hello, Mrs. Fisher," he said.

"What's wrong?" she said.

"May we come in?"

She opened the door wider and let us in. We walked into the living room. Alice turned on a light and stood behind a recliner, her arms crossed under her chest, the robe wrapped tightly around her. "Would you like to sit down?" Rich said.

"No," she said. "Please tell me what's wrong."

"It's about your husband, Paul. We found his car wrecked in Herring Run Park. It's in northeast Baltimore. I—"

"I know where it is. What's wrong?" The light on the end table reflected in the tears welling in Alice's eyes. She had to know where this was going.

"Mrs. Fisher, I'm very sorry to tell you this, but your husband is dead."

"No!" Alice cried. "No, no, no, no, no." She ran to me and buried her head against my shoulder. She kept muttering denials through her tears. I put my arms around her and let her cry. This poor woman had been through a lot. First, she thought her husband was cheating on her, then I discovered her gambling problem, and now her husband was dead. Right now, I wished Paul Fisher had been a rotten and unfaithful husband. It might have kept him alive.

Alice cried on my jacket for several minutes before pulling back. "You're . . . sure it's him?" she said, wiping her eyes.

Rich nodded. "We are."

"What happened?"

Rich told her the details. "We need you to come with us to identify the body."

Alice shook her head, looked at me, and sobbed again. "Why did this happen?" she said. "You were supposed to follow him." She punched me in the shoulder, the same one she had been crying into up until a moment ago. "Why weren't you there? Why weren't you there!" Alice drew her fist back to punch me again. I caught it when it got near me, looked at her, and watched her dissolve into tears again. She put her head on my upper chest and cried for a few more minutes.

When she finished, she looked at Rich. "I'll go with you. Just give me a few minutes to get dressed."

"Take as much time as you need," Rich said.

Alice went upstairs. Rich and I sat in the living room and

waited. I couldn't find anything to say. The room felt so empty it didn't seem right to talk. Rich must have felt the same way because we sat in silence. All I heard was our breathing and a clock ticking in the next room. About ten minutes later, Alice came downstairs in a sweater and jeans. It looked like she had been crying some more. She grabbed a tissue, wiped her eyes, blew her nose, and threw the tissue away. "Can we go now?" she said.

"Of course," Rich said. "You can ride with us. We'll have someone take you home."

"All right," Alice said, and we left.

* * *

ALICE WENT to see the medical examiner. Rich offered to go with her, but she declined. She asked me to go with her. I looked at Rich, who shrugged at me. I agreed to go along. Alice needed the moral support. She knew what happened, but only on the surface. She would have more questions soon, and a look at the body would do nothing to alleviate them. If anything, it would only create more.

We entered the medical examiner's office. I noted the lack of a putrid smell in the air. This place must have had a ridiculous ventilation system. The ME on duty was a lanky, fiftyish man named Dr. Sellers. He had a full head of gray hair and horn-rimmed glasses. He gave us a sympathetic smile as we walked in. Alice simply looked at him. I didn't think she knew what to say. "This is Alice Fisher," I said. "She's here to identify her husband's body."

"I'm sorry for your loss, Mrs. Fisher," Dr. Sellers said. He had a slight Boston accent. We walked to the tables. Three had bodies lying atop them, all covered by white sheets. Dr. Sellers pulled back the sheet on the right. I stood a few steps back, but

I could tell it was Paul Fisher. Cuts and bruises covered his face. I took a deep breath—this was my first dead body. Alice saw him and bawled again. "Is this your husband?"

She nodded a few times and tried to say something through her tears, but I couldn't understand it. It must have been good enough for Dr. Sellers because he frowned and draped the body with the white shroud again. Alice turned around, took a few steps toward me, and slumped forward. I caught her and let her sob on my shoulder some more. Dr. Sellers looked at us for a moment, then went back to his work. Alice cried for a few more minutes and then straightened, wiped at her eyes, and smoothed her hair. I found a box of tissues and gave her a couple. "Can you wait for me in the hallway?" I said. "I'll only be a minute."

Alice nodded and walked out the door into the hallway. Dr. Sellers took a break from his work and regarded me. I took another deep breath and showed him my ID. "Can I ask you a few questions?"

"Sure."

"I'm suspicious due to her husband dying in a car accident."

"You shouldn't be," he said. "I've only done a prelim, but injuries are consistent with that kind of trauma. Broken bones, contusions, lacerations. His face is bruised and cut from the windshield, and I found some glass in it. Looks like a car accident to me."

I frowned. I had hoped Dr. Sellers would support my suspicions. The car crash still felt wrong to me. "Any drugs in his system?" I said.

"We won't know for a few days."

I nodded. "Is there any chance he was dead before the accident?"

"You mean, like a heart attack?"

"No, Doctor. I mean, could he have been killed, then the accident staged?"

Doctor Sellers sighed. "I doubt it," he said. "The body was pretty fresh when it got called in."

His opinion was discouraging. "I presume your full findings will be in your report?"

He nodded. "I'll have it finished in a day or two, pending the tox screen."

"All right," I said. "Thank you, Doctor."

I left the ME's office, collected Alice Fisher, and walked back into the police station. Rich handed Alice off to an officer who would arrange a ride home for her. I went to Rich's desk with him. Once we sat down, he looked at me. "He had your business card in his pocket," Rich said.

"So you said."

"I'm going to need to ask you about it, about him, about his wife, all of it."

I rolled my eyes. "I didn't kill him, and I wasn't sleeping with his wife. Happy?"

"I'm afraid we'll need more," Rich said.

"Fine. We doing it here?"

"A room down the hall."

"Lead the way," I said.

\* \* \*

DESPITE SOME ADVENTURES IN COLLEGE, I had never been in an American police interrogation room before. It looked like I expected it to from the myriad TV shows and movies I had seen. A table sat in the middle of the room with a set of handcuffs attached. The chairs both looked uncomfortable, but the one nearer the handcuffs more so. A long mirror ran down the right-hand side of the room. A window covered in bars split the back wall. I walked in and sat in the slightly better chair.

"Other side," Rich said.

I traded chairs. Apart from being a little smaller, it didn't feel any different. Rich sat on the business side of the table. I saw a camera mounted in the corner to the left of the door. The red light below the lens was lit.

"Turn the camera off," I said.

"What?"

"Turn the camera off."

"Why would I?" Rich said.

"Because I'm not a criminal."

"Not in this country, at least."

I smirked. "When cheap shots are all you can afford, I guess you need to take them," I said.

"Not even two minutes," Rich said, "and you're already pointing out how wealthy you are. Or were before your China trip."

"We all have our crosses to bear."

"You're here to answer questions, C.T."

"Then maybe you should start asking me some," I said. "After you turn the camera off, of course."

Rich slapped the table with the palms of both hands. I had seen it coming so it didn't surprise me. He looked at me as he did it, and I met his stare the entire time. "I spent nineteen days in a Chinese prison, Rich," I said. "There is nothing you can do in here to scare me."

My comment made Rich frown. "What happened to you over there?" he said, his voice low.

I thought about it, and my chest grew tight. My vision narrowed. If I were to tell someone, Rich would be a fine candidate. As a veteran of the Army and the BPD, he had seen a lot and survived more. Rich kept staring at me. Now wasn't the time to answer his question. "I'm here because I'm cooperating," I said after a moment, "not because I have to be."

"Did they torture you?" I didn't answer. I wanted to but I said nothing. "I know someone you could talk to if they did. He's worked with a lot of soldiers who have . . . been through a lot."

The shrink my parents foisted upon me had been useless. Would Rich's guy be any better? I might ask him for the referral sometime, but not now. While I appreciated Rich's concern, I had a murder to solve. He didn't need to see me sweat. "I thought I was here to talk to you," I said, "and I thought you were turning the camera off."

"Fine, fine." Rich got up and crossed the small room to the camera. I let out a slow breath while his back was turned. My vision returned to normal as my breathing eased. Rich reached up and unscrewed a coaxial cable from the back. The red light winked out. "Are you happy, sire?"

"It'll do."

Rich sat down and sighed. He looked at me. I looked back at him. He had eschewed his usual clean-shaven appearance and sported a Van Dyke I pegged as a few days old. A couple gray hairs encroached on the dark brown. "First time trying to grill someone?" I said.

"What if it is?"

"Hey, I went to my first crime scene tonight. Or whatever you're calling it until you realize I'm right."

"Accident scene," said Rich.

"Anyway, it seems fitting that you're getting your first interrogation." I offered a small smile.

Rich gave a slight grin. "A night of firsts," he said.

"I guess it means you should make your first question a good one."

"I'll do my best." Rich paused, cleared his throat, adjusted his tie, and cracked his knuckles.

"Want a breath mint, too?" I said.

"No, I'm good." He paused. "Do I need one?"

"Just trying to be polite."

Rich breathed into his hands. "I think I'm good," he said. "Don't you?" He leaned toward me as if to breathe in my face. I put up my hand and pulled away. Rich leaned back.

"No complaints."

"OK, here we go." Rich took a deep breath. "How did the dead guy end up with your business card?" he said.

"Really?" I said. "Your first question in your first interrogation has to be lame?"

"What?"

"Seriously?"

Rich frowned. "It's a valid question," he said.

"It's boring and predictable, too," I said. "You never get a second chance to ask a first question."

"Can you just answer it already?"

"How do you think he got it?" I said.

"I suppose you gave it to him," said Rich.

"See? You could have led with something else."

"Why did you give him a card? Didn't his wife hire you?"

"She did."

"Because she thought he was cheating on her," Rich said.

"Yes," I said.

"And yet he has your business card."

"Because I don't think he was unfaithful." I went over the events leading me to my conclusion.

"It doesn't sound like he was a cheater," said Rich.

"I told you he was devoted to his wife," I said.

"Still doesn't explain why he had your business card."

"Because his wife is hiding something. She told me they were underwater on their house, and they're not. I—"

"Wait, how do you know they're not?"

"I checked," I said.

"Checked how?" Rich glared at me. "Did you hack into their financial information?"

I put my hand to my chest and feigned indignation. "Moi?"

Rich shook his head and sighed. "OK, so she lied about their degree of financial peril. Big deal."

"It bothered me. It would bother you, too. I figured she was hiding something having to do with money, like maybe a drug problem. Not what I was hired to investigate, but I found it while I poked around. I chose to pursue it. I wanted to keep it from Paul, but I thought maybe he had some insight into what was going on."

"I take it he didn't?" Rich said.

"If he did, he didn't tell me." I said.

"What do you think it is?"

"I don't know. She doesn't seem like a druggie, so it's probably not drugs."

"You wouldn't be holding out on me, would you?" Rich said.

"Would I do something so unprofessional during your first interrogation?" I said.

"Yes," he said and stared at me.

I spread my hands and grinned. "OK, you have me there."

"So you're holding out on me?"

"You know what I know."

"But I don't know everything you know."

I chuckled. "True about a great many things," I said.

Rich smirked and shook his head. "Touché," he said.

"Now I want to know something," I said.

"You think you get to ask questions?"

"You're in plain clothes tonight, and I doubt you normally get so involved with investigations like these. What's going on?"

"I was going to tell you soon." Rich paused and smiled. "I'm up for detective. I already took the exam, and now I'm doing a few ride-alongs."

"Great." I smiled, too. "You'll be a natural. Did you pass the exam?"

"They haven't told me yet."

"Well, if I can puzzle this thing out, you'll get to make a key arrest. Might earn you your shield right there."

"What's there to puzzle out?" Rich said. "You think this is a murder?"

I said, "I told you something about it bothers me. I don't know if it's a murder yet, but I'm going to keep looking around."

"You talked to the ME?"

"I did. He said injuries are consistent with a car accident and his final report will be out in a day or two."

"I don't think it's a murder, C.T. You might be wasting your time."

"Maybe, but I think I owe it to Alice to find out. She thought he was cheating on her, and he ended up dead. He got involved in something a lot worse than adultery and I want to know what it is."

"Good luck," Rich said.

"I might need it," I said.

* * *

It barely turned one o'clock when I turned off the engine. This had been a long day, and not one I would soon forget. More questions had been raised, and I would tackle those in the morning. For now, I wanted to go to sleep. I walked from the recesses of the parking lot to my apartment building and went inside. I collected a few envelopes from the mailbox and unlocked my door, then locked it behind me. No sooner had I left the foyer, tossed my mail on the table, and started down the hall than someone knocked on the door.

I frowned and looked at it. Who the hell would be knocking at this hour? When I looked through the peephole, I saw Jessica Webber standing in the hall. She was about to knock again when I unlocked the door and opened it. "Jessica, it's late," I said.

"You look tired," she said. She had a business suit on, with a matching skirt and blazer, professional heels, and a white shirt unbuttoned just far enough to be interesting. I liked this one spectacular habit about the way she dressed.

"Because I am. What brings you by?"

"I was working on a story not far from here and decided I'd see if you were awake. When I turned the corner, you were walking inside. How goes the case?"

I shook my head. "Not well," I said. "The woman's husband is dead."

"Dead?" Jessica said. "Oh, my gosh. Did that just happen?"

"Tonight, yes. She's a wreck, and the whole thing has become a mess. It's gone from possible adultery to . . . I don't know what."

"Well, since I'm sort of chronicling this case for you, maybe I should talk to her, get her reaction."

I frowned. "No, you shouldn't," I said.

"It sounds like you think he didn't die of natural causes," Jessica said. She had me there. Jessica picked up on things people said—and didn't say, no doubt—very well. "That makes the story so much more interesting. She should—"

"Jessica, her husband is dead. She's in shock, and she's grieving. I don't know if you've ever lost anyone you loved, but the last thing you want is people in your face. Especially a camera and a reporter asking you how you feel. It's a time for mourning and privacy. Who cares about your story?" Jessica frowned and recoiled like I struck her, but I kept going. "Her husband is dead. Have some goddamn respect."

She was about to say something, but I slammed the door in her face.

## CHAPTER 10

THE NEXT MORNING AFTER A RUN AND A SHOWER, I MADE breakfast in the kitchen. Blueberry pancakes seemed too elaborate for only me, so I went with sausage and toast. It won no awards for originality, but it tasted good. I washed it all down with a mug of red bush tea sweetened with a teaspoon of honey. I lingered at the table, sipping my tea until it had grown tepid.

The car accident still bothered me. It was entirely possible Paul Fisher decided to take a drive down Chesterfield Avenue late on a Friday night for reasons currently unknown. Was he having an affair and I simply whiffed on it? I would have to check his coworkers and see if any of them lived on Chesterfield. I really didn't think he cheated on Alice, but I also didn't expect him to end up dead. Maybe I had been wrong all along.

Poor Alice Fisher didn't need to know any of this. Regardless of her husband's possible infidelity, he died, and she was devastated. Even if I discovered he diddled half the office, I couldn't tell Alice. Let her bury her husband with the good memories she had of him. Since Paul died, I wondered if talking to anyone at Digital Sales would now prove more fruitful. Some people didn't want to speak ill of the dead, but more people didn't want to speak ill of living coworkers because of office gossip and politics.

I changed into more professional attire and headed to Digital Sales.

* * *

BASED on the dearth of cars in the parking lot, Saturdays brought only a small crew to Digital Sales. Sally Willis was still there, though, and she smiled at me as I walked in the front door. "You must be working overtime," she said.

"I could say the same about you," I said at the reception desk. "You don't have any better way to spend your Saturday?"

Color rose in her cheeks. "I work a half-day in the morning every other Saturday."

I leaned on the low wall at the front of her desk. Now I could tell she dressed more casually than during the week. Her professional skirts had given way to a well-worn pair of jeans, and her plunging necklines had taken an unfortunate day off in lieu of a red University of Maryland sweatshirt. "What can I do for you?" said Sally.

"So quick to get back to business today, Sally?" I said. "Color me disappointed."

"I only have a few hours." She smiled. "That doesn't leave a lot of time for flirting."

"If you insist. Have you heard about Paul Fisher?"

"What about him?"

"He's dead," I said.

Sally frowned, and her mouth fell open. She sat mouth agape for a few seconds. Finally, after some head-shaking, she found her voice. "Dead? He's really dead?"

"I saw the body myself."

"Wow," she said. "I hate to say it, but I didn't much care for him. Never wanted to see anything bad happen to him, of course. How's his wife holding up?"

"She's destroyed."

"I can imagine." Sally shook her head some more. "Do you want to talk to someone here about Paul?"

"I do, yes. It looks like you're running a skeleton crew today, but if anyone here worked with Paul, for him, supervised him, whatever, I'd like to talk to them."

Sally nodded. "Yeah." The frown remained on her face, "How did he die?"

"Car accident," I said.

"In his own car?" Sally said.

"Yes."

"Wow. That's . . . that's just really hard to believe." Sally sighed and indulged in yet another round of shaking her head. "I'll see who I can find. You can take a seat over there." She pointed to a short row of leather chairs about halfway between the entrance and her desk. I walked to the chairs and sat in the one nearest Sally's desk while she worked the phones.

A few minutes later, she waved me back. "Jake Driscoll is going to talk to you," she said. "He worked for Paul up until recently when he became an account manager, too."

"Thanks," I said. "Where's his office?"

"Third floor, room three-oh-five."

I got in the elevator and punched the "three" button.

* * *

JAKE DRISCOLL's office was to the left of the elevator, second on the right. The nameplate on his door shone like it had been minted that very morning. I could smell traces of fresh paint from his office. Jake had a surfboard hanging on the wall along with a couple of posters for classic surfer movies (if there could, in fact, be such a thing). Jake himself let his long blond hair hang down to his shoulders. He wore a teal collared shirt unbuttoned about a third of the way down, light khaki pants, and sandals he should have packed away two months ago. I wondered if he presented this kind of image to his clients during the week. Maybe Jake managed the accounts for skateboard and beachwear manufacturers. He would fit right in at Tony Hawk's boardroom.

"Hey, man, how are you?" Jake said, extending his hand from across the desk.

I shook it and sat in the guest chair. It felt significantly less comfortable than my own. "I'm OK, considering I'm making the rounds here on a Saturday morning. How are you?"

"Good, I'm good. So what's up? Sally said you needed to ask me some stuff about Paul."

"Paul's dead."

The news wiped the surfer look from Jake's face. A deep frown creased his brows. "Dead? What the hell? I just saw him yesterday. What happened?"

"Car accident."

"Wow." Jake shook his head. There was a lot of it going around today. "Hey, however I can help."

"You worked for Paul until recently, right?"

"Yeah. He's a good dude. Real easy to work for, you know? I mean, he expected me and everyone else to do the work, but he didn't hound us about it. We got our stuff done and everyone was happy."

"Did he ever seem unusually stressed out?"

"No, he was an even keel sort of dude."

Jake's surfer lingo had already grown annoying. I got the feeling he wouldn't be able to tell me much I could use, but I needed to hold out in case he possessed some nugget of wisdom to pass along. My patience grew thin, however. "Did you ever hear him complain about money?"

"No way, not Paul. If he had money problems, none of us heard anything about it."

"Did he talk about his wife at all?"

"Alice? Sure, he talked about her plenty. Most married guys talk about their wives, you know?"

I noticed the absence of a ring on Jake's left hand. "Did Paul ever say anything bad about Alice?" I said.

"Not to me," said Jake. "I never heard him say anything but good things about her. You ever meet Alice?"

"I have."

"She's a good lady, man. A good lady. How's she taking the news?"

"Like you might imagine."

"Gotta be tough."

"Did you know Paul worked overtime for a while? He's been moonlighting downstairs as a technician."

Jake frowned again. "Why would he? Paul did good work here. He had to be making a lot of cash"

"Not enough, apparently. You guys ever socialize outside of work?"

"Here and there, you know? He didn't like to socialize with the folks who worked for him because of the appearance it might create. A bunch of us went out when I got promoted, though. It was pretty epic." He smiled at the memory.

"I'm sure it was," I said. "You know where Paul lived?"

"I never went to his house, but he told me about it," Jake said.

"Then maybe you can answer this for me. Do you know why Paul would be in northeast Baltimore, a good half-hour from his house, late on a Friday night?"

"No, man, I got no idea."

"Any of your coworkers live around there, maybe?"

"I don't know. You think Paul was messing around?"

"I'm only trying to gather as many facts as I can."

"Who hired you?"

"I'm afraid I can't discuss my client," I said. "Did Paul manage a lot of accounts here?"

"I guess," Jake said. "He'd been doing it long enough."

"Lucrative accounts?"

"I don't know. Probably."

"More lucrative than, say, your accounts?"

"You think I killed the dude?" Jake said.

"I'm simply asking questions and exploring possibilities. Any ambitious people here who stand to gain from Paul no longer being on the payroll?"

Jake shook his head. "We're not like that here, man. We're all good people who work together."

"There's ambition in every workplace."

"Not the kind you're talking about. Not here, at least." He paused. "You obviously don't think Paul died in an accident."

"No, Jake, I don't. It means someone is responsible, and I'm trying to find out who." I didn't think Jake lied to me. He remained calm throughout. Of course, his stoner surfer demeanor would probably allow him to remain calm if a terrorist cell stormed the building and strung up the CEO. He would keep saying "dude" and "man" right up until someone shot him to shut him up. I still had problems with Paul Fisher's car accident, but I wasn't going to get any answers about it here. "All right. Thanks for your time, Jake."

"Sure, man, glad to do it. I hope I helped."

We shook hands, and I left without addressing the matter of his helpfulness.

\* \* \*

As I ATE lunch at home, I realized my trip to Digital Sales proved fruitless. I could talk to someone else there Monday, but I didn't think I would learn anything new. Paul Fisher had been a good company man, consistent with his image as a good man in general. Digging up dirt on him would be difficult. Those facts convinced me even more about his accident not being an accident. A good man stumbling into something unsavory made for an easy mark.

Earlier, I decided to look into Paul's coworkers at Digital Sales. I didn't expect my visit to lead to much, but it made for easy due diligence. Anyone can learn the IP address attached to a website. Hackers can run with the information, footprint the network, and figure out how to attack it. Within about ten minutes, I found a file server I could get into without much trouble. From there, I spent about ten more minutes finding and breaking into the human resources department files. I copied all the personnel files to my external hard drive, took care to erase any footprints I may have left, and disconnected from Digital Sales' network.

Going through the personnel files took time. Digital Sales used a database, but the one piece of information I wanted (the address) had been left out. I didn't care about department, service time, and salary. Without the ease of a complete data-base, I had to go through the files one by one. No one lived on Chesterfield Avenue, and only one employee lived within a stone's throw of there: Sally Willis. She lived on Walther Avenue, an easy walk away. The fact by itself didn't mean anything, of course. It may not even be interesting. Then again, it may be. Had I more experience as a detective, I could predict with certainty how much it meant. As it were, I tossed it onto a small pile of curious facts. Perhaps that pile would add up to something more interesting to help me crack the case. I wondered if conventional detectives worked this hard for their epiphanies.

What else could I look into? I ran Alice Fisher's phone records earlier, which is how I discovered her connection to Vinnie Serrano. Maybe Paul's phone records would turn up something similar. The Fishers didn't share a plan even though they had the same cell carrier. The hacks I breached the network with before got me in again now, and I had Paul Fisher's phone records coming out of my printer in a matter of minutes. I collected the printouts and pored over them.

It didn't take long. The night he died, Paul Fisher had two conversations with Vinnie Serrano. Those were two among many.

I needed to pay Vinnie another visit.

Vinnie was a creature of habit: he ate his late lunch at Donna's even on a Saturday. I went on a lark, in the hopes he might be there. I half-expected him to be at his house, huddling with his little baby bookies and going over everyone's college football bets. Instead, Vinnie sat in a remote booth at the back of the restaurant. He had a notebook in front of him, a cell phone in his hand, and a goon at the table. Sam was nowhere to be seen, but considering his size, he could have been hiding under a table waiting to ambush someone.

The goon stared at me as I approached. He didn't stand, probably because it would look too suspicious. He wasn't the same one I tangled with a few nights ago. The personnel swap disappointed me. He kept staring at me as Vinnie talked on the phone. I decided not to wage a staring contest with him. His dyed blond hair made him look silly, which I guessed wasn't the desired effect. A bulge under his sport coat showed he carried a gun. I did, also: the .45 rode holstered at my side, well concealed by my short leather trench coat.

Vinnie hung up and looked at me. A salad sat on the table in front of him, which looked like it had barely been touched. "What brings you by?" he said.

"I'm taking a survey for Legbreakers Incorporated," I said. "We heard you were dissatisfied with your midget goon and traded him in for a larger model."

The new goon looked at Vinnie, who smiled and waved him off. "Sal is another one of my boys." Vinnie picked up his fork and took a bite of the salad. "What can I do for you, C.T.?"

I sat at the booth. "Paul Fisher."

"Who?"

"Come on, Vinnie. We talked about Alice Fisher recently. Paul was her husband."

"Did they divorce?"

I decided to play along. "He's dead."

"Well, I'm sorry to hear that. Are you sorry to hear the news, Sal?" Sal nodded. His lack of a neck made it look like his head rocked back and forth on a hinge. "Sal's sorry to hear it, too."

"Great. I'm sure the two of you will send a wonderful bouquet to the funeral home. Interesting thing, Vinnie—the night Paul Fisher died, he talked to you twice."

"So? Lots of people talk to me and live to tell about it."

"How many don't?"

"I don't kill people, C.T."

"Sure, you have goons like Sal do it for you." Sal narrowed his eyes at me. "No offense," I said to Sal. "I'm sure you're really good at goonery."

Sal balled his hands into meaty fists. Vinnie cleared his throat and shook his head. Sal went back to glaring at me.

"Why do you think I had something to do with Alice's husband's death?"

"I think he knew she was in deep with you. Maybe he threatened to go to the police. A man in your line of work can't have the cops snooping around."

"While what you say is true, you have it wrong. Paul didn't make any threats."

"So you admit you talked to him."

"Of course. I just didn't kill him. Paul knew about Alice's gambling. He'd known about it for a while, actually. He worked overtime for extra money to pay down her debt." It explained a lot of things. "The problem was Alice would always make some stupid bet. Paul made payments, but he didn't . . . knock the principal down much, if you will."

"And he never threatened to go to the cops? Reporting you seems a lot easier than working himself to the bone to pay you forever."

"He was smarter than you think. And you know what, C.T.? I'm smarter than you think, too. You ain't the only one here with a brain. Paul was a regular source of money. Not quite as much money as I'd like, I admit, but he paid when he said he would. I got no problems with people like him. Hell, I wish everyone paid me when they said they would. It would eliminate a lot of the unpleasantness in the job."

"But then you wouldn't have charming fellows like this in your employ." I looked at Sal. He raised his fist at me. "You're going to make a scene, Sal. I'm sure your boss wouldn't appreciate a kerfuffle at his favorite restaurant." Sal glared at me but didn't slam his fist down or take a swing at me. I wondered if he knew what kerfuffle meant. I saw a waitress approach, but she looked at our table and turned back around. Smart girl.

"Here's the bottom line, C.T," Vinnie said. "I don't kill people who are paying me regularly. It's bad for business. I didn't get to be where I am today by doing things bad for business."

I looked at Vinnie. He ate his salad and stared back at me. His gaze was steady. He had always been a good liar, so he could have been lying right now. His story made sense on some level: why would he wipe out a steady source of money? The fact Paul could never really get his head above water on what Alice owed simply meant he would keep paying Vinnie, and keep paying him some more. Killing Paul would have indeed been bad business for Vinnie.

"All right," I said.

"We're good?" Vinnie said.

"I went to school with you, Vinnie. I know you have a good head for business. You wouldn't kill someone who gave you a steady income stream."

"Glad you came to your senses."

I stood. "I'm going to keep looking into Paul Fisher's death. Maybe we'll talk again."

"I don't think we should."

"Is this how you treat all your old friends?" I said.

"Just the ones whose jobs cause them to annoy me," he said.

"Always good to be appreciated. See you around, Vinnie."

"Vincent."

"Yeah, yeah," I said. "Good luck with that."

* * *

VINNIE HAD BEEN AN EASY SCAPEGOAT. He was Alice Fisher's bookie, and by his own admission, didn't like to menace women. I doubted if the same compunction would apply to handsome private detectives. Paul Fisher paid regularly; killing him would be bad for business. Yet Paul talking to Vinnie had to be significant. When I got back home, I looked over his phone records again. Paul had been talking to Vinnie for about two months.

I thought Vinnie told me the truth: Paul worked overtime to make extra money so he could pay down Alice's debt. Alice suspected him of cheating when he had been trying to help her. If only he had told her. No, it wouldn't have mattered. She wouldn't have come to me, but everything else could have unfolded exactly as it did, except Alice Fisher wouldn't have me to save her and figure everything out.

A fine job I had done in the matter. I needed Vinnie Serrano to tell me he hadn't killed Paul Fisher and why. When a choice suspect acquits himself through perfectly good logic, the investigation needs work. I felt out of my element on this one. I still believed what I told my father: hackers were the new detectives. Unfortunately, I found myself doing at least as much traditional detective work as hacking. I was ill-suited for old-school sleuthing. Everything I knew came from novels, movies, and TV shows, and I doubted they painted an accurate picture. Spenser never experienced these problems. I could call Rich for help, but then I would never live it down.

This case was bigger than me and my pride, however. Alice Fisher lost her husband, and while she hadn't hired me to solve the matter of his death, I needed to see it through—for her as much as for myself. At some point, I might need Rich's help. Of course, he recently started working as a detective, but he also had his years as a uniform and sergeant with the BPD, plus his time in the Army. If I had to, I would call him in from the bullpen. For now, I decided to press onward. Pride goeth before the fall, and I have enough pride to goeth before a lot of falls.

If Paul Fisher had been killed, I needed another suspect besides Vinnie and his goon squad. Vinnie had made a convincing argument, but I knew him to be a good liar. Right now, his connection to Paul Fisher was the only thread I could pull. Logical argument or not, I decided to stick with it and see what unraveled when I kept tugging. My decision meant I would need to start watching the people in Vinnie's organization again.

Hopefully, I could manage to avoid getting waylaid by a goon this time.

## CHAPTER 11

MY PHONE RINGING AT QUARTER AFTER EIGHT WOKE ME from a deep sleep. I pawed at it from the comfort of my warm bed, almost knocking it off the nightstand before I finally corralled it. I answered without even checking the caller ID. "Hello?"

"It's Alice."

"Alice . . . what can I do for you?"

"I'm not sure why I'm calling you, really." Her voice sounded like she had been crying recently. "I just . . . I just wanted to talk to someone."

"You must have family."

"I do. I do. It's just . . . we're not exactly close. Do you know anything about planning a funeral?"

"Unfortunately, no."

"Neither do I. Do you know anyone I can call about this sort of thing?"

"Maybe I can have someone call you."

\* \* \*

I ROPED my parents into brunch at Sofi's Crepes, a restaurant in downtown Baltimore. They were eager to hear about the case. I was not eager to share many details about it. However, as long as my mother and father served as my benefactors, I would have to talk to them about my cases, and maybe even get them involved from time to time. If I got breakfast out of the deal here and there, it was at least some compensation.

They beat me to the restaurant and got a spot as they normally do. In this case, our place to eat meant three consecutive seats at the small counter. For once, they hadn't ordered. My mother looked at her watch as soon as I walked in the door. "I'm only four minutes late, Mom," I said. "For me, I'm early."

"Coningsby, you don't live far away," my mother said. "It shouldn't take you more than five minutes."

My father laughed. "June, have you tried to drive any distance up Charles Street? There's a traffic light every five hundred feet. In five minutes, you might be able to go ten blocks, maybe fifteen if you really hit the lights."

"Thanks, Dad," I said. "Maybe Mom would understand if she didn't think driving were something best left to you and the little people."

My mother's face colored, and she frowned like she wanted to scold me. "Coningsby, the fact that I don't drive has nothing to do with this."

"Can we eat?" I said. "I didn't have much breakfast." Unfortunately, Sofi's doesn't open until noon on Sundays, so a crepe at breakfast time is out. Even I wake up too early to consider noon a good time for breakfast.

"Yes, let's eat," my father said. We all looked over the menu at the counter. My mother still looked unhappy, but she would get over it. I went with the bacon and maple syrup crepe. My mother wrinkled her nose at my choice. Both opted for traditional sweet crepes.

"How is the case going, son?" my father said.

"It's certainly gotten interesting." I filled them in on a decent percentage of recent events. Benefactors or not, they didn't need to know everything.

"I can't believe that poor woman lost her husband," my mother said. "This case has certainly drifted away from where it was when you took it."

"You've put your finger on one of the reasons I wanted to see you guys today. Alice called me this morning. She's not close with her family, and she's never planned a funeral before. Mom, I know you've helped some of your friends with theirs. Do you think you could call her and give her some advice?"

"I'd love to," my mother said with a smile. If nothing else, it gave her a feeling of being involved in my case.

"Keep in mind she's not rich. She's on a budget, and I doubt it's big. None of your elaborate ideas."

"Coningsby, I know how to do things cheaply."

"You do?" my father and I said at the same time.

"Of course I do. You boys are just being silly."

I wrote Alice's number on a napkin and slid it along the counter to my mother. "I'll tell Alice you'll call her later," I said. "I'm sure she'll be grateful for the help."

"Are you still looking into her problem?" my father said.

I nodded. "For now, I'm not convinced that Paul's car accident was an accident."

"You think he was murdered?"

"I think the possibility shouldn't be ignored, even though I don't really have a good suspect."

"Maybe you should talk to Richard about it," my mother said.

"No. He'll see it as me coming to him for help with my very first case and never let me live it down. I'll call Rich if I figure enough out to make an arrest. I'm hoping I don't need to call him beforehand."

"You call him if you need to, Coningsby. We want you to help people, and if that means you need some help from Richard, it's all right. The important thing is helping the people who come to you in need."

"I know." And I did realize the situation. For my self-esteem, I had to make sure my pride didn't get dinged if I found myself in a spot where I did need Rich's help.

The fellow behind the counter said our crepes were ready. I got them, and my parents eyed mine suspiciously. They didn't even cut into their own crepes, instead waiting for me to try mine. I thought about keeping them in suspense, but they were picking up the tab, so I cut into it and tried a bite. Considering I had no idea what to expect of a crepe filled with bacon and maple syrup, I found it delicious. The sweetness of the maple syrup offset the saltiness of the bacon. My parents waited until I gave the thumbs up before they started eating their own.

While I ate, I thought of a way I could involve Rich without making it seem like I had gone running to him for help. I resolved to call him after lunch.

* * *

"You're lucky the Ravens have a bye this week," Rich said over the phone.

"It's good to know your pursuit of justice stops for nothing but the NFL," I said.

"If you were a fan, you'd understand."

"I've been gone for three and a half years. Give me some time to soak it all in again since I'm back."

"Whatever," Rich said. "You said you wanted to do a stakeout today?"

"Yes."

"Do you even know what a stakeout is?" I could hear amusement in Rich's tone.

"Yes," I said.

"You know no one serves you a steak, right?"

"You're enjoying this."

Finally, the laughter slipped out. "Of course I am. You don't know the first thing about being a detective, and now you want to have a stakeout." Rich paused. "Wait a minute. Is this related to that woman whose husband wrecked in Herring Run Park?"

"Yes."

"You still think it wasn't an accident?"

"I think there's a decent chance it wasn't, and I want to pursue the idea."

"What aren't you telling me?" Rich said.

"There's an easy way to find out: do the stakeout with me. I'll fill you in on what I know so long as you promise not to charge in and screw everything up."

"Because you have everything under control."

"As a matter of fact," I said, "I do."

Rich chuckled. "This should be interesting," he said. "Since my ride-alongs are over, I have a few days off. I had hoped to spend them more productively, but you know what? This might be better entertainment. Sure, I'll do this stakeout with you. When were you planning on starting?"

"Meet me at my building at seven," I said.

In the meantime, I tried to watch the NFL games on TV. Without the Ravens being involved, though, I couldn't get into the games. I hadn't seen much football during my time in Hong Kong, and while I wasn't the type to paint my face and run around in a jersey, I had been a fan. Maybe I would be again, but I wasn't going to make a lot of progress on my fandom this week.

*  *  *

RICH CAME by sharply at seven o'clock. I insisted he drive, since his unmarked police car looked a lot more official than my Lexus. My car would let us be stealthy, but the police cruiser would get us out of more binds. I didn't plan on landing in the soup but I hadn't planned on trouble in Hong Kong, either.

Armed with two bags of food in a cooler, a thermos of hot tea, and two bottles of water, I rode along and directed Rich where to go. We ended up in Canton Square, about half a block from Margaret Madison's front door. Rich looked at the cooler full of food on the backseat. "Planning on being here a while?" he said.

"You never know," I said.

"Usually, someone will make a food run while they're on a stakeout. So you know in case you ever rope me into this again."

"I figured bringing good food would be better."

"Only you would haul such a huge cooler to a stakeout," Rich said.

"Hey, you can't spell 'stakeout' without 'takeout.'"

Rich rolled his eyes. "Whatever. As long as the food is good, I'm OK with it."

"Do you think I would bring lousy food?" I said.

"No," Rich said. "You're too much of a food snob for mediocre grub."

"And a snob in general, right?"

Rich shrugged. "Hey, you said it, not me." He paused and sighed. "Whose house are we watching, anyway?"

"Her name is Margaret Madison. She's a pretty girl in an ugly business. She works for a bookie."

"Do you know which upstanding gentleman employs her?" said Rich.

"Remember Vinnie Serrano?"

"Hmm." Rich frowned in thought. "The guy you went to school with?"

"The same," I said.

"How does he fit into all of this?" I explained Vinnie's connection to Alice Fisher, what Paul did to pay off his wife's debt, and the fact Paul and Vinnie being in regular contact. "Doesn't mean Vinnie killed Paul," Rich said.

"Of course it doesn't, but it's the only real lead I have, so I'm following it."

"If anything, he doesn't figure for bumping off the husband. The guy was a source of money. Guys in the business of squeezing people for cash don't do things to make the well go dry."

"Vinnie said pretty much the same thing."

"You went and talked to Vinnie?" Rich frowned.

"What?" I said. "We have a history. He's not going to have me shot in public. Besides, I can take care of myself."

"Vinnie probably has thugs working for him."

"At least two. Not counting Miss Madison, who seems to be his principal bet-taker. I saw her get rough with a guy around here—she can definitely hold her own."

Rich watched Margaret Madison's house. We hit a lull in the conversation, so I did the same. One light remained shining on the second floor. I wondered if she had gone out and left a light on when it suddenly went out. A few seconds later, a light on the first floor came on and shined through the bay window. A minute after, Margaret Madison walked out of her house, locked the door behind her, and headed up the street.

"She *is* a looker," Rich said. "Seems an odd choice of business for a pretty girl."

"Not really," I said. "Think about it—men are suckers for girls they want to sleep with. If she can bat her eyelashes or show some cleavage and get a guy to make a bet he wouldn't otherwise make, it's all good for the business."

"Fair point. She could probably talk me into a bet or two."

We watched the house for another few minutes. When it became apparent Margaret wasn't returning quickly, I unlocked my car door. "I'm going to see if I can get into her place," I said. "There might be something useful in there. Keep an eye out. My phone's on vibrate—call me if she comes back, or if someone else comes by."

"You're going to break in?" Rich looked at me as if I had grown a second head.

"I think we'll learn more inside than we will out here in this car."

"Breaking and entering?"

"What if she left the back door unlocked?" I said.

Rich sighed. "And you wonder why I question you and your methods."

"I'm not bound by all the same rules you are."

"B and E is illegal for you, too," Rich said.

I gave Rich a smile. "Like I said, maybe she left the back door unlocked. Then I'm only guilty of entering. Are you going to keep an eye out for me while I'm in there?"

Rich shook his head and sighed again. "Why am I not surprised? Yeah, I'll keep an eye out. Hurry back."

I got out of the car and closed the door behind me. "I hope not to be gone long."

* * *

BALTIMORE IS a city full of rowhouses. Many of them have stood for ages, predating even the families who handed them down. Within the past generation or two, rowhouses got reborn as townhouses, but these very Baltimore structures still use and deserve the old name. Few have anything in their front or back yards except steps, clotheslines, and concrete. A good feature, because limited street parking means most have alleys running behind or alongside them.

Margaret Madison's row featured such an alley behind it. I went into it and looked around. I didn't see anyone milling about or taking an interest in me. Margaret's back gate opened simply by lifting the latch. I ducked so my head didn't stick up over the chain-link-topped stone fence, entered the backyard, and closed the gate behind me. The backyard was mere concrete broken by grass growing in the cracks.

The rear entrance had a storm door covering it. It wasn't locked. I took my special keyring out of my pocket. This was something I couldn't let Rich see because the police would consider it a set of burglar's tools. While in Hong Kong, I learned a lot about burglary and received two identical sets of special keys as a gift. Even though I broke into businesses and a few homes overseas, I could never bring myself to steal. I only wanted to know how to do it.

This lock was an older Schlage Margaret should have replaced a couple years ago. I took my small LED flashlight out of my pocket, turned it on, and held it in my mouth. I got the lock to click open in under a minute using a tension wrench and a slender steel rod. Before rushing in, I waited to hear if anyone stirred inside or if a large dog came thundering in my direction. To be safe, I knocked on the door and waited a few seconds more.

The house sounded empty, so I went in, relocking the back door behind me. I didn't want to turn the lights on because any neighbor who saw Margaret leave would become suspicious. The LED flashlight would have to be enough. I walked into the kitchen, which Margaret hadn't bothered to straighten. Two pans sat on the counter and another two in the sink along with a bunch of used plates and utensils. The dining room looked immaculate by comparison. The table had a white floral print tablecloth atop it. A small china cabinet filled with average dishes stood in the corner of the room.

I continued into the living room. Margaret left the light on in here, so I put my flashlight away. I still didn't know what I was looking for. Margaret may not have been involved with Paul Fisher at all. Even if she had been, she wouldn't leave a smoking gun lying around for some dashing and ingenious detective to find. Maybe I could learn more about her from her house. Maybe there would be something I could use to uncover more about what happened to Paul Fisher. The police would do this with a warrant. They would also have a better idea of what they were looking for.

Margaret had a nice flatscreen TV mounted onto the right-hand wall. A thin bookshelf packed with DVDs sat to the right of it. A glorified TV stand held a DVD player and a game console, along with a few games I never would have fired up, even in my videogame heyday. Her leather couch looked and felt like it came from a department store and was set against the wall opposite the TV. A dark wooden coffee table didn't go with the couch at all but was positioned about a foot away. I sat on the couch and looked at the coffee table. It held a pile of papers and envelopes. I leafed through Margaret's mail. It was mostly bills, the occasional magazine, and some envelopes of indeterminate origin. Judging by the pile, it looked like Margaret routinely tossed the mail there and went through it when the mood struck her. I did the same with my mail.

I stood up to look around some more when I heard the storm door open at the back of the house. "Shit," I said under my breath. Why hadn't Rich called me? I could go out the front door, but my exit would make noise and be suspicious to the neighbors. As quietly as I could, I went toward the rear of the house. The door to the basement was between the dining room and kitchen. I heard laughter coming from the back door as a key went into the lock. I opened the basement door, went down two steps, and pulled it shut behind me. I heard the back door open.

The laughter continued into the kitchen. The back and storm doors both swung closed. "Looks like you need to hire a maid," I heard a male voice say. It sounded an awful lot like Vinnie Serrano.

"Maybe you need to pay me more, then," came Margaret's response.

"Why don't we go upstairs and negotiate your raise?" It figured Vinnie would sleep with her—or at least try. For someone like Vinnie, the good thing about running an illegal business is workplace harassment laws can't be enforced. Vinnie could paw at Margaret all day and what could she do about it?

Right then, Rich decided to call me. My phone vibrated on my hip. I grabbed it and turned it off quickly. They probably heard the noise.

"What was that?" Margaret said.

Yup. They heard it.

## CHAPTER 12

"I KNOW I HEARD SOMETHING," MARGARET SAID.

"I didn't," Vinnie said.

"It sounded like it came from the basement." Footsteps pounded toward the door. I considered going down the stairs. They could be old and creaky, which would give me away even more. Of course, if Margaret opened the door, I had a big problem. Vinnie wouldn't let me talk my way out of this one. Stairs are noisiest and creakiest in their centers. I kept to the side and backed down, trying to be as quiet as possible while still getting to the basement floor at a good pace.

"You probably have a rat. Everyone in Baltimore has rats in their basement."

"I do *not* have rats in my basement," Margaret said, her voice full of indignation. Vinnie had to be careful, or there wouldn't be any negotiation of raises tonight. I got to the bottom of the stairs and crawled off to one side.

"Do you want me to go down there and see what it is?"

A set of wooden walls, open at the rear, framed the staircase. I crawled under the stairs. I didn't see anything I could use to cover myself. If anyone came down, I had to hope they didn't see me. There was plenty of room under the steps, so I situated myself as far into the shadows as I could.

"Could you, Vinnie?"

"Sure."

The door opened. Vinnie flipped on a switch. The stairs were off center in the basement. The bulb was off to one side. Luckily for me, it happened to be the far side. It didn't shed a lot of light on the other side. I could see the ceiling was barely high enough for someone of average height, let alone someone as tall as me. Good thing I had been crouching the whole time.

Vinnie came down. I heard him reach the bottom and walk toward the light. I still couldn't see him; the wooden walls under the stairs blocked my view of most of the basement. I pulled my sweater up over the lower half of my face. The .45 dug into my hip. I hoped I wouldn't need it. Vinnie prowled around the far side of the basement, passed in front of the stairs, and then puttered about on the near side for a minute. "There's nothing here," he said.

"I was sure I heard something."

"I'm telling you there's nothing down here."

"All right, come on up, then. I opened a bottle of wine."

Vinnie bounded up the steps and closed the basement door behind him. He didn't even turn the light off. I let out a breath I had been holding. "Looks like a nice red," Vinnie said when he got back to the kitchen.

"It seemed like a nice way to begin negotiations."

I rolled my eyes. They chatted for a few more minutes as they drank wine. Then they retired to the second floor. At that point, I couldn't hear them anymore. I crawled out from under the stairs and stood up as far as I could. This basement had been made for someone five-eight; I stood six inches too tall for it. Even the gap between the wooden beams didn't allow me to stand straight.

This seemed like a good time to leave. Vinnie and Margaret were two floors above me and obviously distracted. A few moans from up there pierced the silence. Negotiations were going well. I crept up the stairs, got to the basement door, and opened it an inch at a time. It didn't creak. I stepped out into the hallway and closed it behind me. Now I heard the moans louder. I padded toward the back door, opened it, and eased my way outside.

\* \* \*

I walked from the backyard, closed the gate behind me, and entered the empty alley. I kept low so the fence would hide me from prying eyes, only straightening when I hit the street. I jogged back to Rich's car and opened the door.

"I called," he said right away.

"Yeah, after I hid in the basement," I said. "The vibration almost gave me away. If they hadn't been horny, I might be in a bind right now."

"Well, maybe you shouldn't go breaking in to people's houses."

"Maybe you should keep a closer eye on things."

"They hit the alley from the far end. I couldn't be sure it was them. I only knew when they turned the porch light on."

"You could have called and given me a heads up."

Rich shrugged. "I didn't want to worry you for nothing," he said.

I rolled my eyes. "It's almost like you wanted me to get caught."

"Of course not. If there's something to investigate here, I want to see it investigated."

"But . . . ?"

"But there's a right way and a wrong way to go about it."

I looked at Rich. "Tell you what," I said. "I'll keep poking around and making the case my way. You can follow your little police manual and make sure all the Is are dotted and the Ts are crossed. When I figure out what happened before you, I'll call you in to make the arrest. We'll see how strong your principles are then."

"Why would you call me in for the collar?"

"It might help your career. You get to arrest a murderer, or a manslaughterer, or whatever the lawyers figure out that it is. You broke a case your fellow detectives didn't. It'll make you look good. You might even get a commendation."

"You assume you're going to solve this case. Hell, you assume there's a case to be solved."

"Of course I do. I can't work from the assumption this is all too much for me, and I'll never put two and two together."

"You have to roll with the punches." Rich looked at me and frowned. "It's the part you don't understand. You think you can sit behind your computer, maybe venture out here and there, and figure everything out. That's not how it works. You have to hit the streets. You have to put in your time. You can't go out and party every night. You can't sleep in all the time. You'll have days where you can solve every problem and others where the smallest thing trips you up. I don't think you understand the basics."

I nodded. "I believe you've laid out how it is for a lot of very smart people."

"But not for you," Rich said. "You're different. You're special. You don't play by the same rules or have a little police manual."

"Exactly the reason I think I'll be able to do some good work," I said. "I learned a lot in Hong Kong. You and my parents will say I fell in with criminals, and you'd be right. But I learned things over there they don't teach in classrooms or police academies. I don't come from your background. I think I can solve things the police can't because I think differently."

"Like a criminal?"

I shook my head. "Black and white. Everything is black and white with you. Everyone is a sinner or a saint. There's a lot of gray in the world, Rich."

Rich shrugged. "I guess we'll see about you, won't we?"

"If there's a case to be solved here, I'm going to solve it."

"Why are you doing this?"

"Alice hired me."

"Not this case. *This.* Your line of work. Why are you doing it?"

"I told you already," I said. "I think it's something I'm good at."

"No." Rich shook his head. "You're smart enough to be good at a lot of things. Why this?"

"I have some good skills."

"Not buying it."

"What do you want?"

"I want the truth!" Rich said. "Not a dodge and not a joke. Tell me the truth, C.T. Why are you doing this?"

"I'm tired of people thinking Baltimore's just Freddie Gray, or the city they saw on *The Wire*." I sighed. "Warts and all, I love this city. I know what you think of my time in Hong Kong, but I helped people. Americans trying to get out, Chinese nationals looking for family members the government didn't want them to find. I made a difference for them, Rich. I can do it again."

"Now we're back to your time in China."

I let out a slow breath. This conversation bumped against the edges of my patience. "You may think what I did in China was bullshit. Great. You're entitled to your opinion. There are people who would tell you you're wrong."

"We have police to help people," Rich insisted.

"No. You're handcuffed by the commissioner, the city council, the mayor . . . a lot of people. At best, you might not be part of the problem."

"But you're part of the solution."

"I'm trying to be," I said.

"Good luck," Rich said.

"You know, I don't think I want to do this stakeout anymore."

Rich looked at me and shook his head again. "You haven't changed a bit. You needed to learn a few things when you graduated college and took your entitled ass overseas. The shame of it is, despite all your talk, you still need to learn the same things now. I really shouldn't be surprised. Why would I expect you to change?"

I grabbed my cooler from the backseat and my thermos from the floor in front of me. "You can keep the bottled water."

"Don't you want a ride back to your building?"

"I'll get an Uber." I closed the door to Rich's car and walked up the street, away from Margaret Madison's house. After about two blocks, I took out my phone and summoned a ride.

* * *

A FEW MINUTES after I walked inside and put the food into the refrigerator, my cell phone rang. I looked at the number; it was Jessica Webber. I let it ring a couple more times before I answered. "What do you want, Jessica?"

"Wow, aren't we in a good mood?" she said.

"Not especially."

"Can I come by? I want to talk a little after . . . the other night."

"If you like, sure." I really didn't feel like seeing her, but it sounded like she wanted to talk about things. Whatever she said, I had no intention of apologizing to her. She needed to have some respect for a grieving widow.

"OK. I'm not far away. I'll be by soon." It felt like Jessica was stalking me. She showed up unannounced two nights ago, and now she was nearby on a Sunday night, only a few minutes after I returned. I pondered the problem and decided there are worse fates one can suffer than having a sexy, uninhibited female reporter for a stalker. If this became my cross to bear, I would take it up every day.

A few minutes later, I heard a knock at the door. I looked through the peephole to be certain and saw Jessica. I opened the door and beckoned her in. "Thanks," she said. "I wasn't sure how eager you'd be to talk to me after the other night."

"I admit you're not high on my list of favorite people right now."

"I'm a reporter, C.T. I go after the stories. It's what I've been trained to do. We all have. We want to get the story before the other guys do. If it's a big enough story, every news station and paper in town will be there. But when you're the first one on the scene, that's a good feeling."

"And the hell with what the people you're reporting on feel?" I said.

She shook her head. "No. No, I'm not usually like that. I think I got caught up in the surprise factor. I mean, you had a case of possible adultery, and now the husband is dead. And you didn't think he cheated."

"He didn't."

"Then it's very surprising he ended up dead. Admit it, that's a compelling story." I nodded. "And since I'm chronicling your first case, I think I got caught up in breaking a story." Jessica paused and sighed. "The reality is, I don't want to shove a mike and a camera into the face of a grieving widow. I know I came across like some heartless newshound, but that's really not who I am."

"Good to know."

She smiled. "I think it took you cursing at me and slamming the door in my face for me to see it." She didn't sound like she angled for an apology there. "So thank you for that."

"I don't think I've ever been thanked for something rude before." I smiled back. "You're welcome."

"Can I ask you a question, though?" Jessica said. "Off the record."

I said, "sure."

"Who did you lose?"

"What?"

"When you were yelling at me, you said you weren't sure if I ever lost someone I loved. I guess I've been lucky in that respect, but I haven't. I get the feeling you have, though."

I looked at Jessica and let out a slow, deep breath. I kept looking at her, and she simply returned my gaze, not saying anything, giving me whatever time I needed. "My sister," I finally said.

"What happened?"

"She was nineteen, and in college at Penn. I was in my junior year of high school. She was home for a long weekend." I paused and collected myself. I couldn't even remember the last time I told someone about her. Why was I telling Jessica now? She must have picked up on my trepidation.

"If you don't want to say, it's OK," she said. "I'm sure it's not an easy subject."

"It's not." I took another slow breath. "The doctor said it was a heart defect. Something they'd never found before. They didn't find it when she was a baby. Medical technology improved a lot in nineteen years, but not enough to save her." There really wasn't any more to say, and I don't think I could have spoken another syllable had there been. I wiped at my eyes.

"What was her name?"

"Samantha," I said after a few seconds. "Samantha Elizabeth Ferguson."

Jessica got up and sat on the arm of my recliner. She patted my shoulder, and I offered her a small smile. I didn't cry, but I knew it would come soon if I kept talking about my sister. It had been almost twelve years, but I never really got over it. My grades slipped after Samantha died, and my parents sent me to see a couple of different therapists, but none of them delivered the breakthrough their boasts and diplomas implied. Eventually, I rallied and finished the school year strong, but I carried her death with me every day. It wasn't something I talked about. Jessica had a habit of getting me to say more than I wanted.

"I can stay, if you want me to," she said.

"I'll be OK," I said.

"You sure?"

"Yeah. It's been years, Jessica. It's still raw, but it's not a gaping wound anymore. Go on, I'll be OK."

She stood, looked down at me, and smiled. "You're deeper than you appear, Mr. Ferguson."

"And you have a bigger heart than you show, Miss Webber."

She gave me another pat on the shoulder and walked out. I sat in the recliner and took another deep breath. After I went down the hall and got ready for bed, my cell phone rang again. I didn't recognize the number, which I figured could happen often in my chosen profession, but I answered anyway.

"C.T.?" The feminine voice sounded familiar.

"Yes, who's this?"

"Gloria Reading. We met at the art show the other night."

Now I pictured a face and a body—and what a body it was —to go with the come-hither voice. "I remember. How are you?"

"I'm good. Are you working tonight?"

"Unfortunately."

"That's too bad. I was hoping to see you."

"I don't think I'd be great company tonight, Gloria."

"Your case?"

"Yeah."

"This is more than you signed up for, isn't it?"

"You have no idea."

"I'm a night owl," Gloria said. "If I'm not going to see you tonight, let's talk a while. I'm feeling a little lonely."

"Yeah, I am, too." In a city of over six hundred thousand people, and with the closest thing I've had to a brother working beside me, I still felt lonely. Welcome back to America, Mr. Ferguson.

"Then I'm glad I called," said Gloria.

"Me, too," I said.

*CHAPTER 13*

Gloria and I talked for over an hour. She sounded like someone who never should have been lonely but still suffered the fate often. I understood. She didn't come across well to a lot of people. Her looks would open plenty of doors and start a ton of conversations, but there would be no depth to them. She needed someone who understood her, and she thought she found said someone in me. Maybe she did. We would have time to explore the idea later. For now, I had a case to work and a murderer to catch. More immediately, I had breakfast to make after going to bed late and waking up hungry.

I pondered what trouble to get myself into today. I knew Vinnie was diddling the help, but I didn't know how to use the information. If I told him, he might deduce Margaret Madison in fact heard something in her basement and the specific something in fact was an old friend turned nosy private investigator.

I still didn't know what to make of Vinnie's meteoric rise from simple bookie to advanced bookie. He needed the blessing, if not the backing, of Tony Rizzo. I hadn't seen Tony since before I went overseas. He had been friends with my parents for as long as I could remember, and before his rise to power, they actually loaned him part of the money he needed to open

*Il Buon Cibo.* I would pay Tony a visit at his restaurant at lunchtime. Before that, however, I resolved to eat breakfast, take a run through Fells Point, and get a shower.

\* \* \*

IL BUON CIBO was one of many Italian restaurants in Little Italy. Sabatino's enjoyed the reputation and tourist business, but people who knew Little Italy ate at places like Chiapparelli's and *Il Buon Cibo.* Tourists be damned. Let them eat Sabatino's. I found a parking spot on the street about two blocks from the restaurant, paid the machine, and walked to the front door.

The maitre d' only worked the dinner crowd. I walked past the sign asking me if I could please wait to be seated. I could not. Tony always had a table in the back. It was the closest to the fireplace and isolated from those nearby by about ten feet. He employed a goon to sit close just in case, and the brutish bodyguard stood when I approached. Tony looked up from his salad, his eyes fell on me, and he did a table take. "Jesus Christ," he said.

"I flew back," I said. "He could have walked across the ocean."

Tony got up, held his arms out, and we embraced. "It's good to see you again, C.T."

"You, too, Tony."

"I heard you got yourself in a little hot water overseas."

"You hear a lot of things."

"A man in my line of work likes to stay connected."

"What about you?" I said. "You're looking good. A little thinner since the last time I saw you. What happened to your legendary Italian appetite?"

Tony snorted. "Fucking doctors. I need to watch what I eat now. I told the doc I always watch what I eat—from the plate to the fork to my mouth." He laughed, like he probably laughed every time he told the story, and I gave a chuckle to be polite. When the crime boss laughs, the minimum response is a snicker. "But enough about me. What happened to you in China?"

I knew Tony wouldn't carry tales, but I didn't want to tell him everything. I let him know the big details about the hacking and piracy ring, leaving out the burglary, self-defense, and learning the language. He shook his head when I finished. "Fucking gooks couldn't be rid of you quick enough by the sound of things," he said.

My thirty-nine months away from America had dulled my memory of conversations with Tony. He always had an ethnic slur ready for non-Italians. I let it slide. "They made it clear they didn't want to see me again. I assured them the feeling was mutual."

"Your parents must have been pissed."

I smirked. "You hit the nail on the head."

"You doing anything with yourself these days?"

"I am." I told him the conditions my parents imposed on me when I got back. "So I'm using what I learned overseas and working as a private investigator."

For the first time, Tony's happy demeanor cracked. "You? A PI?"

"It's a living," I said.

"I can't believe it." Tony frowned. "I've known you since you were an infant. After all this time, we gonna be at odds?"

"I don't see why we would, Tony. I'm not out to hassle you. What you do is your business."

He nodded. "All right. What brings you by?"

"Vinnie Serrano."

"What about him?" Tony still frowned and regarded me

skeptically now. A man like him didn't spend a lot of time talking to people in my line of work.

"He's a . . . person of interest in the case I'm working on. When I knew him, he was a nickel-and-dime bookie. Now he's a bookie with muscle, and I have a hunch he's looking to add 'loan shark' to his business cards next. I would imagine he needs your blessing for something like he's into now."

Tony picked up his glass of red wine and swirled it. "Vinnie and I are acquainted," he said after some consideration. "He's not one of my boys. He's only an asset. What do you mean he's a person of interest?"

"He has some role in the case. I'm not sure what it is yet. But my client is also one of his clients."

"And you're here checking up on him."

"Again on the head of the nail, yes."

"You always were thorough. You wanna stay for lunch? It's on me."

"Sure, I'd like some lunch."

Tony snapped his fingers, and a waitress rushed to our table with a menu. My run had given me an appetite, so I ordered gnocchi with meat sauce. Tony suggested a basil pesto, but I stuck with my first choice. We chatted for a while before my meal came and while I ate. It felt good to catch up with Tony, but he got a little frosty once he learned I became a PI. I couldn't blame him; it still made me a little frosty to think about it. While we ate, Tony asked about my parents. "I haven't spoken to them since you got back," he said.

"Why not?"

"Hell, I don't know. We never talked every day or anything. It's probably nothing. Old friends can go weeks and months without talking and things are still the same when they pick it up again, right?"

"Right."

Despite his history with my family and me, I knew Tony wouldn't hesitate to send some muscle after me if I turned out to be bad for business. Considering I still had to deal with the threat of Vinnie and his own goons, I hoped to avoid any new trouble.

\* \* \*

LESSON FROM LUNCH with the mob boss: I could get to Vinnie if necessary. If he enjoyed Tony's protection, the problem would have been much harder. While I pondered this, my cell phone rang. It was Alice Fisher. Maybe she needed more funeral-planning advice. "Alice, how are you? Did my mother help you?"

"Yes, she did." I heard Alice's voice brighten from its dreariness of the past few days. "I don't think she understood the idea of doing a funeral on a budget, but she was a great help. That's part of the reason I'm calling, actually."

"Do you need me to do something?" I said.

"Come to the viewings today?" she said. "The first is from two until four, and the second is from seven until nine."

"I can be there, but I'm wondering why you want me to be. I'm sure you have friends and family you can lean on."

"I do. It's just . . . I'm worried Vinnie or one of his cronies might show up." She sighed. "I don't think he's that ghoulish, but . . ."

"But you owe him a lot of money."

"Yeah."

"Honestly, I don't think Vinnie is quite the type, either, but if you want me to be there, I will. Tell me where the viewings are."

"Ruck's Funeral Home in Towson," she said. "You know where it is?"

"I do," I said. "I'll see you there at two."

\* \* \*

PAUL FISHER's two o'clock viewing was somber and uneventful. I met Alice there a few minutes before two. She introduced me to her parents and her sister. When they asked who I was, she said I was a private investigator friend of Paul's who decided to make sure his car accident was truly accidental. I didn't think they liked her explanation. It raised more questions than it answered, and it was more than I would have told someone. They didn't press for any further details, but I figured they would grill Alice later.

I didn't see any of Paul's coworkers at the early viewing. Several of Alice's stopped by, including her boss. He frowned at me every time he saw me but never said anything. Most of Paul's family made an appearance; I heard the rest of them would arrive in time for the late viewing. Alice introduced me to Paul's relatives as her friend who happened to be a private eye. She really needed to learn about oversharing. I hoped the families didn't swap stories about the dashing stranger in the expensive suit. If they did, I hoped they confined their conversations to how I was the best-dressed man in the room. Even the funeral director wore something off the rack.

Between the early and late viewings, I went home and grabbed some carry-out for dinner. While I ate, Rich called. I considered not answering the phone, but snubbing him would have been juvenile, even for me.

"I wondered if you'd pick up," Rich said.

"Mystery solved. Sure you're not already a detective?"

"Are you still working the case today?"

"I am." I told Rich about the viewings.

"Do you think anything will happen at the evening one?"

"I doubt it," I said, "but I guess you never know."

"Well, it's a Monday night, and I still have a couple days before I go back to work. Want another pair of eyes?"

"If you're willing to come, sure."

"All right, I'll see you there."

"Try not to look too much like a cop, if you can help it."

"I don't have your wardrobe," Rich said, "but I'll see what I can do."

When I got to Ruck's for the evening viewing, Rich arrived a few minutes before. His suit looked off the rack without appearing too cheap, and if I hadn't known he was a cop, I might not have guessed him for one. He looked at me and shook his head. "Armani?" he said.

"How'd you know?" I said.

"I know you. You get it recently?"

"After college. It still fits like the day I got it."

Alice's family was there again. They all looked at me a little suspiciously, but no one ventured close to talk to me. Paul's folks tried their best not to look at me, which I found puzzling. If they believed Alice, I was her friend who had resolved to look into their relative's death. Why avoid me? I hoped I wouldn't have to talk to them about Paul and Alice at some point.

As I scanned the room, I stood near Alice. She talked to a few more well-wishers I recognized from her job. When someone from Paul's side of the family approached her, I moved in a little closer. The man was Paul's uncle Randy, and he and Alice exchanged pleasantries and condolences. She introduced me as her friend the detective, and we shook hands. "Do you think Paul's death wasn't an accident?" he said in a quiet voice.

"I believe in being thorough," I said. "I'm only making sure the police don't overlook anything."

"Paul was a good driver. He rarely drank." His comment

reminded me I wanted to see the ME's report. Anytime there is a one-car accident, the police suspect intoxication, and with good reason. I remembered hearing some chatter about it at the accident scene. The ME would have sent Paul's blood out for a toxicology report, and the results would be included with his final report. After tonight's viewing, I would try and find it on the BPD's network.

"Why has Paul's family been avoiding me?" I whispered to Alice.

"I don't know," she said.

"Do you think he told them?"

"Told them what?"

I gave her a look one should refrain from giving widows. "Why he worked overtime."

"Oh." She shook her head. "No, I don't think so. Paul was close with his family, but we kept our business between us."

"Did your family know?"

"I never told them."

"They could lend you money."

"I wouldn't trouble them for that," she said. I couldn't pursue it any further because more guests made their way to Alice. Among them, I recognized a few of Paul's coworkers, including Jake Driscoll and Sally Willis. I wondered if Jake left his surfboard tethered outside. Neither of them said anything when they saw me. I gave Alice space to greet the well-wishers. Rich sipped a soda toward the back of the room. I saw Sal walk in through the door right next to where Rich stood. When Rich looked at me, I nodded at Sal. Rich gave a nod back and followed him.

Vinnie sent someone after all. He said he hadn't put undue pressure on Alice because he didn't want to have his guys beat up a woman. Why send someone like Sal to the funeral home, then? If Alice noticed him, she didn't give any indication. She may not have known him. Sal made no move toward Alice while people gathered around her. He circles the room and looked at the three picture collages of Paul setup on stands throughout.

A few minutes later, Alice had a free moment to take a breath. She wiped her eyes and sighed. Sal took the moment to walk near her. I moved closer, and Rich stayed near him on the other side. Sal looked at me and smirked. I glanced at Alice. She didn't react; either she didn't know Sal, or she decided to play it cool in front of friends and family.

"Alice, how are you?" Sal said.

"I'm doing as good as I can," she said. "Are you one of Paul's friends?"

"Not exactly. Vinnie wanted you to know he sends his condolences, and he'll be in touch."

I watched the color drain from Alice's face. Her knees wobbled. I took her arm, walked her to a nearby chair and sat her down. "Stay with her," I whispered to Rich as I passed him. Sal didn't move, though he watched me with an amused smile.

"A man can't come and pay his respects?" Sal said.

"You're not here to pay your respects," I said. "You're here to intimidate Alice. At her husband's viewing. Mission accomplished, asshole."

"I don't think you should say those things in a funeral home. It's disrespectful."

"Your presence is disrespectful. Why don't you leave?"

"You gonna walk me out?"

"If it means we'll be rid of you, yes."

"Let's go." Sal started toward the door, and I followed. Alice watched us walk past. Two family members huddled around her, along with Rich, who sat right behind. We walked from the viewing room into the hallway and out the back door of Ruck's into the rear parking lot. A few people stood outside and smoked, while a few others made toward their cars.

We had walked more than halfway into the lot when Sal turned around and threw a wild haymaker. I had been expecting him to do something and stepped to the side as the punch whistled past me. Sal looked confused when he hit only air, and I capitalized on the moment by kicking him in the side. He staggered back a step, then charged at me again.

I expected another punch, but Sal grabbed me in a bearhug my ready forearm couldn't block. Complicating matters, I now had my left arm pinned against me. Sal squeezed, and I groaned as the pressure built on my ribs. My right hand remained free, and I used it to hammer Sal in the nose. It snapped with a satisfying crunch on the second hit. Blood poured out of Sal's nose, and his grip slackened. I got my left arm loose and boxed Sal's ears. He took a step back and covered his face. I kicked him in the groin.

Sal doubled over, now protecting his family jewels. I gave him a quick snap kick to his damaged face to straighten him back up, then kicked him in the stomach without putting my foot down. Sal staggered back a few steps and reached inside his jacket. I sprinted the distance between us and grabbed his wrist when he got it free from his coat. He had a nine millimeter in his hand and tried to bring it to bear. Sal was bigger than I and no doubt stronger. This would require leverage, which I learned plenty about in China. I barred Sal's elbow and twisted his wrist until he shouted in pain.

"Let go of the gun," I said, keeping the hold. He didn't let go. "Let it go, or I'll break your arm."

"All right, all right," Sal said, wincing through clenched teeth.

He dropped the gun. It rattled against the asphalt. Sal

glowered at me. I let go of his wrist, then kicked him in the face and knocked him out. Then I called 9-1-1.

* * *

WE FOUND a couple of witnesses for the altercation in the parking lot. Both were outside smoking during the fisticuffs portion of the evening. One was a funeral home worker and the other a mourner at a different viewing. They backed up my story of what happened. Rich stayed with Alice while I gave my statement to two of Baltimore County's finest. We managed not to disrupt the viewing, but the police cars and ambulance drew the attention of people leaving the room, as well as those arriving late. Onlookers gathered despite the best efforts of the cops.

The ambulance took Sal away, a couple marked cars followed it, and two others drove off in the other direction. Word of the parking lot incident must have spread because everyone looked at me when I walked back in. The blood on my right hand and sleeve from Sal's broken nose gave it away.

"You'd think these people had never seen a guy win a fight in a parking lot before," I said to Rich.

"You didn't have to fight him," Rich said.

"He threw the first punch."

"What happened to him?" Alice said.

"If Sal comes around to menace you again, he'll have to breathe through his mouth. More than he usually does."

"Do you think Vinnie sent him?"

"I don't think he's smart enough to show up on his own," I said.

"Now what?"

I hadn't thought much about consequences. "Now Vinnie

knows I beat up his goon," I said. "I'm not sure what he's going to do now."

"Do you think he's going to come after you?"

"Maybe, but I'm more concerned with him coming after you. Sending someone like Sal to an event like this isn't a good sign."

"Neither is sending him to the hospital," Rich said. "Sal may not have been here to start trouble with anyone. He was probably only delivering a message. Someone else will deliver it next time, and it probably won't be so friendly."

"So I should let Sal beat me up next time?" I said.

"I think Sal only got physical because you were here. If you hadn't been, he probably spooks Alice and leaves."

"Right. It's Batman's fault the Joker is a criminal." Good rule in life: when the opportunity arises to compare yourself to Batman, take it.

"Should I expect another visit from Vinnie's people?" Alice said.

"I think so," said Rich.

"I'm sure it gets worse from here," I said.

CHAPTER 14

RICH AND I STRATEGIZED AFTER THE LATE VIEWING. WE both followed Alice home to make sure she arrived safely. When we left her house, we went to a coffee shop and tried to strategize the next move. Rich could draw on practical experience with this sort of thing, whereas I went with a combination of instinct and whatever I learned watching police shows and movies. I didn't mention the second part to Rich because I knew he would laugh me out of the coffee shop.

"We could go after Vinnie," he said. "He's running a book-making business and maybe more. His activities are illegal."

"True," I said. "It's not a lot, though. If he's behind Paul Fisher's death, you probably won't find out just because you popped him for running a book."

"Al Capone went down for tax evasion."

"Vinnie isn't Al Capone. Besides, Capone might have gone down, but what about the families of the people he killed? They didn't get any closure."

"Now you're concerned about Paul Fisher's family?" Rich said.

"Alice hired me," I said. "I'm sticking with the case because of her."

Rich nodded. "All right. I'm still not convinced of your altruism, but the attempt is encouraging."

"Fair enough. I want to talk to Vinnie again. He's going to see this thing through because Alice owes him a lot of money. Maybe we can give him enough rope to hang himself along the way."

"Let's hope he doesn't hang Alice first," Rich said, frowning.

I raised my cup to his sentiment.

\* \* \*

ONCE I GOT HOME, I looked for the ME's report. The BPD's network still accepted my computer as one of its own. Before I left for Asia, the BPD modernized and put their case files online. The benefits were obvious, and the only downside was the chance of hackers getting in, which is why they secured the system (or tried to). The average hacker didn't care enough to risk getting caught breaking into the network merely to read whatever case file he or she deemed important.

The police updated Paul Fisher's case file today. The notes mentioned the official cause of death was trauma from a car accident, which meant the ME's report was finished. I couldn't find it, though. It wasn't attached to the case file, and I didn't see it by browsing. Did the ME maintain a separate network I would have to crack? Did someone at the BPD want to keep the ME's report from me? Rich would have told me if he did it. I think.

After a few more minutes of not finding the report, I gave up. I needed to visit the ME's office in person. I called the office and learned Dr. Sellers wouldn't be back on duty until tomorrow afternoon. The delay gave me a chance to talk to Vinnie earlier in the day. He might tell me to buzz off, but I hoped he would listen to reason. He would have back in the day, but the intervening years changed him. He became more of a calculating businessman, one who had goons working for him and might be quite averse to someone—even an old friend —trying to reason with him when a lot of money was on the line.

I felt obliged to try.

* * *

IN THE MORNING after taking a run and eating breakfast, I called Vinnie. "What the hell do you want?" he said.

"Good morning to you, too," I said.

"Cut the crap, C.T. What do you want? I got a guy in the hospital because of you."

"Send a better guy next time."

"Fuck you."

"He picked the fight, Vinnie."

"I don't care. I'm hanging up now."

"Vinnie, wait," I said. "We need to talk. Whatever it is, this thing is way beyond us and out of control. I think we need to figure something out before it gets too bad. Before someone important gets hurt."

"You don't think Sal was important?"

"If he had been, you wouldn't have sent him alone yesterday."

Vinnie didn't say anything for a few seconds. I thought he might have hung up on me until he finally said, "Fine. Where do you want to meet?"

"Meet me at the Field at one o'clock," I said. "I'll bring lunch."

"You coming alone?" Vinnie said.

"Yes. You should, too."

"All right. One o'clock. This is the last time I'm going out on a limb for you like this."

"I'll make sure lunch is good, then," I said.

\* \* \*

VINNIE and I both went to Roland Park Middle School. Ages ago, students had dubbed the athletic field there "The Field," instead of whatever snooty donor-sponsored name it had. When I got there a few minutes after one o'clock, Vinnie sat in the bleachers. I didn't see anyone else around. Maybe Vinnie came alone after all. I carried a gun under my jacket, and I presumed he did, too.

I sat next to Vinnie in the second row of the bleachers. His black Oxfords rested on the front row. Vinnie came in dress pants and a nice coat. I felt underdressed in my jeans and Timberlands. He shot me a disdainful glance, then looked down at the bag of food. "Where'd you go?" he said.

"Nick's Fish House," I said.

Vinnie smiled. "You always knew where to eat well."

"Still do."

"What'd you bring?"

"Two shrimp salad sandwiches and two orders of coleslaw."

"No fries?"

"They use peanut oil," I said.

"You remembered," he said.

I reached into the bag and tossed Vinnie a sandwich. "You were the only kid in school with a peanut allergy, Vinnie. People couldn't bring peanut butter and jelly sandwiches because of you. How could I forget?"

"Thanks for reminding me." He unwrapped the sandwich and took a bite. "You never brought PB and J, did you?"

"Are you kidding? My mother thought servants ate such

stuff. I used to love it when I went to friends' houses and their parents would fix us PB and J."

"No shit?" Vinnie took another bite of the sandwich. I set out both containers of coleslaw, two forks, and a pile of napkins weighted down with two bottles of water. "This is good. I haven't been to Nick's in a while."

"I've only been twice since I got back." I took a bite of my sandwich. Nick's had great shrimp salad because of two factors: large chunks of shrimp and liberal use of Old Bay seasoning, a local favorite whose popularity was confined mostly to Maryland because my state is surrounded by Philistines.

We ate in silence for a few more minutes. Both of us devoured our sandwiches, drank some water, and started on the coleslaw before we talked again. "So what do you want to talk about?" Vinnie said.

"What do you think?" I said.

"I think you still have it in your head I killed Paul Fisher."

"The idea occurred to me."

"I told you it would be bad business. I don't do bad business."

"Sending Sal to the funeral home was a nice touch," I said.

"I wanted to pay my respects," Vinnie said.

"If what you say is true, you would have come in person instead of sending a goon."

"I'm a busy man."

"I'm sure you are."

"Look, I don't want to shake Alice down," said Vinnie. "She's been through a lot recently, but she owes me money, and I think she should be able to pay it off."

"Why should she be able to pay it off all of a sudden?" I said.

"Her husband died. He must have had life insurance."

I hadn't thought about whether Paul Fisher owned life

insurance and if it paid any kind of reasonable sum upon his death. Maybe Alice could be free of Vinnie once and for all. Why hadn't she mentioned it? Why did she turn pale when Sal talked to her? She had been through a lot, but if her husband's life insurance paid for the funeral expenses, she should have made the association. "I'll talk to her about it," I said.

"I think you've done enough already," Vinnie said. "Alice is burying her husband tomorrow. I'll leave her alone. Afterward, though, she's going to get a reminder she owes me money. Her husband isn't making regular payments anymore."

"I'm sure you'll offer her a sweetheart deal."

"I'm a businessman. Everything is negotiable." Vinnie looked at me. "You want to be such a fucking white knight, why don't you pay her tab?"

"She needs to learn people aren't going to bail her out," I said. "Her husband working overtime to help her is one thing. Me writing her a check to cover her problems doesn't teach her anything." I also didn't have a spare thirty grand, but Vinnie didn't need to know my finances, even though I knew he could deduce it.

"Yeah, you've always been about people learning for themselves. Your lessons all came the hard way."

My sister's death flashed into my mind. I thought about punching Vinnie in his very punchable face, but that wouldn't help Alice. I took a breath and said, "I've learned a few. Besides, this isn't about me. This is about Alice and what you plan on doing."

"I plan on getting my money. So far, I've been nice and patient. I can't keep being a nice guy forever. If she doesn't want to pay up, other clients might get the idea they can skip their payments, too. I can't allow it."

"So your midget enforcer is going to pay her a visit after the funeral?" I said.

"Maybe I'll send Sal again. Maybe I'll bring in someone new. I'm going to get my money. You should stay out of it. I don't want to hurt you, but my people can get . . . zealous when they're making collections. Anyone in the way tends to get injured."

"I'm not going to abandon Alice."

Vinnie shrugged. "I can't guarantee your safety, then," he said.

"Thanks for the threat. At least I know to look under my table for midgets with guns."

"Don't take Sam so lightly."

"The cops know your business, Vinnie. I came here to try and make sure it doesn't get to be *their* business."

Vinnie frowned. "You should keep the cops away from me," he said.

"Why?" I said.

"My people have instructions to get the money from Alice and some other clients if I get arrested. Without me to keep them in check, things could get ugly. I don't think it's the way you want it to go."

I shook my head and looked out at the lacrosse field. Grass always a vibrant green in season now lay mottled with brown where the dirt poked through. "We made a lot of plays on this field, you and me," I said.

"We did." Vinnie cracked a smile. "I was always the better player."

"The hell you were."

"I scored more goals, C.T. Here and in high school. You can look it up."

"You're ten months older. Didn't you read Malcolm Gladwell and his theory about early birthdays?"

"They stopped being important by eighth grade."

Vinnie could have his theory; I would stick with Gladwell.

"I had more assists," I said.

"Assists ain't on the scoreboard," said Vinnie.

"Not many goals come without assists."

"And now your giving nature manifests itself again with your devotion to Alice."

So much for the memories. "Yeah," I said.

We lapsed into silence again. I had almost finished my coleslaw. Vinnie worked on the last bit of his sandwich. He looked at the lacrosse field again, then glanced sideways at me. "You know the difference between you and me?" he said.

"How much time you got?" I said.

He smirked. "You have to be the good guy. It's why I never let you work for me in college."

"You assume I would've wanted to."

"Whatever. I didn't want you to. No matter what you're doing, you always have to throw something in to remind everyone you're a nice guy after all."

"It sure beats being a prick and menacing women," I said.

"How's it working out for you?" Vinnie said. "I'm guessing you burned through most of your money overseas or you wouldn't be doing this job and bothering me now. Your parents were always nice. I know they used to want you to be involved in their charity shit. They put you up to this?"

I forgot how smart Vinnie was. "Doesn't matter why I'm doing this," I said. "I'm trying to do what's best for Alice." I put my coleslaw container in the empty food bag, downed the last of my water, and added the empty bottle to the bag. "I hoped we could come to an arrangement."

"I make arrangements good for business."

"I'm sure you do. You're on trash detail. I don't care if that arrangement is good for your business or not. See you around, Vinnie."

"Vincent!"

"Yeah, well. Throw the fucking trash away when you're finished, *Vincent*." I got up and walked away.

* * *

NOT LONG AFTER I got back from my chat with Vinnie, Rich dropped by. I keep the front door locked and made a point to double-check it after Vinnie's threat. When Rich knocked, I took my .45 to the door with me. "I take it your chat with Vinnie didn't go well," Rich said, eyeing the gun when he walked in.

"Not particularly, no," I said. "He wants his money from Alice, and he's going to get it. She's safe until the funeral tomorrow, at least. Afterward, he's going to try and collect."

"And she can't pay."

"Vinnie thinks she can. Paul should have had life insurance."

"Even if he did, the payout isn't instantaneous. The insurance company could do their own investigation if they think Paul's death was suspicious. They might wait for the police investigation to end."

"Vinnie doesn't strike me as too patient right now."

"What are you going to do, then?" Rich said.

"I don't know," I said. "I can't watch Alice around the clock."

"Do you think Vinnie is going to send someone after her?"

"Maybe not right away. I'm sure someone will contact her, but I don't think he has breaking her leg on his list of goals for the week."

"Have you said anything to Alice yet?" Rich said.

"No," I said. "I need to talk to her but this is just such a bad time. She had two viewings yesterday and has a funeral tomorrow. I don't want to burden her with things Vinnie might do."

"She deserves to know."

"So I'll tell her . . . after the funeral."

"What are you going to do in the meantime?"

"Well, I'd love to read the ME's report, but I can't find it anywhere. It's not in Paul Fisher's case file."

Rich frowned and shook his head. "You read his case file?"

"Rich, don't insult me. Of course I read the case file. I also wanted to read the ME's report. Where can I find it?"

"They're kept on a separate network. You have to authenticate to it separately."

I shrugged. "I'll figure it out eventually."

"Maybe you shouldn't be poking around on the police networks," Rich said.

"Maybe you should share information with me," I said.

"If I thought you were in this for the long haul, maybe I would."

"You still think this is all about getting back into my parents' money, don't you?"

"Isn't it?" Rich said, folding his arms across his chest.

"At first," I admitted. "Now I'm invested in this case. I want to see it through. You know I don't quit something when I start it."

"Yeah. You're still a hacker. Being in a Hong Kong prison didn't teach you anything."

I rolled my eyes. "Whatever. I'm going to talk to the ME. Show yourself out when you've finished feeling self-righteous." I put my coat on and started toward the front door.

Rich grabbed my arm. "The ME isn't going to help you."

I looked at Rich's hand, but he didn't let go. "Why, because you talked to him and told him not to?"

"No, because his office is a resource for official business," he said.

"I'm on official business. I have my license and everything. Want to see it?"

"I want to see you do the right thing for the right reasons."

"Then let go of me and give me the chance," I said.

"You're not off to a good start so far."

I grabbed Rich's wrist, but he pulled back before I could do anything. He made a grab at my arm, which I avoided, and then I returned the favor. Then we both realized what we were doing. He put his hand up and so did I.

"I'm doing good work," I said. "I don't give a damn if you like my reasons or not. You're not the morality police. I'm going to do my job. It'd be easier if I had your help, but if the last four years have turned you into an asshole, I'll survive without it."

Rich looked at me and sighed. "Fine. I'll go along with you on this one. When the case is over, we'll see where things stand."

I nodded. "Fair enough."

"What about Vinnie?" Rich said.

"He said his people have instructions in case he gets arrested, and he might not be able to rein in their zeal in pursuing debts while he's behind bars."

"Sounds like it could go badly for Alice."

"Yeah. We need to lay off him for now," I said.

"For now," said Rich.

\* \* \*

I TOOK some time to look into a dojo where I could train, then headed to the ME's office. Dr. Sellers had arrived by the time I got there, and he had a body on the table when I walked into the room. I stopped and waited inside the door. I had seen one corpse so far working on this case and didn't wish to make a habit of it. Dr. Sellers looked up, saw me, and nodded. He worked on the deceased for another few minutes. I watched him make some careful incisions. Then he took his mask and gloves off and walked to me. "You were here a few nights ago," he said.

"Yes," I said. "My name is C.T. Ferguson, and I'm a private investigator." I showed him my ID while noticing I'd gotten used to saying my name and title. Great.

"I remember. What can I do for you?"

"Paul Fisher. I brought his wife in to ID his body. You mentioned you might have your full report done in a couple days."

"Yes, I finished it. Have you read it?"

"No, I wasn't able to. I came here to read it."

"I have a hard copy. Let me dig it up." He walked to the other side of the room and looked through a pile of file folders sitting atop an old metal desk. Dr. Sellers pulled one out from about the middle of the stack and carried it over to me. "Here it is. If you don't want to read it in here, you can use my office. It's out the other door, down the hall, and on the left."

"Thanks, I think I will read it there." I walked past the body on the table, out the other door, and along the corridor. Dr. Sellers's office was the second on the left. I entered, turned the light on, and sat at the desk with Paul Fisher's file. I didn't know if it would tell me anything I didn't already know (or suspect), but I had to see. Maybe I would find a smoking gun that pointed right at Vinnie and his crew.

The first thing I came across was the toxicology report. I read it until it got boring and then skimmed the rest. Paul Fisher had not been drunk or otherwise impaired when his car smashed into the tree. Some over-the-counter medication was in his system, but the report said common cold medicine in such quantities would not impair anyone. This information took driving while impaired off the table.

Dr. Sellers made a comprehensive list of Paul's injuries. I winced reading some of them. He suffered a laundry list of broken bones, plus a lot of bruises and cuts. His face had been torn up by the glass as he went through the windshield. Dr. Sellers concluded Paul's wounds were consistent with someone having been traveling at a good speed, stopping, and being battered about on impact.

I leafed through the rest of the report. Nothing jumped out at me. Dr. Sellers concluded the crash had been an accident based on the toxicology results. Anything else would be a matter for the police—and extremely intelligent private investigators—to puzzle out. I looked at the photos and saw nothing new.

Nothing in the report suggested Paul Fisher's car accident had been anything else. He seemed a devoted husband who wanted to help his wife in her hour of need. Guys like him don't drive their cars into trees. I supposed he could have fallen asleep at the wheel, but his file didn't indicate any medical conditions to cause that, and he hadn't been taking any strong medicines.

"I'll figure out how you did this, Vinnie," I said as I reassembled the file. I took it back to the prep room and left it on the table, giving Dr. Sellers a wave as I departed.

## CHAPTER 15

I PUT ON A BLACK ARMANI SUIT, BLACK SHIRT, AND A black and silver striped tie. The suit would have been appropriate for a funeral or an Oakland Raiders fundraiser. I added silver cufflinks and a pair of highly-polished black shoes. To combat the November chill in the air, I wore my Calvin Klein coat. I had amassed a very impressive dry cleaning bill after getting back to the States. Even though I would be going to a funeral, I took my nine millimeter. Vinnie or one of his boys might make an appearance and I wanted to be ready for them if they did.

Paul Fisher's funeral was at a church I never heard of. It would be my first Lutheran funeral. The church itself looked small on the outside, but the modest exterior belied a spacious interior. It featured the fine stained glass, woodworking, and art of Catholic churches without the opulence. The marble altar was the most obvious indication the congregation had some spare coin to toss around.

I took a seat toward the back of the church on the left. From there, I could see people enter and leave and keep an eye on the gathering. I considered asking Rich to come along, but I didn't know how we stood after last night. Despite the near-seven-year age gap between us, we were pretty close when I grew up. In some ways, Rich acted like the older brother I never had. Since my teenage years, however, Rich and I drifted to a distant sort of close, and my working as a detective only made the distance greater. Rich served in the Army, saw combat in the Middle East, got medically discharged, and started his career with the BPD. By comparison, I was the rich loafer who blew most of his money learning shady things overseas and now wanted to be a detective. I could see his trepidation; I had given him plenty of chances to believe the worst about me.

The service started a few minutes late. I rose and sat on cue but didn't take part in any of the singing. Lutheranism definitely wasn't my faith, and I didn't have one to call my own, anyway. Years ago, I had decided I didn't much care about the whole God thing. I would be respectful at the funeral but would participate as little as possible.

One of the songs struck me like it always did. I think I heard "Be Not Afraid" at almost every funeral I ever attended, including my sister's. It was among her favorites, and we played it at the funeral. Today, it lacked the same punch, but the song haunted me like a specter at my window, and a chill crawled up my spine when the first chorus started.

When the funeral mass ended, I accompanied many of the mourners to the cemetery. Paul Fisher's eternal resting place lay in front of a plain gray headstone stating he was a beloved husband and son. Alice and Paul's family stood nearest the casket as it got lowered into the ground. Everyone stayed while the priest said a final blessing.

I followed Alice and the family back to the Fishers' home. She asked me to show up in case Vinnie or one of his people decided to make an appearance at the wake. At some point, I would have to ask her about the life insurance issue. If she already received the check, writing one to Vinnie would provide the neatest solution. If she hadn't, we had to hope we could buy her some time. If Paul didn't have life insurance for some reason, then Alice was really up a creek.

* * *

AT THE HOUSE with my overcoat off, I wished I had opted for a smaller gun. The nine millimeter created a bulge under my suit jacket. I didn't know if anyone noticed, but I felt awkward wearing the gun at my side at a wake. If Vinnie or a goon didn't make an appearance, I would feel doubly silly.

Everyone at the gathering had been to one of the viewings. I didn't know most of the names, but I recognized the faces. Paul's family kept to themselves, Alice's did the same, and she flitted between them like she didn't know where she belonged. Neither group seemed interested in talking to me. For my part, I didn't try to strike up any conversations.

Alice hired a caterer to handle the food. I tried some of the salad, chicken tenders, and meatballs. None of it would make me dash upstairs and write home, but it was adequate food. Wakes were about togetherness and swapping stories, anyway, not food. They were also about alcohol. I didn't see a lot of it; while I hadn't planned on drinking, a houseful of people had varying reasons to drown their sorrows in the bottoms of adult beverage bottles. I found the dry nature of the party odd. Maybe a key family member battled alcoholism. Hell, maybe it had been Alice. She already suffered one addiction she struggled to control.

As the crowd filtered out, I saw Alice in the kitchen. She munched on some food and looked around like she saw her sink and appliances for the first time. This would be my best chance to ask about the life insurance. I walked in. Alice saw me and smiled. "Thanks for coming," she said. She still had trouble meeting my gaze. Some things would never change.

"Of course," I said. "It's been quiet so far, and quiet is good."

"It is. I need that after what happened at the funeral home. Thanks for dealing with that guy, by the way. I think I thanked you already, but it's been sort of a whirlwind these last few days."

"I understand. You're welcome." I paused. This felt like an awkward subject to broach. "Alice, there's something I need to know."

"What is it?" she said.

"Did Paul have life insurance?"

She frowned. "Why do you ask?"

"Vinnie Serrano thinks he can get paid off quickly if Paul had a policy, even through his company. I hate to be the bearer of bad news, but I think Vinnie is going to get more impatient." I wondered if she knew Paul had been working overtime to pay down her gambling debts. Regardless, I didn't think it my place to tell her. Not yet, at least.

"He did at one point," she said, shaking her head. "It used to be free at his company, and then they started charging for it a few years ago. He blamed Obamacare. Tough times and all that. Paul's premiums were expensive because he was a cancer survivor. He'd been healthy for years, and we needed the money to pay for other things." I didn't ask what those other things were. Alice took a deep breath. "We figured we were young. Who needs life insurance when you're still in your thirties?" Tears rimmed her eyes, and she gave a sad smile. "The company had some kind of policy where they'll cover funeral expenses, but that's it. At least I got spared the cost of a funeral."

"I know this is a bad time to talk about all of this, but

Vinnie is going to want his money. We need to decide on a way to deal with him."

"Can't you just have him arrested?"

"He implied something would happen to you if the police were involved. Something about not being around to control his people and their zeal for collecting money."

Alice frowned and shook her head. She put her face into her hands. "I don't know what I'm going to do." Her voice sounded muffled, but I could still understand her. "Can we deal with this tomorrow?"

"Sure. You want me to hang out a while in case Vinnie or his people make an appearance?"

"That would be great, thanks." She gave me a small grin.

"No problem."

Vinnie and his people never made an appearance. I stayed for a few more hours despite being so bored I had started counting pockmarks on the ceiling. Then I devised a robust game of deciding if something was a pockmark or a spot of water damage. The rest of the mourners, including family, left. Alice reheated some food for us, and we watched the local news. Once it and the national news aired, I decided to leave.

"You have my number," I said. "Call me if you have a problem."

"I will," she said.

* * *

My RINGING CELL phone woke me from a sound sleep. I looked at the alarm clock; it was almost four-thirty. I fumbled for the phone, grabbed it on the third try, and answered it in a voice I hoped sounded coherent. "Hello?"

"C.T., it's Alice." Her voice quivered.

"What's wrong?"

"Can you come over? Something has happened. I . . . I don't know who else to call?"

"How about the police?"

"No. I don't want to involve them, not after what you said about Vinnie. Please, can you come over?"

I rolled my eyes and looked at my pillow. Hanging up on Alice and getting more sleep was tempting. But I chose this life —at least for now—and I said I would support Alice. "Sure. Let me freshen up a bit. I'll be there as soon as I can."

"Thank you." I heard a wave of relief in her voice and in the deep breath she released. I hung up the phone, splashed some cold water on my face, brushed my teeth, and ran a comb through my hair. Last night's clothes were already in the hamper, so I put on a jogging suit, got my wallet, keys, and a gun, and left the apartment at four-forty. Thanks to my lead foot and light traffic on the roads, I made it to Alice's house in 15 minutes.

When I got there, Alice had the door open by the time I hit the steps. She looked composed as she offered me a wan smile, but the red and puffy eyes gave away the fact she had been crying. I walked inside, Alice followed me, and she locked the door and the deadbolt. In the living room, I sank into a recliner while Alice remained standing. She looked around even more nervously than normal. Something had her spooked.

"Tell me what happened," I said.

"I was asleep," Alice said. "I haven't slept very well since . . . since Paul . . . anyway. I was sound asleep and something crashed through the bedroom window." Her eyes were open wide as she talked. Alice wasn't getting back to dreamland any time soon.

"Why don't you show me?"

Alice led me to the second floor. The stairs opened into a hallway, which ended with a bathroom on the left. The master bedroom was at the other end of the hall, past two other bedrooms and a laundry room. The first thing I noticed when I entered the bedroom was the walk-in closet. Alice left it open, and I saw a lot of Paul's clothes still hanging, a hard reminder. I wondered when she would get rid of them. On the other side of the bedroom, broken glass covered the carpet, and a brick sat amidst the shards.

"Have you picked it up or done anything with it?" I said.

"No," Alice said, "I was too scared."

I nodded and took a glove out of my coat pocket. After I put it on, I picked up the brick. It looked like any other brick— maroon in color, rough exterior. On the bottom, someone had written "PAY UP" in large letters. The letters looked painted on. I set the brick back down, leaving the printed side up for Alice to see. "Looks like we're seeing the first signs of Vinnie's impatience," I said.

She stared at the brick and began to cry again.

* * *

ONCE THE MORNING hit a more respectable hour (and after I consumed one mug of tea and one mug of Alice's thoroughly mediocre coffee), I called Rich. He grumbled about getting up for an unofficial investigation, offered an uncharitable opinion or two of my methods, then agreed to come by anyway. About a half-hour later, he arrived. I offered him a cup of coffee in the interests of getting rid of it quicker. Rich accepted the mug, added nothing to it, and didn't react when he drank. I decided not to pay Alice the backhanded compliment of saying she made coffee as well as the police did.

We took Rich upstairs and showed him the scene. He put on a latex glove, picked up the brick, turned it over a few times, and put it back down. "When did this happen?" he said.

"I looked at the clock right after I heard the glass break," Alice said. "It was four twenty-three."

"It's obviously a gift from Vinnie," I said.

"We don't know for sure," Rich said.

"Of course. I'm sure the paper carrier is so eager to get paid he would toss a brick through the window right after tossing *The Sun* onto the porch."

"I admit it's likely Vinnie or one of his cronies did this. Without forensics, though, we won't know for sure."

"I don't want to involve the police," Alice said.

"I'm already here," Rich said.

"On your day off," I said, "and in an unofficial capacity. If this turns into an official case, your brethren will want to move on Vinnie and his organization. Right now, I think it's a bad idea."

"Because of his threat."

"Yes. It might be hot air, but we can't take the chance, nor can we guard Alice twenty-four-seven."

"Very responsible of you," Rich said with an approving nod.

"See? I'm not all bad," I said. "I used a glove when I picked up the brick, and I petted a stray puppy on the way here."

"We'll hold off on the beatification until this case is over," said Rich.

"What do we do now?" Alice said. "I don't feel safe here anymore." Her voice quivered again, and I saw her eyes well up.

"It's probably best if you stay somewhere else for a while," I said. "I would suggest family, but Vinnie might still find you there."

"What about Paul's family?"

"He could probably find you there, too. Besides, then you'd need a story about why you need to stay there."

Alice frowned. "Where am I going to go, then? I can't afford to pack up and go to a hotel."

"Does the BPD have any safehouses?" I said to Rich.

"Sure, for official business," he said. "This is still off the record."

"Do you know where they are?"

Rich looked at me. "You're going to break into a safehouse? No. Absolutely not."

"Doesn't mean you don't know where they are."

"I don't. Even if I did, I wouldn't tell you."

"You know I can—"

"Don't. It goes beyond the pale. Breaking into a safehouse will get you arrested. In *this* country."

I winced at Rich's barb, though I deserved it. Alice looked confused, like we exchanged a bunch of inside jokes. "All right. A hotel it is. I'll pay for it, Alice. Don't worry."

"I couldn't impose like that," she said.

"I didn't say I'd put you up in four-star digs. But I can get you away from here for a few days, at least. How quickly can you pack a bag?"

"I want to shower, too. Give me an hour?"

"We'll be downstairs."

* * *

"How many more days off do you have?" I asked Rich.

"Two more after today," he said. "I put it some overtime, so the brass told me to take a couple extra."

"While they ponder your rise to detective?"

"It's more of a lateral move, but yes."

I was curious about the BPD's org chart but tabled the subject for now. "I think one of us will need to check on Alice periodically," I said.

"This is your only case, right?" Rich said. "Can't you look in on her?"

"I can, but I have an investigation to continue. It might be unofficial for you, but it's official for me."

Rich nodded. "All right. We'll come up with some times."

"Good," I said.

"You know, I'm impressed you're staying away from her."

I frowned. I had a feeling I knew what Rich meant, but I wanted to see. "What do you mean?"

"You know . . . widow, vulnerable, pretty good-looking. It's not like you haven't gone there before."

"I was in college then. People change, Rich. Even me."

"All right," he said.

"All right, what?"

"Just wanted to see if you'd done any growing up at all."

"Satisfied?" I said.

"For now."

"Good to know." We waited a while for Alice, talking occasionally about random things. I couldn't get a read on Rich. He would ride me for my shady methods and put down my investigative skills, then help me with the case and test me to see how much growing up I had done. Were these the kinds of things an older brother would do? Neither of us possessed any experience with something like this.

About a half-hour later, Alice came downstairs with a suitcase on wheels and a smaller bag over her shoulder. "I'm ready when you are," she said. "Where are we going?"

"We'll drive a ways and find something," I said. We did. I found the La Quinta Inn on Route 7, at least a half-hour from Alice's house. We got there hours before the normal check-in time. The desk clerk tried to charge me for an extra day, but I showed him my ID and managed to talk him out of it. He ended up being eager to help an official investigation and promised not to tell anyone Alice was staying there. If I had a tinfoil hat, he would have put it on and given me a conspiratorial nod. We registered her under a fake name, and I paid with my debit card. I had to hope the case ended soon. My expenses mounted, and I hadn't gotten paid yet.

Alice settled into the room. We got extra keycards made for me and Rich. "We'll check on you periodically," I said. "You have my cell phone number already, and I'll leave Rich's before I go."

"Will he mind?"

"Of course not." I knew he would, which gave me all the more reason to do it.

"Thanks for all your help." Alice managed a smile. "I don't know what I would have done these last few days without you."

"I'm nothing if not full service," I said.

* * *

I LINGERED in the area until lunchtime when I took Alice to the Bill Bateman's Bistro nearby. She ordered soup and a salad while I opted for the crab cake sandwich. I ordered it without bread, which seemed to confuse the waiter. When it came, it sat on a Kaiser roll. I eschewed the roll and only ate the crab cake and fries. Anyone who ruins a crab cake by diluting it with a bunch of bread deserves what they get.

After lunch, I dropped Alice off at the hotel and drove home. I still hadn't found a dojo to spar and train in, so I checked out a couple more on the list and found both promising. One of them let me take a class for free to see how they ran things. I liked the strikes and holds, which I studied in Hong Kong, but didn't like the number of children in the class. The dojo probably offered private or semi-private lessons. I would have to check on those.

Once I showered and changed back into my civilian clothes, I drove to my place again. I walked toward my building, gym bag over my right shoulder as I fished my keys out of my left front jeans pocket. I heard a footstep from my rear. I got halfway turned around when something hard hit me in the back of the head. My vision swam, and the last thing I saw before the sidewalk rushed up to meet me was a short person standing behind me.

CHAPTER 16

I FLUTTERED IN AND OUT, EVENTUALLY BECOMING AWARE of lying on a cold, hard surface. I felt like I had been shaken from a dream but still existed halfway inside its alternate reality. Sound came back next in the form of two voices speaking Cantonese. I lay there and tried to discern as much as possible without opening my eyes. No point in revealing my consciousness to my captors.

The solid, chilling ground felt like the concrete I lay on during my days in the Chinese prison. The memory got my heart racing. My hands were bound behind my back with what felt like a plastic zip tie, also something the Chinese had done. This was hitting too close to home. I took deep breaths as quietly as I could. I noticed the absence of the .45's heft at my side. I never thought I would miss the feeling of a gun holstered on my belt until I needed one to be there. The feeling of my arms against my back told me my coat had been taken from me as well.

I listened to the conversation in Chinese. One of the voices definitely belonged to the short man Vinnie called Sam; I hadn't heard the other one before. They discussed what they were supposed to do with me. Sam said they were waiting on his boss to deal with something else first. The other fellow seemed eager to be rid of me. I wondered if he were related to any of the bastards who served as my jailers and tormentors in Hong Kong. They had been eager to have a rich American in their prison. Images of the prison guards played on my closed eyelids. My heart raced anew, and I struggled to remain calm. After a minute, Sam said he was going outside to smoke.

His footsteps echoed leaving the room. Wherever they held me had to be large. Sam took fifty steps, each resounding gradually less than the previous before he pushed a heavy door open. It groaned like a loud wind in winter and slammed shut like a giant pushed it from the other side. Where the hell was I? The other fellow milled about. I wanted to see where he was but didn't risk opening my eyes. For now, he and Sam thinking me unconscious sounded better than the alternative. They would probably leave me alone if they thought I was still out.

A few minutes later, the door opened with another groan and a squeak. Sam walked in, and the door slammed shut behind him. His footsteps echoed again as they came back toward me. He shouted to his friend about me still being unconscious. The other guy suggested a rather rude way of waking me, but Sam vetoed it. He said they were waiting for his boss, and since he was paying the other fellow, he was the boss in this room. A brief argument ensued, but Sam's logic overcame his friend's desire to do me harm.

I didn't know how long my respite would last; I needed to get out of here. Working free from a zip tie under observation would be impossible without some way to cut it. I carried a knife in my pocket, if my captors hadn't taken it. Could I grab it without them noticing? Sam suggested turning the TV on. The other fellow agreed but lamented the fact the show would be in English. While they fussed with the channels, I decided to try and make my escape. I felt my pocket. The knife was still there. It was small, which made it hard to find and also difficult to reach in my current circumstances.

It felt like the right time to risk opening my eyes. I squinted from one at first. Both Sam and his friend were turned the other way and messed with the small TV. I opened my other eye and looked around. They stood on a raised platform. I lay on a concrete floor. A vaulted ceiling yawned overhead. Scraps of dark wood were strewn about on the floor. Large windows on the side of the building had been covered in plastic and boarded up. I didn't risk rolling over to look behind me, but based on what I had seen so far, I had to be in an abandoned church. There were enough of those in the area.

I closed my eyes when Sam and his bloodthirsty friend got the TV figured out. They had dropped me on my right side, which enabled me to try and reach into my left front pocket for my knife. I shifted to lie a little more on my back to hide the fact I was awake and digging for a weapon. The zip tie bit into my wrists as I reached into my pocket. I got one finger in there on the first try, but couldn't reach the knife. The second try got a second finger into the pocket. I felt something warm and wet run over my right wrist. The zip tie bit into my skin again as I got the tips of my index and middle fingers around the knife. I couldn't let it go because I didn't know if I could reach it again. I pinched the handle and pulled it out of my pocket. Now I had to transfer it to my other hand without dropping it.

I got the lock-blade knife all the way out of my pocket and let it fall into my hand. It didn't hit the floor. I used my right hand to pull the blade out, then worked on the zip tie, moving the blade back and forth. Sam and his buddy chatted occasionally over the sounds of a TV show I didn't recognize. It took about a minute to cut through the zip tie. I caught it and let it hover at my wrists rather than shedding it completely. No point in giving away all my secrets.

Now free, I wondered what to do next. My head still hurt, I was armed with a small knife, and I still had two people to deal with. Sam was short but stocky, and if he worked for Vinnie, he had to be a decent enforcer. His friend had loose and easy movements. He lacked Sam's bulk, but I could tell he knew how to take care of himself. I had to wait for them to split up again.

I got my chance when the show ended. Sam said he was going outside to smoke again. He walked past me, down the aisle of what used to be the pews, and out the door. When it shut behind him, I opened my eyes. Sam's friend sat on a milk crate in front of the TV. I transferred the knife to my right hand and stood. He didn't notice me as I crept closer.

The dim lighting and candles reflected on the small screen. As I got closer, I noticed my own reflection. Sam's friend did, too. He turned. and I rushed him. He threw a quick left jab, which I blocked. I slashed at him with the knife, and he grabbed my wrist. We struggled back and forth. He threw an elbow, I blocked; I threw an elbow; he blocked. He tried to knee me in the groin, which I blunted with an upraised leg. I couldn't get my right wrist out of his grip. He threw another left at me. I blocked it and headbutted him. It took him right in the forehead, staggering him back a step. I got my hand free. Sam's friend shook away the cobwebs, but not in time. I led with the knife, stabbing him a few times in the left side below the ribs. He grunted and slumped to the floor.

I looked for a side door and saw one past what had once been the altar. Sam's friend clutched his side and bled onto the marble. I wondered if he'd survive the stabbing. Internal bleeding could still be his undoing. His fault for throwing in with Sam and being a bloodthirsty prick. I saw my coat and gun in another milk crate, grabbed them, and sprinted toward the side door. I threw it open and ran out. It closed behind me at the same time I heard the large front door open. In a minute, Sam would discover what happened, but by then, I already hit the sidewalk and took off down the street.

## CHAPTER 17

IT TOOK A FEW BLOCKS TO REALIZE IN WHICH UNSAVORY part of town I found myself. I holstered the gun, put my coat back on, and made sure my cell phone and keys were still there. If I pegged my location correctly, I was about three miles from my apartment. I walked into a generic fast chicken restaurant, sat at one of the many open tables, and summoned an Uber. While I waited, I ordered a large drink, didn't get any soda from the machine, and held the cup of ice to the back of my head. It earned me several funny looks, but I didn't care.

The car came about ten minutes after I used the app. Ten more minutes and seven dollars later, I stood in front of my building. I kept one hand on my gun and looked around. The last time I was here, Sam waylaid me. I hadn't seen him, wherever he hid. The fact he was short enough to stand up under a car didn't help. I didn't see anyone and went inside.

After I got upstairs and double-locked the door behind myself, I went into my office and sat. I hooked my cell phone to the charger and saw four missed calls on its screen: one from Alice, two from Rich, and one from a number I didn't recognize. I called Rich back first. "Where the hell have you been?" he said when he picked up.

"I got waylaid by a Chinese midget," I said.

"You're going to have to explain that one."

I did.

"Goddamn," he said," sounds like you were lucky to get away."

"I prefer to think of it as a skillful, daring escape."

"What about the guy you stabbed?"

"It's probably not fatal," I said. "I didn't go for a vital area, but if you're wondering if I care whether he bleeds out, I don't."

"I think I would feel the same way. Do you know where they held you?"

"An abandoned church. I think I could find it again if I had to."

"What do you want to do now?" Rich said.

"I'm going to be more vigilant in looking for midgets. Other than that, I'm still working the case. I want to get Vinnie even more now."

"Let me know if you need more help."

"I will. How's Alice?"

"She was OK a few hours ago. I took over some carry-out and had dinner with her."

"Good," I said. "I'll check on her in a little while, then."

"You still think Vinnie and his crew killed Paul Fisher?"

"I don't see any reason to change my theory. If anything, tonight convinced me of it even more. Why?"

"Because," said Rich, "they probably didn't come upon that old church all of a sudden. Maybe they kept Paul there, too."

Rich had a good point. "I'll check it out later, too," I said.

* * *

I PUT a bag of frozen peas on my head for a while. It felt good, and when I checked the knot, it had gone down a little. It would be as good as I could expect for a while. I took some aspirin, got a shower, and pondered dinner. My fridge, freezer, and pantry held few appealing options. I wanted something quick, so I called ahead to Hull Street Blues and ordered a Caesar salad with tilapia and a baked potato. When I got back home, I covered the baked potato in marinara sauce, a delicacy I discovered in college.

After my late dinner, I drove to the La Quinta Inn to check on Alice. I knocked on the door to her room and heard her milling around inside. "Who is it?" she said in a voice deeper than her own.

"C.T."

She turned the lock, took the chain off its slot, and opened the door. I walked into the room. Alice had opened and emptied her suitcase. The TV played some sitcom. Bed covers were rumpled like someone had been lying on them. The trash can held two Styrofoam containers. "I tried calling you earlier," she said. "I got worried when you didn't answer."

I told her what had happened. "It's why I gave you Rich's number, too," I said.

"Vinnie had you kidnapped?" Her eyes went wide, and she sat on the edge of the bed, shaking her head. "This is getting really bad."

"It's an escalation from throwing a brick through your window. I've been a thorn in his side for a while now. He probably thinks getting me out of the way makes you more likely to knuckle under."

"It would."

"We don't need to tell him," I said.

She smiled a small smile. "Thanks for sticking around, C.T. I know this isn't the case you signed up for."

I shrugged. "I told you I see things through."

"I'm glad you do," Alice said. "What are we going to do now?"

"First, we're going to keep you here until this all blows over. I'm going to continue working angles. I'll have to deal with Vinnie at some point, and in the meantime, I'll keep dodging his goon squad."

"Be careful." Alice's face took on a somber look. "One person already died because . . . because of . . ." She trailed off into tears. Before I could do anything, she walked to me and buried her face in my shoulder. I patted her head as she sobbed.

"I'm not going to die, Alice," I said.

After another minute of crying, she found her voice. "You can't promise that."

"Yes, I can. Vinnie's not good enough to take me down. Even his most trusted man couldn't keep me prisoner. They can't kill me." I hoped she believed it. Hell, I hoped I did.

"Are you going to kill them?" Alice's eyes were still wet, but a hardness shone through the tears now. If she hadn't grabbed me, I might have stepped back.

"Bloodthirst doesn't become you," I said. "Besides, I'm not a killer."

"You carry a gun," she said.

"And I'll use it if I have to." I decided to omit the part where I stabbed Sam's friend and left him there to bleed. Alice's bloodlust didn't need to be fed. "I may be a lot of things, but I'm not a killer."

She nodded. "All right. Just don't get yourself hurt or kidnapped again."

"I am ever vigilant," I said.

\* \* \*

WHEN I GOT HOME, I had to park my car in the same area as last time, when Sam had jumped me. After I turned the engine off, I sat in the car with the doors locked, looking all around me. The lot and street looked free of hooligans, miscreants, and ne'er-do-wells—or at least as free of such people as any lot and street in Baltimore can look. Thankfully, Fells Point streets were freer than most, at least when one lived a few blocks from the bars. Drunk hipsters and boozed-up bros posed the largest threats, and I knew I could deal with them. I checked around again, taking care to look in all three mirrors before getting out of the Lexus.

I kept my right hand inside my coat on the handle of my gun as I walked across the parking lot toward my building. The occasional car went by on the street. I didn't see any random white cargo vans, and no one jumped out of any vehicles with a tire iron and a rope. There weren't a lot of people on the streets, but this was the residential part of Fells Point. A block or two over, the streets would be more crowded, even on a weeknight.

I got to my building. The good thing about large apartment complexes is they provide few places for people to hide. I never considered it a selling point before, but getting waylaid and kidnapped changes one's perspective on a few things. Maybe the management company could put a blurb in their brochure: *Convenient to downtown and nightlife. Brick front and spacious for a downtown feel. Fewer places for people to hide and waylay you as you arrive at your new apartment!*

Maybe not.

Satisfied I wouldn't get jumped, I went inside and upstairs and checked my door. I left it locked, and its condition hadn't changed. I turned the key and walked inside. The foyer light came on as I entered. I had my gun in my hand as I closed the door. I went through each room and didn't see anyone.

I put my gun back in the holster, took the whole thing off,

and set it on the nightstand. After being tied up for who knows how long in some abandoned church, I wanted a long, hot shower. I took one, downed a couple more aspirin for my headache, put peroxide on my wrists, and got into bed. Rich made a good point about the church. I wanted to check it out early in the morning, so I set my phone to rouse me at an obscene hour and went to sleep.

* * *

THE BUZZ WOKE me at the beastly hour of five-fifteen. I couldn't remember the last time I got up so early not involving an exam or a girl who needed to leave. I got dressed, ate some fruit, drank a tall glass of milk, and walked out the door. On my way to the church, I stopped for a much-needed vanilla latte. The pounding in my head had gone down along with the knot, which had shrunk to about the size of a pea.

I drove back into the sketchy neighborhood I ran away from only yesterday. At this hour, I didn't expect any problems. Even criminals have to sleep sometime. I had the .45 with me in case any kept odd hours. I put my hand on the grip to be sure I had it holstered at my side. A few minutes later, I parked across the street from an abandoned church.

It was about six o'clock, and the sun's first rays peeking over the horizon illuminated things so I could see. The dark red brick exterior had faded in spots and suffered damage due to abuse and disuse in others. The erstwhile stained glass windows had been boarded up with weather-beaten wood. This church didn't have a steeple, but it did have a tower above the building proper. If a bell had once been there, it was long gone. I saw a window up there covered by a piece of wood appearing much newer and fresher.

I decided not to try the front doors. Going in the regular

way made me too visible to anyone wandering by and would give anyone inside way too much notice. The door I used for my hasty retreat last night would do nicely. I tested it and found it locked. Maybe Sam secured the place before taking his bleeding buddy to the hospital. I took out my special keyring and went to work. The lock wasn't complicated, just unusual to work with because of all the ornaments and garish doodads on the outside. A minute later, I opened the door and walked inside.

The hallway was pitch black once I closed myself off from the street. My LED flashlight lifted the darkness. I scanned the floor but didn't see a blood trail. I drew the .45, opened the next door, and walked into the church. The only sounds I heard were my breathing and my heartbeat. My first steps didn't echo much, but it got more pronounced as I got closer to the center. I walked past the altar to where I had stabbed Sam's friend. They did a pretty good job of cleaning up the blood; I only saw a few stray specks of crimson dotting the marble.

I walked around the church until I felt confident I was the only one inside. Now I needed to get up to the tower. I hadn't seen another door down the hallway, but there was one past the altar on the other side. In my younger, more pious days, I learned they called this the sacristy. I felt like an interloper in a house where I was no longer welcome as I walked into the sacristy. I flipped the light switch expecting it to be futile, and it was.

The flashlight showed me a sacristy in ruin. Whatever had been here was long gone. Now, only kindling, scraps of cloth, a few broken wine bottles, and pockmarked walls covered in peeling paint remained. It looked like the godliness had left this place and taken the cleanliness along with it. The carpet had once been a deep red but now had stains, splotches, and patches of other colors all over it. The room smelled musty and faintly of urine.

A doorway yawned ahead. I shined the flashlight past it and looked around before walking through it with the .45 leading the way. Exploring dark places is a lot easier with a gun. The doorway led to a corridor which ended in an ornate door which could have been on the front of the church. On the right side of the corridor, I saw another door. I walked to it, checked the lock, and opened it.

Jackpot. A staircase led above. I used the flashlight to peer up as far as I could. The steps stopped at a landing. Then a spiral staircase went up what looked like the full height of the church, ending at another landing. I went up. Almost every step creaked when I stepped on it. Somewhere above me, rats chattered and scurried. Chunks of wood had fallen away over the years, and I skipped some of the steps because they were in such disrepair. The landing was about eight feet square. The spiral stairs continued up, and I saw another closed door in front of me, probably leading to the balcony where the organ player and chorus would perform.

I went up again. The staircase squeaked but its sturdy metal looked to be in good shape apart from some cracking paint and the occasional spot of rust. The next landing had to be two stories up. I like winding steps as an eclectic architectural choice. As something to climb in an abandoned church in the dark, they were more like an obstacle. I put the .45 away so I could keep one hand on the railing as I ascended.

This landing looked to be the same size as the other, and like the other, a door faced me on the opposite side of the landing. I checked it and found it unlocked. I turned the knob, drew the .45, and shouldered the door open. The flashlight illuminated a small room. On the right side, old plywood covered the center of the wall. I checked the nails and noticed the rust covering their heads. The room itself couldn't have been more than ten feet square.

I didn't see anything of interest on the walls. The floor, however, proved to be another story. Dried blood stood out against the unadorned concrete. It hadn't formed large pools but rather into several small ones spaced apart, mostly on the left side of the room. I guessed someone had been beaten there —not enough blood for anything more severe. The blood went all the way up to the wall across from me where new plywood covered a broken window. I saw no glass on the floor in here, so the window had broken outward.

I went to one of the small blood pools, crouched, and took out my improvised CSI kit. This always looked easy on the TV shows. The photogenic CSI—or private investigator, in my case —would swab the blood with a long Q-tip and deposit it in a longer plastic tube. I brought regular Q-tips from my bathroom and didn't have any fancy plastic tubes for evidence collection. I did have plastic sandwich bags, and they would have to do. When this case began, I never expected I'd be breaking into an abandoned church in a rundown neighborhood to collect blood samples.

I swabbed the bloodstain until I could see residue on the cotton. I swabbed the other end to be sure I had a good sample, dropped the Q-tip in a plastic bag, and zipped it shut. One blood sample would probably be enough. It occurred to me I should have taken some photos of the scene before I collected evidence. My future as a CSI looked bleaker by the moment. I took out my smartphone and snapped some pictures, being sure to focus on the blood and the broken window.

I put my phone away and surveyed the scene. Sam and his friend used this church to hold me hostage, so it stood to reason they used it before, like Rich suggested. The blood was Paul Fisher's. I would have to wait for a forensic test to make sure, but I felt sure of it. Sam and maybe others worked Paul over, leading to the red splotches on the floor. They punched him in the face until he bled on the concrete. I frowned; punching took a toll on the hand, too. What if the puncher had busted his hand open in the process? Maybe one blood sample wouldn't be enough after all.

I collected two other blood samples and dropped those Q-tips into their own bags. Good thing I had grabbed a handful before I left. There didn't look to be anything else of interest in the room. I had to check out the ground below the window. Even if Sam and whoever else had been careful, they had to clean things up in a hurry. Haste makes waste.

Even though I probably didn't need to lead with the .45 anymore, I still did as I left the room and went down the spiral staircase. Having traversed it once, I didn't feel the need to hold onto the railing. I would have felt like a gigantic ass if I had gone tumbling down, but no such catastrophe (and resultant loss of dignity) befell me. I got to the first landing, went back down the conventional staircase, and ended back in the hallway past the sacristy. Curiosity almost got me with respect to the ornate door, but I ignored it and walked back through the sacristy. A minute later, I went outside toward the area below the broken window.

The window was on the side of the church tower to the left of the building's center. Below it, damaged concrete steps yielded to grass. I had the sun to light things for me now, but I wanted to be sure of what I saw, so I still used the flashlight when I crouched. Sure enough, Sam and his crew of at least one minion had neglected some of their clean-up duties. I saw bits of broken glass, varying in size from tiny all the way to pieces attaining full shard status. The window had been plain glass, not stained, so the bits with dried blood on them stood out from the rest. I used my tweezers, gathered a few, and dropped them into another plastic bag, my last one. I added it to the other plastic bags in my small satchel and walked back to my car.

I would need to get these samples examined. But how could I get the job done without turning the whole thing into an official police investigation, thus alerting Vinnie and endangering Alice?

CHAPTER 18

ONCE I GOT HOME, I WENT UPSTAIRS, TOOK OFF MY GUN and holster, and lay down for a nap. Getting up at five-fifteen is a fate I did not wish to suffer often. While I was still young enough to rise early and go on with my day, a nap would be preferable. Rich and Alice wouldn't be up for a while yet, and Vinnie didn't know where Alice went. I set my phone to rouse me in ninety minutes, and I don't remember being awake long after my head hit the pillow.

Ninety minutes later, at the more reasonable hour of five after nine, the hard-rock strains of the alarm pulled me from my nap. I went downstairs and made sausage and toast for a second breakfast. At some point, I had to go to the grocery store. Man cannot live on carry-out alone, unless he also makes frequent trips to the gym. When I finished, I called Rich.

"Hello?" he said.

"I'm wondering how far we can push the unofficial nature of this investigation," I said.

Rich's sigh hissed in my ear. "What did you do now?"

"Always so negative, dear cousin. I discovered some evidence which might break the case."

"You did?"

"Yes."

"You?" he said.

"You seem surprised."

"Please don't tell me you went and messed up a crime scene."

"Of course not," I said. "I'm a licensed investigator."

Rich snorted. "And I'm the fucking commissioner. What did you find?"

I told him about the church where I had been held, what I found there, and what I did in terms of evidence gathering. "Looks like you were right—they held Paul Fisher there. They probably worked him over in the upper room. Then I guess they threw him out the window." I paused. "Huh."

"What?" Rich said.

"It explains the injuries in the car crash. Hitting the pavement from four stories after being beaten and thrown through a window probably looks a lot like crashing your car and exiting through the windshield."

"It probably looks worse, but I think the injuries would be similar enough. We'll have to ask the ME once we know more. You have this evidence in plastic bags?"

"Yes," I said. "How are we going to get it analyzed and keep this whole thing off the books? We don't want an official investigation yet. If Vinnie gets spooked, things could go poorly for Alice."

"He doesn't know where Alice is, though," Rich said.

"True, but we can't presume he'll never find out," I said. "She might slip up and do something to get herself noticed somehow."

"How?"

"She's a compulsive gambler and emotionally traumatized," I said. "I'm sure clear thinking isn't first among her virtues right now."

"Good point," said Rich. "I can ask one of the CSI guys to run the evidence for me. He owes me some money from a poker game."

"All right. Have you checked on Alice yet?"

"No, I was going to take some food over there for breakfast."

"OK," I said. "I'll take her lunch. Then I can give you the evidence, and we can strategize going forward."

"You're really taking to this, aren't you?"

"It's a lot more interesting than the simple adultery case I got handed at first. I can handle interesting."

"We'll make a real detective out of you yet," Rich said.

"Don't wish such a fate on me," I said.

* * *

ALICE DESERVED to know what I found. I don't know if she shared my suspicion about Paul's murder; I think she simply got caught up in the tragedy of it all. In the end, it doesn't matter how someone's loved one died, only the fact the person's not there anymore. Car accident, murder, or heart defect, the cut feels the same. Still, Alice deserved to know, especially because Vinnie might try and take her out, too.

I made sure to run a few miles between breakfast and lunch since I would be doing carry-out again. Bill Bateman's was the most convenient place to go, and I liked the menu, so I went there again. When I got to the room, Alice opened the door with a small, resigned smile on her face. I took the carry-out inside. She ate on the bed while I ate on the desk.

"How are you doing?" I said.

"Bored," she said, her eyes landing on me a little more often than normal. "I'm getting tired of being in this room all the time. The TV and books can't keep my interest."

"I'm sure it's frustrating. I wouldn't like it, either. Right now, though, you're safe here."

"But I want to leave the room, C.T. There's a shopping center across the street. I want to wander around Wal-Mart and look at all the random people who shop there. I want to have a dessert in the Dairy Queen. I want to feel sunlight and wind on my face." She shook her head. "I can't do any of it in here."

I nodded. "I'll take you across the way to Dairy Queen for dessert."

"Thanks," Alice said. She smiled a bigger smile, one looking happier and less defeated. "It's a start."

We ate a little while longer until we both almost finished our lunches. I wanted to tell her what I found, but how could I work such a thing into the conversation? *I'm sorry you're cooped up in this hotel room. By the way, a Chinese midget beat your husband to a pulp and threw him out a third-story window. Can you pass me a mustard packet?* There had to be an easier way. While I pondered my lack of bedside manner, Alice solved the problem for me.

"You seem a little troubled," she said. "Something happen in the case?"

I finished my mouthful of food. "Yes," I said. "You know a couple of Vinnie's guys held me hostage for a while." She nodded; I continued. "They were holed up in an abandoned church. It occurred to me they probably used the same building before. Since I already suspected they had done something to your husband, I went back early this morning and looked around."

Her eyes widened. "Were they still there?"

"No, they left. Once I got away, they must have abandoned the place. They left in a hurry, though, and haste makes people sloppy."

"What did you find?" Alice leaned forward on the bed. Her eyes stayed on me for a change.

"A lot," I said. "There's a room in the church tower right next to where the bell was. I found dried blood on the floor and collected some of it. I also saw a window boarded up. The other windows were covered with old wood. This wood was brand new. I looked at the ground and saw pieces of broken glass. A few had some bits of dried blood on them. I collected those, too. I'm going to give everything I found to Rich and have it analyzed."

Alice didn't say anything for a minute. She looked at me with a constant gaze I found a little unnerving. I had gotten used to her eyes never landing on anything for more than a second or two. Finally, she let out a slow, deep breath. "They killed him," she said.

"Looks like it," I said.

"Why would they do that?"

"Vinnie thinks Paul had life insurance. You'd get a windfall, and he'd lean on you for his cut."

She shook her head. I saw her eyes well up. "Why did I have to place all those bets?" said Alice.

"Don't blame yourself. It's Vinnie's fault Paul is dead. Rich and I are going to prove it. He'll get what's coming to him."

Alice wiped her eyes and nodded. "All right," she said. "You two be careful, though. Vinnie is dangerous."

"We're trained professionals," I said. At least it was half-true.

* * *

AFTER FINISHING LUNCH WITH ALICE, I drove to Rich's house in Hamilton. He owned a very nice Victorian with a huge screened-in porch and large front and back yards. Rich's parents—my paternal aunt and uncle—died a few years ago. They left Rich and his brother decent sums, and willed the rest of their money to various charities. Rich used the money to buy the house and invested the rest toward his retirement.

I gave Rich the brown bag holding my evidence Ziplocs when he opened the door. He looked in the bag. "This almost looks professional," he said with an approving nod.

"Well, I'm almost smart enough to pull CSI stuff off," I said.

"You did a good job considering you're not trained for it and don't have professional tools."

"I've watched years of cop shows," I said.

"Did those shows tell you the value of taking pictures?"

"They did. I'll email them to you so you can print them."

"All right," Rich said. "The guy who owes me money doesn't start his shift for a couple hours. I'll take everything to him then and tell him to put a rush on it."

"How much does he owe you?" I said.

"Two fifty."

"Must be some poker game. High stakes for a bunch of public servants."

"We do it once a month. Maybe I'll invite you sometime and win back my money from your stack."

I snorted. "Please. You're not winning anything from me. I can handle your little game."

Rich grinned and shook his head. "Maybe we'll see one of these months," he said.

"Maybe we will."

* * *

Rich and I both went to the hotel room for dinner. On the way, I told him about Alice going stir crazy. We could only hope she wouldn't wander outside and get herself noticed by the wrong people. I wanted to think she had more sense, but with all she had been through recently, I couldn't be sure. We all wanted a change from Bill Bateman's, so we stopped for food at Panda Express. Alice looked a little disappointed when we got there, but she shrugged it off and ate. I got an assortment of food, including pepper steak, sweet and sour chicken, vegetable lo mein, and hunan chicken. American Chinese food always reminded me how much better real Chinese food in Hong Kong had been, and Panda Express reminded me more than most.

We left about an hour later, after stressing to Alice the importance of staying in the room and not being seen. I offered to loan her a tablet, but she said she would be OK. I drove us back toward downtown. "What now?" Rich said.

"How long until we get those results?" I said.

"Tomorrow at the earliest."

"We need to go after Vinnie's people if we're going to keep this off the books. They have to roll over on him when the time is right."

"Want to start tonight?" Rich said.

"No time like the present, right?"

"Sure. Who first?"

"Might as well go after his lover."

Rich grinned and shook his head. "Of course you want to go after the girl first."

"You know me all too well, dear cousin," I said.

* * *

I STOPPED at my apartment and made a pot of coffee for the thermos. We were still sated from dinner, so we snagged some snacks at a convenience store and headed to Canton Square. I parked the Lexus around where I had the last time Rich and I staked out Margaret Madison's house. When we got there, she had only the token light on in the front of the house. I looked up her home number and dialed it. No answer.

"Looks like she's not home," I said.

"Good thing we have coffee, then," said Rich.

"This time, I think we should avoid breaking in. You have your badge and gun on you?"

"Of course."

"Good. When we present our case, I think having a real cop in the house will make it that much more convincing."

"You think you can get her to roll on Vinnie?"

I shrugged. "I don't know. I think she's OK with collecting bets and maybe beating someone up here and there, but she may draw the line at murder."

"We don't know the blood is Paul Fisher's," Rich said.

"She doesn't know we don't know," I pointed out.

Rich nodded. "All right, we'll see what we can do about turning her."

Novembers in Baltimore can be brisk, and this one was no exception. I fired up the engine periodically for some heat, but we didn't want a running car to give anything away. Rich and I had each had a cup of coffee within the first half-hour. I looked around at the holiday decorations. Margaret Madison had eschewed any festive accoutrements on her house, but her neighbors showed more holiday spirit. I counted three Santas, a handful of illuminated reindeer, one large and tacky Nativity scene, and a bunch of lights strung around bushes and draped over doorways and gutter spouts.

It was almost nine o'clock when Margaret Madison walked to her front door. Rich and I got out of the car once we saw she had gone inside. We ambled the half-block to her house, climbed her three front steps, and knocked on the door. She opened it, and we both showed our IDs. Margaret looked better up close. She had bright blue eyes and a face that belonged on magazine covers. "We need to talk," I said.

She frowned and looked at us in turn. Margaret had taken her coat off and now wore a purple sweater atop a pair of black jeans. At least she wore the Ravens' colors. "What's this about?" she said.

"Your boss," I said. "There are some things going on you might not be aware of. Can we come in?"

"All right," she said and stepped aside. We walked into the small foyer, which yielded to the living room. I admired the new hardwood floors and leather furniture. Margaret sat in a leather recliner. Rich and I seated ourselves facing her on the comfortable sofa. "What's going on?" she said.

"We know you work for Vinnie Serrano," I said, "and we know what he does. We know you take illegal bets, and I've seen you beat up a man in a parking lot not far from here." She looked like she wanted to say something, but I held up my hand and continued. "Your boss and his cronies killed a man, though, and now they're terrorizing his wife."

Margaret leaned back in the chair and sighed. "Vinnie isn't a killer. He's a simple bookie."

"He's trying to get into loan-sharking, too," Rich said.

"That's why he has the new guy," Margaret said.

"Sal?" I said.

"Yeah."

"Sal might have killed a man. The victim got roughed up and thrown out a window. Then they staged a car accident to cover it."

Margaret stared at us with wide eyes. "You're serious."

"We had some evidence tested," I said.

"Why hasn't Vinnie been arrested, then?"

"He's made it clear his arrest would spell bad news for the

dead man's widow. We're keeping this off the books as long as we can."

"Basically, Vinnie is going down," Rich said. "If you want to go with him, it's up to you. If you don't, we can make things easier for you."

"I've never killed anyone," Margaret said. "Vinnie never asked me to. I just take bets and make some collections. Sometimes I have to rough the marks up, but I've never done worse than break a bone here and there."

"Would you be willing to testify against Vinnie?" Rich said.

She sighed again. "I don't know. How can I be sure you're not just giving me a bunch of shit?"

I took out my phone and called up the photos. "Here," I said, standing and walking to her recliner. "These are the pictures I took of the room where they beat up a man and threw him out of a fourth-story window." I handed her the phone. She scrolled through the photos and frowned.

"It's not exactly a smoking gun," she said.

"We had the evidence tested. You see those pools of dried blood? I had them and some glass samples analyzed. A man is dead and your boss did it."

"Or ordered people to do it," Rich said. "Legally, they're the same. Anyone who works for him is going to go down with him."

Margaret looked at us for a minute and didn't say anything. Her lustrous blue eyes looked between us, then closed as she shook her head. "I don't want to go to jail with him or because of him," she said. "I'm not a killer. I don't want any part of that."

"You've made the right decision," Rich said. "If you testify against Vinnie, the state's attorney will go easy on you. I can't promise you anything now, of course."

"What am I supposed to do until Vinnie gets busted?"

"What you normally do," I said. "Act like nothing has changed. Try not to make him suspicious."

Margaret nodded slowly. "OK, I think I can do it."

"Here's my card," I said, giving her a business card from my wallet. "Don't let Vinnie see it. Call me if anything unusual happens or if you think he's on to our plan."

"I will."

Margaret showed Rich and me out and closed the door behind us. We walked back to my car. "What's the next move?" I said once we were in the car and I had turned the heat on.

"We hope she's not calling Vinnie right now," Rich said.

"Let's presume she's not."

"Try to flip someone else, then, I guess. Sal's new. He might be easy."

I shook my head. "I think Sam should be next. Something makes me think Sal will be a harder sell."

"You want me to help?"

"Only if I really need it. Keep an eye on Alice. I'll worry about the Chinese midget."

"Try not to get waylaid again," said Rich.

"Everyone's a critic," I said.

## CHAPTER 19

When I got home, I realized I knew nothing about Sam, not even his real name. Vinnie only called him Sam because Vinnie was a jackass. How could I find someone whose name I hadn't a clue and didn't know much else about? I knew he worked for Vinnie, and that could be enough. They would have to talk. I could run Vinnie's phone records, see who his frequent calls to and from were, and run those numbers to see who owned them. There didn't appear to be another way to find Sam.

Tracing him could wait for tomorrow. Even with my nap earlier, I felt tired. I had brushed my teeth and changed into my silk pajamas when my cell phone rang. I didn't recognize the number except to note it was the same caller who rang while I had been held prisoner. Might as well answer it. "Hello?"

"C.T.?" said a female voice I thought familiar.

"The one and only. Who's this?"

"It's Gloria. Gloria Reading."

"Of course. How are you?"

"I called you last night but didn't get an answer."

"Yeah, I was tied up."

"Busy with the case?" she said.

"Well, yes. And literally tied up." I told her what happened, leaving out the part where I got waylaid by Sam. Gloria didn't need to know all my secrets.

"Wow, you must have been terrified."

"I'm not too proud to admit I was scared," I said. "But I got free, and I'm still working on the case. It takes more than a zip tie to keep me down."

"Your job is certainly interesting."

"More than I thought it would be."

"How are you feeling now?"

"I'm OK," I said. "My headache is pretty much gone."

We made small talk for a few more minutes. Then Gloria said, "I like you, C.T. You get me. Not many people do."

"Chalk it up to my impressive people skills," I said.

She chuckled. "I'm not looking for anything serious right now."

I wondered where this conversation was headed. "Neither am I."

"But if you want to have a good time here and there, I think we can work something out."

Now knowing the direction of the conversation, I liked it. "I definitely think we can," I said.

* * *

THE NEXT MORNING, I showered and shaved, then went downstairs to do some work. It was already past ten. I had Vinnie's cell phone number from my inquiries into the Fishers, so I went online, found his provider, and broke into his phone records. I downloaded the last three months, dumped the data into a spreadsheet, and perused everything while I ate a bowl of cereal. The glamorous life of a private investigator. Next time, I might live on the edge and add a sliced banana.

Several numbers showed up frequently. I highlighted all multiples, filtered out the random one-offs, and then looked up the important numbers. One belonged to Margaret Madison, two to people whose names I didn't recognize, and one belonged to Chaoxiang Ngai. Unless Vinnie had acquired a spate of friends with Chinese names, it had to be the man he referred to as Sam.

I ran Chaoxiang Ngai and got his address. It didn't look right to me. When I plugged the address into a map program, I got the American Visionary Art Museum. Sam—I'd already fallen into the habit of thinking of him by his asshole-bequeathed nickname—had a fake address. I would need another way to find him. Vinnie's house would work.

* * *

VINNIE BOUGHT a house in Rodgers Forge while we were still in college. It gave him an easy commute to Loyola—until he got kicked out, of course—and provided a nice private place to run his gambling enterprise. Vinnie's parents had some money, but he paid for the house with the proceeds from his bookmaking business. I parked on his street about four houses up on the other side of the road. I had no idea what Sam drove, but a short Chinese man walking into and out of the house would be easy enough to spot.

Shortly after twelve-thirty, Vinnie left. He had to be taking his usual lunch at Donna's. I grabbed some lunch at Pei Wei and returned to my surveillance spot. While I waited for Vinnie to return, Rich called. "How goes the case?" he said.

"I'm looking into Vinnie's shortest henchman," I said.

"Find him yet?"

"He has a fake address, so I'm staking out Vinnie's house in the hopes he shows up here. How's Alice?"

"She's OK. I took her out for a while this morning. She really needed to be somewhere other than her hotel room."

I didn't like the risk involved, but I trusted Rich. I knew he could spot someone snooping on him, and trusted he would keep Alice safe. "Where did you take her?"

"White Marsh Mall. She was out of clean clothes, so she walked around and found some sales. Then we had lunch in the food court and walked around outside. I dropped her off before I called you. She looked a lot happier for getting out in the sun and doing something in fresh air."

"Good. I know she was going stir crazy in there." I saw Vinnie's Mercedes come down the street and pull into his driveway. A small import followed it and parked at the curb. "Looks like Vinnie is home." Sam got out of the import. "So is his Chinese friend. I'm going to follow him when he leaves."

"All right. Good luck."

Why would I need good luck following someone? "Thanks."

* * *

ABOUT A HALF-HOUR LATER, Sam left. He drove the other direction down Vinnie's street. I let him get past me, turned around in a driveway, and set off behind him. He had a lead of several houses on me. Sam left Rodgers Forge, got back onto I-83, and headed downtown. I stayed with him on 83. Early afternoon traffic allowed me to linger a few cars behind, even in the next lane, and still keep his car in sight. Watching all those cop shows paid off. Sam took 83 all the way to its terminus, where it became President Street, turned onto Fleet Steet, and headed into Fells Point.

He drove around the area, eventually parking on a dinky side street and walking into a bar. I couldn't risk following him in there because he would recognize me, which left me to wait outside. In my car. In the cold. The high temperature today was set to be a robust 37. I could run the car and the heat periodically but ran the risk of arousing suspicion.

Most people paid for their lunches and bar tabs with credit cards. The problem people like me had with modern credit card machines was they only spit out the last four numbers. I wanted Sam's whole card number. Getting it would lead me to his real address. I took my special tablet—loaded with a suite of hacker scripts and tools—out of the glove compartment and fired it up. I scanned for local networks and found the bar's wi-fi. They still used WEP for alleged security. I cracked their WEP key in a couple minutes and got onto their network.

The credit card machine must be tied to a computer, which would use the network. Like most small businesses, the bar used the modem given to them by their service provider to function as a router as well as a bridge to connect the wired and wireless networks. I zeroed in on the router and took it down with a simple yet persistent denial-of-service attack. They would try rebooting the router. It wouldn't help. I got out of my car and walked into a bar across the street so I could keep an eye on Sam.

An hour later, he got into his car. I put down my soda, walked to the bar he patronized, and went inside. The décor made the bar look more like a tacky American restaurant from my youth. Lamps with square shades sat in the middle of every table. I noticed two tables still needing to be cleared of empty glasses and debris. The bar itself was made of dark wood designed to look like mahogany. Closer inspection revealed it to be a stain job faded and chipped in splotches. Posters for hair metal bands hung on the walls. Four men and one woman sat at a bar large enough to accommodate a crowd three times their number. I waved the bartender to me.

"What can I get you?" he said. He had a crew cut and a short black moustache. His voice sounded friendly enough, but his small smile never reached his eyes.

"Information," I said. I showed him my ID.

"Not on the menu."

"Neither is modern atmosphere by the looks of things."

"Sorry we don't meet your high standards. You drinking anything? Maybe some top-shelf liquor?"

"Sure. I'll take a shot of Patron and a chaser of information." I took a fifty out of my wallet and put it on the bar. "You can keep the change."

"I think my memory is improving." He took out a clean shot glass, pulled down the bottle of Patron, and poured me a shot. He set the glass in front of me. "What do you want to know?" he asked, pocketing the fifty.

"A few minutes ago, a Chinese midget left this place. Did he pay by credit card?"

"I don't think he's a midget. He's just short."

"I'm doing the bribing; I'll do the stereotyping, too," I said.

"Have it your way, man," he said, raising his hands. "I'm only trying to keep the oppression down."

"Your social consciousness is noted. Now, can you tell me if this Asian man of small stature paid with a credit card?"

"He did."

"May I see the receipt?"

"You gonna drink your tequila?"

"Consider it rent for the barstool. The receipt?"

"Sure." The bartender turned around and looked through a small pile of slips near the cash register. "You're in luck," he said. "Our network is down, and we had to dig up this old machine." He looked at the receipt. "Huh. Jerk didn't put his address on there." He slid the receipt across the bar to me. While it didn't have the address, it listed all of the credit card numbers instead of only the last four. I recorded the digits into a note on my phone. Sam couldn't get his credit card bills at a fake address.

"Thanks," I said, pushing the receipt back across the bar.

"You gonna drink or not?"

I pushed the glass across the bar toward him, too. "You can have it. Bottoms up and all that."

The bartender downed the shot as I walked out the door.

TRACKING the address attached to Sam's credit card proved easy. Sam lived on a side street in Fells Point about four blocks from my building. At least assaulting me had been convenient for him. I wondered how many times Sam had observed me before whacking me over the head. I also wondered how long it would take me to stop thinking of him as Sam.

Vinnie called Chaoxiang Ngai "Sam" as some sort of pejorative. He had to hate it. While he may have been a small Asian man, Chaoxiang must have bristled at being reminded of it by someone like Vinnie. I hoped to exploit the probability; I only hoped I could do it before he shot me. I drove up Sam's street, went a few doors past his house to find a parking spot, and turned off the engine.

Walking directly to the door and knocking struck me as a poor idea. Waiting would be similarly poor; I didn't want to spend another cold day on a stakeout for who knew how long? This time, I didn't even have any coffee or snacks. While I pondered my next move, Chaoxiang walked out of the house with a smallish dog on a leash. The petite pooch was tan with pointed ears, a classic long snout, and a long, curled-up tail. If I cared about dog breeds, I might have been able to identify it.

I slid down in my seat, but Chaoxiang walked in the opposite direction of my car. Once he had gone about 100 yards, I got out of the Lexus and closed the door quietly. I flattened myself against the other parked cars in case Chaoxiang turned back. He went around a corner, and I walked to his front door. Fells Point rowhouses offered few places to lie in wait for someone. I didn't want to linger on the front steps, so I tried the door. Chaoxiang left it unlocked. I went inside, took out my .45, and sat in a chair in the living room.

Chaoxiang's front room fit the definition of Spartan very well. He had a 40-inch TV mounted on the wall and a small entertainment center used for DVD and Blu-Ray storage beneath it. I sat in the only chair; a matching brown sofa sat at a right angle to it. A coffee table atop an ugly—though authentic —Chinese area rug rounded out the furnishings. The hardwood needed some work. My chair faced the side of the house, allowing me to watch both front and back.

I heard rustling from the front. I turned in the chair to face it. The door didn't open. Did Chaoxiang know I sat in his living room? The blinds were drawn, so he couldn't see in. What had the rustling been? It sounded like someone walked on the grass. I heard a dog bark. Then I heard footsteps on the hardwood behind me. By the time I turned, I saw Chaoxiang, without his dog, pointing a gun at my head.

## CHAPTER 20

CHAOXIANG STARED DOWN THE BARREL OF HIS GUN AT ME. I hadn't turned all the way to face him, but I had a heck of a shot at the wall of the house. I knew if I completed the turn, I would be dead. How had Chaoxiang managed to sneak around the house and get behind me? He didn't blink as he kept staring at me.

"Would you like to buy a vacuum cleaner?" I said to break the tension. I hoped my voice didn't betray my nerves. My heart pounded in my chest. Flashbacks to the Chinese prison swam before my eyes. I fought them down.

"No," he said.

"Some encyclopedias?"

"No."

"How did you know I was in your house?"

"I happened to look back as you walked in. Saw your coat trail behind you. I tied the dog in the front yard and came around." Chaoxiang's English had an accent, but I understood him easily. He must have lived in the States for years.

"You're stealthy," I said. "You keep sneaking up on me."

He shrugged and managed to keep the gun pointed at my head while he did. "You're pretty easy to sneak up on."

I would need to work on my situational awareness, if I survived. "I came to talk," I said.

"Don't need a gun to talk."

"Sometimes they help."

"Not this time."

"I'll drop mine if you drop yours."

"Why don't you say what you wanted to talk about?" he said. "Then I'll decide if I want to shoot you or not."

I needed to be careful here. Saying the wrong thing could get me shot. I hoped my theory supposing he really didn't like Vinnie was right because it was all I had. The only thing separating me from a bullet was a cold read of a Chinese man I knew from a brief chat at gunpoint and from hitting me over the back of the head. What the hell did I get myself into?

"It's about your boss," I said.

"My boss?"

"Vinnie. He's going down. Whether you take the fall with him is up to you."

"Vinnie isn't going anywhere."

"He's not as smart and careful as he thinks he is." Chaoxiang frowned. He hadn't pulled the trigger yet, which meant he held at least some interest in what I said. "There's no reason you need to share a cell with him."

"He's my boss."

"But you hate him."

"Do I?"

I answered him in Cantonese. "I think you do, Chaoxiang. Vinnie doesn't respect you. You're nothing but a thug to him, and he demeans you by using the nickname."

Sam stared at me. Now the malevolence in his eyes yielded to wonder. The gun lowered as his arm fell to his side. "You speak Cantonese."

"Lived in Hong Kong for three and a half years. Unless I'm wrong about your name, I think you lived there even longer."

"I did. Almost thirty years."

"The rug on your floor comes from Hong Kong. I saw many like it while I was there."

"Yes, it was a gift from my uncle."

"Vinnie doesn't care about your rug, Chaoxiang. He doesn't care about your uncle, and he doesn't care about you. You're a means to an end. Your name means 'expecting fortune.' You can't expect much in the way of riches from Vinnie."

"I do hate him," Chaoxiang said with a nod. "What can I do, though?"

"Testify against him. With what you know, I'm sure he'll go to jail for a long time."

"What about me? I'll go to jail, too."

"Probably. I can't speak for the law. I'm not official enough to make deals, but I would try to get you the best one possible. Maybe they'd send you back home."

He smiled. "I would like that."

"Why haven't you already gone back?"

"Vinnie threatened my family. He said he knows Tony Rizzo."

"He does, but he's only an errand boy. Tony doesn't protect him, and I don't think Tony would go after your family."

Chaoxiang's shoulders relaxed. He put the gun back in a holster at his side. Having spoken his native tongue, I had no problem thinking of him as Chaoxiang. "Why is Vinnie going down?" he said.

"The death of Paul Fisher."

"You know."

"I know enough. I know he was beaten in the church tower and thrown through the window, which probably killed him."

"The other guy did it. The big one."

"Sal," I said.

"Yes. We were supposed to rough Paul up. Sal got . . . carried away. I think he thought Paul would survive the fall." Chaoxiang closed his eyes and shook his head. "I don't mind beating people. I'm good at it. But I'm not a killer. Vinnie takes bets and now he loans money. It shouldn't require killing."

"No, it shouldn't." An image rushed into my head. I remembered it from the crime scene and from my recent perusal of all the photos thereof. Paul Fisher's wrecked car made an abrupt stop against a tree. The passenger's seat had been moved pretty far forward, as if someone Alice's height had recently been in the car. The driver's seat matched it—dead even. Paul had about ten inches on Alice. He couldn't have driven so cramped. "You drove Paul's car into the tree. Maybe you bailed out before it hit, but you were behind the wheel."

Chaoxiang nodded. "I was," he said. "We had to cover it up. Vinnie said he couldn't have a homicide come back on him."

"Now it's about to anyway."

"I didn't want to do it. It was Sal's fault the guy was dead. Vinnie's fault we had to hide it."

"I believe you."

"What now?"

"My cousin is a detective with the Baltimore police. I'll talk to him, and he'll talk to the DA. We'll see what kind of break we can get for you."

"What about Vinnie?"

"Try to act like everything is normal for now. If you don't, he may suspect something, and we don't want him getting suspicious."

"All right. Have you talked to the others?"

"We have Margaret on board," I said. "Still have to talk to Sal."

"He'll be a tough one," Chaoxiang said.

"He's loyal to Vinnie?"

"Not really. He likes money, and he likes hurting people. Doesn't mind killing. He has it good with Vinnie. Wouldn't want to give any of it up."

"I'll have to be persuasive."

"Make sure you're careful."

"I will." I stood and offered Chaoxiang my hand. He shook it. "I'll be in touch when I know more about a deal."

"All right," he said.

* * *

AFTER TALKING TO CHAOXIANG, I grabbed a late lunch at The Abbey and went home. I didn't know much about Sal, but I could use Vinnie's phone records to find him, too. A scan of the data showed many calls to one Salvatore Mancini. Unlike Chaoxiang, Sal had a real address when I ran a search for him. I expected him to live in Little Italy, but his address was a few blocks from Vinnie's in Rodgers Forge. I didn't want to drop in on him there in case I ran into Vinnie.

Rich would have taken lunch to Alice by now, which left me on dinner detail. I wanted to find Sal before then. Alice needed a shot of good news, and telling her we had flipped Vinnie's little organization would be the best news of all. We would still have to deal with Vinnie, but without his people behind him, he wouldn't pose much of a threat. Right now, he had only Sal, even though he didn't know anything would be amiss. It still made him dangerous.

I was pondering how best to search for Sal when Rich called. "Hello?" I said.

"C.T., they got her," Rich said.

"What? What are you talking about?"

"Alice. She's gone. I think Vinnie got her."

"Goddamnit." I pounded the steering wheel. "How did he know where she was?"

"I have no idea. You should meet me at the hotel, though."

"I'm on my way," I said.

## CHAPTER 21

I PULLED INTO THE LOT AT LA QUINTA AND PARKED NEXT to Rich's blue Camaro. When I got to Alice's room, the door was open. Even a novice like me could spot the forced entry. The jamb splintered, most likely from a boot when Sal kicked it. The frame showed extensive damage, the wood ripped away and lying in small shards inside the room itself. The chain lock had flown a few feet and settled near the foot of the bed. Rich stood in the center of the room, his arms crossed under his chest. "How did he find her here?" he said.

"I don't know," I said. I had asked him the same thing a scant few minutes ago. Neither of us had an answer. I looked around some more. The room appeared lived-in but undisturbed. Nothing was toppled over or damaged. Sal's snatch and grab had been a smooth one.

"Do you think he would hurt her?" Rich said.

"Maybe. He wants money out of her, and he wants it badly enough to kidnap her to get it. Vinnie thinks Alice got a nice life insurance check and can pay him off. He's going to be disappointed."

"We have to find her."

"We have to do something about this room. No one's noticed it so far. I guess the hotel isn't very crowded this time of day. Sooner or later, though, a guest or a staff person is going to see the door."

"This is the county, so their people would investigate." Rich frowned. "This is getting harder to keep unofficial. Now we're in another jurisdiction. I can't do anything here."

"Then let's go," I said. "We'll close the door and hope it doesn't get noticed. Put the DND sign up to make sure house-keeping walks on by. Maybe they won't spot it for a while and give us time to find her."

Rich nodded and grabbed the "Do Not Disturb" sign off the floor. We walked out, closed the door, and put the sign on the handle. The door would open if someone bumped into it, and anyone looking would see evidence of damage. We had to hope no one did anything about it. "How are we going look for her?" Rich said when we left the hotel.

"Vinnie doesn't realize we know she's missing. Does his ignorance give us any kind of advantage?"

Rich shook his head. "Not really. He has to figure we'll find out at some point. If he knew to find her here, he has to know you're involved."

"But not that you're involved. So we can investigate twice as quickly as I could on my own. It works in our favor."

"OK, but we have to work out where to start. You know Vinnie. Where would he take her?"

"I went to school with Vinnie, but I wouldn't say I know him. Not anymore. The old Vinnie never would have done something like this." I paused. Maybe Chaoxiang would have an idea. It couldn't hurt to ask. "I'm going to see if his Chinese associate knows anything."

"The midget who waylaid you? You talked to him?"

"Yeah, he'll play ball. I told him you'd try to get him a

decent plea bargain from the DA if he tells us everything about Vinnie." I took out my phone.

"I wish you wouldn't make promises for me," Rich said, rolling his eyes. "He might not get any break at all."

"He would be happy to get deported back to China." I called Chaoxiang, who answered in Cantonese.

"Hello?" he said.

"Chaoxiang, Alice is missing," I said in his language. "We think Vinnie took her. Do you know where he might keep her?"

"He called me right after you left. Said he wanted to get the girl. I told him I was too far away. He must have used Sal."

"Do they kidnap people a lot?"

"No."

"Do you know where Sal might keep her? Anyplace he frequents?"

"I try not to hang around him. Sal is tight with Vinnie. He likes him. I don't."

He wasn't telling me anything useful, but I didn't think he had been lying to me. It sounded like Chaoxiang really didn't know where Sal took Alice. "All right, thanks," I said and hung up.

"Did all of the Chinese you babbled end up with anything useful?" Rich said.

I shook my head. "He doesn't know where Sal would take her."

"You believe him?"

"Yes."

"All right. We should split up and start looking, then. You poke around downtown. I'll see what I can find out in Vinnie's area."

"All right." Rich and I got in our cars and drove off. We didn't have much of a plan past looking for Sal and Alice in our respective areas. How would I find them? I couldn't ask random people downtown if they had seen a burly Italian guy pushing an unhappy woman around. It might happen every day on The Block. I had to figure something out. I sped toward downtown in search of Alice, Sal, and an idea to help me find them.

* * *

I CAME out of the Fort McHenry Tunnel when my cell phone rang. I didn't recognize the number. "Hello?"

"Is this C.T.?" said a quiet female voice. Slight pauses betrayed the caller's nerves. I heard a background noise I couldn't place.

"It is. Who's this?"

"Margaret Madison." I expected her to say something else there—namely, the reason she called me—but she didn't. Something had her out of sorts, and she didn't strike me as the type to be out of sorts often.

"What can I do for you, Margaret?"

"The woman, Alice? She's here."

"What? She's at your house?"

"Yes, Sal brought her. I'm in the bathroom with the water running so he won't hear me. What should I do?"

"Stay there and act as normal as you can. I'm on my way." I already missed the Key Highway exit. The exit for I-395 to Howard Street would have to do. I stepped on the gas, zoomed in front of a few cars, and hit the exit ramp at 85. Traffic on I-395 hadn't gotten heavy yet. I swerved between lanes, getting ahead of as many cars as I could. Horns blared at me, but I drove onward. I ran a yellow light to turn at Conway, made the left at Light Street, then made a fast right turn onto Pratt.

I had to hope to catch the green lights on Pratt. Running a red in downtown Baltimore can lead to catastrophic results. I blew through a couple yellows, but had to stop at Calvert Street. As soon as the light turned green, I took off down Pratt. Traffic held until President Street, which turned red as I made the right turn at a speed not recommended in driver's ed. The left turn arrow went red at Fleet Street, but the signal to go straight remained green. With light traffic coming the other way, I made a sharp left from the center lane. No one honked at me, but I imagined there were a few uncharitable expressions hurled my way.

Once on Fleet, I got through all the necessary lights, then made the right onto Boston Street. I decided to call Rich in case I needed him. Calling earlier would have been a better idea, but I became wrapped up in Alice's abduction and driving like a maniac. Rich picked up right away. "What is it?" he said.

"Alice is at Margaret Madison's," I said. "She called me. Sal took her there. I'm a few minutes away."

"I'll turn around and head your way." He hung up.

A few minutes later, I stopped three houses from Margaret's. I called her house number and she answered. "Hello?"

"It's C.T. I'm on your street. Act like this is a normal call."

"Oh, hi. I haven't heard from you in a while."

"I don't want to run in there while Sal has Alice. Is he leaving soon?"

"I think that would be great."

I got out of the car, crossed the street, and put my free hand on the grip of my .45. "He doesn't suspect anything, then. Can you send him away? Tell him you'll handle it."

"I'd love to. Let me call you back when I have more time."

"Great, thanks."

"Nice talking to—" she said, but I hung up. I put my phone away, drew the .45, and started down her alley. I stopped and put my back against the house. Sal rounded the corner of the stone fence a few seconds later, saw me, said, "Shit!" and ducked back around the corner. I saw the barrel of his gun poke out from around the corner.

"What the hell are you doing here?" he said.

"Looking for stupid goons who like to kidnap helpless women," I said. "What a break to find one so quickly."

"Get the fuck outta here before I hurt you."

"You tried to hurt me once, remember? It didn't go so well. Sure you want to try again?"

"I got a gun."

"So do I, genius."

"We have a standoff, then."

"You want to try and hurt me again? Throw down your gun. I'll do the same. Then you can try all you want."

"Yeah?" Sal took a step from around the corner. My finger tightened on the trigger. I didn't want to shoot him, but if it looked like he might shoot me, I definitely would. Sal held a revolver in his hand that could have come straight from a Dirty Harry movie.

He looked down the long barrel of his .44 at me. I watched his hand for any sign he was about to fire. Despite the cold, I felt a drop of sweat run down the side of my face. My finger grew sore. The .45 felt heavy in my hand. Sal looked at me a few seconds longer, then held his gun out to the side and tossed it up the alley. "Let's settle this, then," he said.

I felt tempted to shoot him where he stood. It would be so easy, and the son of a bitch deserved it. I couldn't do it. The legal nightmare aside, I knew I wasn't a killer, and I wouldn't change my principles (such as they were) for someone like Sal. I lowered the .45 and tossed it toward the far side of the alley. Sal stayed away from the open end. He didn't want to attract attention. I was happy to play his game, so I walked toward him.

I shook off my trench coat and flung it up the alley atop my gun. Sal took off his heavy coat and pitched it to cover his gun. The stone and chain-link fences would hide us from a lot of prying eyes, but anyone walking by could still see us fighting in the alley. At least the guns were out of sight. Sal backtracked toward the intersecting alley running behind Margaret's house, and I followed him. Once we turned the corner, he took a swing at me. I saw it coming and avoided it. Sal threw another haymaker, which I also dodged. I felt like I was playing Punch-Out, and I had to weather the initial barrage from the champ.

Sal had the size and strength advantages. His bulk meant he carried too much weight for his frame. If I could dodge or block his haymakers, I could tire him out and win this fight. He stopped throwing the haymakers, however, and instead went with a hard jab. I blocked it with my left forearm and gave him a good right to the stomach. Sal grunted but didn't slow his assault. He threw another jab, then another. I blocked both, but didn't have a chance to counter. Sal took a step back, lowered his head, and charged. I stepped to my left. He didn't grab me, but his right arm still hit me in the midsection as he ran past. I staggered back a step, then recovered enough to turn and face Sal again.

He tried the same bull rush. Before Sal could build a lot of momentum, I snapped off a quick kick to his face. He slowed and straightened partway, so I kicked him again—harder this time—in the belly. Sal grunted and doubled over. I took a step forward, then drove my elbow down onto the back of his neck. Sal's neck crunched, and he crashed to the concrete. He rolled over onto his side.

"Your boss is done," I said. "Whether you go to jail with him is up to you. I know you killed Paul Fisher."

"So what?" he said.

"So give up Vinnie. Say he ordered you to do it. Testify against him."

"Why should I?"

"Unless you want to be cellmates for twenty-five to life, it's in your best interests."

"What if I don't care what you think?"

I shrugged. "It's your future—such as it is."

Sal raised his knee and bent his leg. He gave me plenty of warning for the kick, so I made sure to be well out of his reach when he actually delivered it. He scrambled to his feet faster than I would have thought he could and assumed something resembling a boxing stance. His earlier footwork and punching technique made me think he had a boxing background. The silly bull rush ruined my first impression. Maybe Sal was out of practice. I was, too, when it came to fighting boxers. Now I had added motivation to stay out of his reach.

He advanced, moving his feet carefully and keeping good balance. I took a defensive stance, keeping my side to Sal. He snapped off a jab, which I blocked, and followed it with a hook. I blocked it with my forearm and paid for it when my lower right arm went numb. I tried to hide the wince, but a glint in Sal's eye told me he saw it. He pressed the attack now, throwing jabs in quick succession. I blocked them all, mostly with my left arm. A strong hook I couldn't block took me in the stomach.

I almost fell over from the blow, managing to stay on my feet through some combination of balance and good fortune. Sal rushed again. I couldn't let him unleash another telling barrage, not with one and a half arms to work with. I kicked at his legs, hitting him in the knee and the quadriceps. He stopped in his tracks. I had to press this momentary advantage while feeling returned to my lower right arm. I kicked at Sal's legs again and again. He blunted a couple, but the majority hit him. I gave him a good kick in the back of the leg and drove him to one knee. Sal tried to punch me in the balls, but I blocked it with my left arm. The effort almost caused him to topple forward. I drove a side kick right into Sal's face, bending him backward over his right leg and making him howl in pain. Maybe I broke his nose again.

Sal writhed on his back. I rubbed my right arm. It tingled a little, but the feeling came back. Sal had his hands under his back. When he sat up, he had a snub-nose revolver in his right hand. "You think you're fancy with all those fucking kicks?" he said. I froze. Sal got to his feet, favoring his right knee. My pulse, already elevated from the fight, spiked.

"Still time to roll over on Vinnie," I said. "Make sure he takes the fall for this, not you."

"What if I don't want to?" Chaoxiang told me Sal would be difficult to turn. I hoped he would be wrong. Sal took a couple limping steps toward me. I raised my hands, keeping them even with my shoulders. He held the gun a foot from my face. "Yeah, I killed Paul Fisher," he said. "Maybe he won't be the only asshole I kill."

I had to act. My right arm exploded forward, grabbing the barrel of the gun and moving it away from my face. Sal scowled and pushed against me. I figured he would and grabbed his right wrist with my left hand. "Last chance to let go," I said.

"Fuck you," Sal said.

"Eloquent as ever." I pushed up with my right hand and pulled down with my left. Sal's index finger crunched and snapped in the trigger guard. He shouted a curse in pain. His grip on the gun slackened. I kept my grip on the barrel and pulled it from his hand. Sal looked at his broken finger. I whacked him in the head with the butt of his gun. The crack of the grip against his skull sounded so much like a gunshot I wondered if the revolver went off. Sal crumpled to the ground. Blood ran from the side of his head.

"I'm tired of people pointing guns at me today," I said. I reversed the gun in my hand and pointed it at him. Sal made some incoherent groans as a reply. "This time, you might want to stay down, and you probably want to listen, too."

"You don't care . . . what I think?" Sal said, holding a hand to his bleeding head.

"Never have. I'm sure Vinnie doesn't, either. He doesn't pay you to think."

"I'm not stupid."

"Then do something smart. Give up Vinnie. You did kill Paul Fisher, so you won't get a great deal from the state's attorney, but you'll probably get something. Take it. Take the deal and sing like a goddamn canary who doesn't want to go back to the coalmine."

"You want me to give up Vinnie?"

"I think it's in your best interests. He doesn't care about you. If I arrested you, Vinnie wouldn't care. He'd just hire some other guy with a gun fetish and no neck. If he's not going to care about you, why care about him?"

He nodded. "Yeah, OK. OK. I get you. Fuck Vinnie. I'll give him up."

"Good. Here's the thing: you need to act like everything is normal for now. He'll go down soon. Until he does, I don't want him to know his people have turned on him. I don't want Alice Fisher to get hurt." Alice—she was still in Margaret Madison's house. I glowered at Sal. "You didn't hurt her, did you?"

"No, she's good. She's inside. I had to tie her up, but she ain't hurt."

"Good." I used my free hand to grab my wallet and fish out a business card, which I tossed down onto him. "I'll call you when the shit hits the fan. Don't burn me on this." I put the gun closer to his face for emphasis.

"I won't, I won't," he said.

I heard footsteps running down the sidewalk. Sal heard them, too. He tried and failed to get to his feet. I stuffed the gun under my sweater. Rich ran to us, his Beretta in his hand. "Everything all right?" he said.

"We're under control, Officer," I said.

"You need this guy arrested?"

"No, he's going to play ball."

"Good." Rich put his gun away, and crouched beside Sal. "I can probably get you something from the DA, but if you burn us, you'll go down hard. Harder than Vinnie. I'll make sure of it."

"I ain't gonna burn you," Sal said. He managed to pull himself to a seated position. Blood stopped running from his head and face, and now it caked in his hair. "I ain't gonna go down for Vinnie."

"All right, then. Get out of here," Sal got to one knee, winced, and pushed himself to his feet. He limped on his dodgy right knee toward his coat and gun. Rich and I both watched him as he put the gun back in the holster, put his coat on, and hobbled out of the alley.

"Alice is inside," I said. "Sal told me he tied her up, but didn't hurt her."

"Let's get her," Rich said.

I put Sal's gun in my waistband, retrieved my .45, and put my trench coat back on. It needed a serious dry cleaning after being in the alley. I frowned at the wet spot on my left sleeve, refusing to imagine it was anything other than water. Rich had gone to Margaret Madison's rear door. When I got there, Margaret stood in the doorway.

"She's in the basement," she said.

"Is she OK?" Rich and I said simultaneously.

Margaret looked between us and smirked. "Yeah, she's fine. Once Sal left, I told her what was going on."

"Is she still tied up?" I said,

"No, I untied her when Sal left. She stayed in the basement in case he came back."

Rich and I walked inside, and I led the way to the basement stairs. Fortunately, no one asked why I knew where they were. Alice rushed forward and wrapped me in a hug. "I'm so glad to see you," she said. Her voice trembled. I put my arms around her.

"It's good to see you, too." I said. "We're glad you're safe."

"Not as glad as I am." Alice let me go, ran to Rich, and they gave each other huge hugs. I guess they had bonded over carry-out lunches in the hotel.

"We need to decide where you go from here," I said.

"Can I stay with you?"

"I wouldn't recommend it. Vinnie knows me. He knows where I live. Hell, he found out where we stashed you." I still didn't know how he pulled it off. "You need to go someplace he's not going to find you easily."

"You can stay with me," Rich said. "Vinnie doesn't really know me. Besides, it shouldn't be for long."

I nodded. "We've flipped his people on him. I think we can take him down tonight."

"Just say when."

"I have a plan in mind. You can make the arrest. I want Vinnie to confess, though."

"We don't need him to."

"Sure, but he doesn't know that."

## CHAPTER 22

WE DIDN'T NEED VINNIE'S CONFESSION. WITH THE information his erstwhile employees could give us, plus the physical evidence recovered from the Paul Fisher scenes, we had enough to put him away. Though I didn't expect him to, Rich went along with me on getting Vinnie to confess. Now I had to deliver the goods.

First, I had other matters to address. Chaoxiang Ngai had a unique name, so finding his bank records didn't take me long. I didn't want his money, though, only knowledge of where he got it. Twice a month, deposits from Serrano Enterprises, LLC, hit his checking account. Vinnie considered his gambling ring an enterprise now. Somehow, he hoodwinked people into thinking it was a legitimate limited liability company. Regardless, I found his corporate bank account easily.

I had previously accessed the Fishers' account and still had his information noted in a text file. Vinnie would pay for Paul Fisher's death in terms of a legal punishment. I decided he should also pay for it financially. Paul didn't have life insurance, but Alice said his funeral would be paid for. She could use that money for other, happier means. I hoped she wouldn't decide to gamble it away, but considering all the trouble her habit had gotten her in, I felt confident her days as a high roller were over.

How much did funerals cost these days? My sister's had cost quite a bit, but my parents had insisted on the finest coffin, a headstone carved from granite with Mjolnir, and other extravagances the Fishers' limited benefits wouldn't cover. I settled on ten thousand as a reasonable figure and decided Vinnie owed Alice at least as much again for pain and suffering. The loss of her husband couldn't be valued in dollars, but her near-term financial comfort had a value. I transferred thirty thousand from Vinnie's account—leaving him with only a few hundred dollars on hand—to the Fishers' joint account. Those funds would completely wipe out Alice's debt and allow her to live a little after the loss of her husband,

It would also piss Vinnie off, which made me happy.

I SKIPPED dinner as I assembled my plan. Margaret called me to say Vinnie checked up on Alice. She said everything was OK. Sal checked in to say he told Vinnie everything still came up aces. I didn't hear from Chaoxiang but presumed something similar had happened to him. Vinnie still thought his people were his people, and Alice Fisher sat in Margaret Madison's basement tied to a chair and afraid for her life. I imagined the smug smile on his face.

I called Vinnie. It was time to kick the plan into motion. "What the hell do you want?" he said when he answered his phone.

"To know where manners have gone," I said.

"I don't have much patience for you, C.T. What do you want?"

"Sal took a shot at me today, Vinnie. I want a truce. At least for tonight. Let's talk. There's no reason we both can't be civil and come out of this unscathed."

"You want to talk?" I heard the mirth, the joy in his voice. He thought he had the advantage. After all, he had Alice Fisher stashed in his girlfriend's basement, and I didn't know anything about it.

"Yeah, just you and me. No guns, no goons. We can meet at The Field again. I'll bring dinner."

Vinnie released a slow, deep breath into the phone. "Dinner is fine. You bring dinner. But we won't meet at The Field. You want to talk to me now, you come to my house. I'm going to have the home-field advantage in this one."

I made a point to sigh into my phone. "All right, I'll do it your way. You have me in a bind here, so I guess I have to."

"Yeah, I guess you do."

"You still have the same house in Rodgers Forge?"

"You remember. I'm touched."

"Of course, I remember. I'll pick up some food and come by at eight-thirty. Is that good?"

"Sure, eight-thirty. Oh, C.T.? Park on the street. I reserve the driveway for my friends." Vinnie hung up.

The smug prick. This would be very satisfying.

* * *

At eight-thirty-six, armed with a paper bag full of delicious carry-out and as much false humility as I could muster, I got out of my car and walked up to Vinnie's front door. I rang the bell. He made me wait in the cold for over a minute before he opened the door. He looked at me like a teacher might regard an uppity pupil—a look I remembered during my school days. "I was beginning to wonder if you'd show," he said, swinging the storm door wide.

"You know how prompt I am," I said.

"Where'd you go?"

"Scotto's Pizza. It gets good reviews."

"I've wanted to try that place for a while." Vinnie walked into the kitchen, and I followed him. The house looked much like I remembered, right down to the maroon carpeting. It had seen more wear since the last time I was here, but the color remained the same. Vinnie's upholstery upgrade money went toward the ginormous TV mounted on his wall. He also had every next-generation console on an entertainment center, along with a slew of movies and games in a tall bookcase. His hand-me-down furniture had become dark brown leather looking and smelling recently cleaned. The bookmaking and loan-sharking business must be a good one.

Vinnie had an oak table in his kitchen. I set the bags down atop it while Vinnie took a seat. "Fetch me a beer, will you?" he said.

"Fetch" indeed. "Sure," I said. I walked to his stainless steel refrigerator and opened the door. Vinnie didn't keep a lot of food on hand, but the drawers and compartments were full of soda, condiments, and beer. I grabbed two bottles of Blue Moon out of the fridge and carried them to the table.

"Care to slice an orange?" Vinnie said. He flashed an insincere smile. That same smug look was still plastered on his face.

"Don't press your luck," I said. "Silverware?"

"Last drawer on the right."

I walked to the counter opposite the fridge and opened the drawer. Vinnie kept his silverware and some other supplies in there. I grabbed what I needed and carried it to the table. "What's the silverware for?"

"Salads came with our sandwiches. I also picked up some marinated potatoes and string beans in olive oil. They sounded good."

"Sounds almost swell enough to turn me into a fucking vegetarian." Vinnie laughed. It sounded sincere, and the accompanying smile reached his eyes. "Almost."

"If you're going to convert, do it after this," I said. "I got us barbeque chicken pita sandwiches and curly fries."

"I've heard the curly fries are divine."

"Who says 'divine'?"

"I do," said Vinnie. "You ever try them?"

"Nope, I just went there because it's sort of on the way and because I read some good reviews."

I sat at the table, and we started eating. "So you want a truce?" Vinnie said. He had eaten a few bites of the pita sandwich, but none of the sides. I speared a marinated potato and tried it. They deserved the reputation.

"Yes," I said. "I'm tired of looking over my shoulder. Tired of getting hit over the head. Tired of people shooting at me. I'm just tired of this case." I sighed and made sure to look down at the table. "I didn't sign up for all of this. It was supposed to be an adultery case."

"Adultery? Paul was fucking around on his wife?"

"No, actually, I guess I should have bailed when I discovered he was innocent, but you know me—I like to see things through to the end."

"But not this time."

I shook my head. "No. Not after everything that's happened."

Vinnie nodded. He put the pita down, grabbed a few curly fries, and shoved them into his mouth. "Then let's negotiate the terms of your surrender."

He must have thought he was Ulysses S. Grant. "All right," I said, lowering my voice.

"Drop the case, first of all. Stop trying to be Alice's white knight. She owes me a lot of money. One way or another, I'm going to get it from her."

"Sounds OK so far."

"You know I have Alice, right?" Vinnie practically beamed at me. "I've been waiting to tell you. You think you're so smart. You think you can fuck around overseas, come back home, and do the job of a real detective. A real P.I. would know not to use a debit card with the same number he had in college." Now I knew how he found Alice. "Yeah, I remember. A memory for numbers helps someone like me. You can't even keep a woman safe from my boys."

I looked at the tabletop, closed my eyes, and shook my head. "I hope you don't hurt her."

"I hope I don't have to. You never know, though." Vinnie picked up his fork and ate a few potatoes, then some string beans. "Damn, these are good. Spiced really well, too. Where was I?"

He knew where he was; he just wanted me to say it. "Something about not keeping Alice safe from you and your boys."

"Fuck, those words sound sweet." Vinnie paused long enough to cough once, then continued. "Yeah, I have her. She's going to get me my money, and you're going to stop looking for her. No cops, either, and no fucking feds. You involve anyone official, and I'll make sure she gets hurt."

I nodded. "I don't want to see her hurt."

Vinnie ate some more string beans. "Of course you don't. You're so fucking noble when you want to be. Always have to be the good guy." He coughed again and took a swig of his beer. I sat there and watched him. "I don't want you sniffing around my operation, either. Me and my people are off-limits to you, you got it?"

"I got it."

"I guess we're good for now. I might think of something else later." Vinnie coughed again. "Damn, I'm getting congested." He dove into his curly fries again, giving me a mocking smile as he shoved each one into his mouth. I ate my sandwich and fries and watched him.

Vinnie finished eating some string beans when it happened. The fork fell from his hand. His eyes opened wide. His breathing sounded labored and ragged like he had to suck in great gulps of air to take a regular breath. "What's wrong?" I said.

"Breathing . . . problems," Vinnie said. He got up and dashed to the counter, opening the last drawer on the right while clinging to the counter to remain upright. I watched him rummage through it. Then he threw his hands up and shouted.

"Looking for this?" I took his epinephrine pen out of my pocket and waved it in the air. He looked at it and glared at me. "I saw it in the drawer. Even someone as stupid as I am figured you might keep it there."

"Give me . . .," Vinnie said, staggering toward me with his hand out.

"I don't think so."

"What . . . the food?"

"Yeah. I went to Scotto's because they cook the fries in peanut oil."

"Peanut . . . oil?" Vinnie clutched his chest. He stopped shambling toward me, halting about three steps shy. His breath came in ragged gasps.

"I know . . . I know. You have a peanut allergy. You were the only kid in school who did. How could I forget? Where was I?"

Vinnie's only reply was a gasp.

"Oh, right, your allergy. I took chemistry in high school and college. I know peanut oil alone won't set it off. You need the peanut proteins too. So I added salt from the bottom of a peanut jar to all the food."

"I'll . . . die." Vinnie sank to his knees.

"Not right away. You'll be in anaphylactic shock for a while."

"I'll . . . die," he said again.

"Then confess. Confess to what you did to Paul and Alice Fisher."

"Or . . . what?"

I shrugged. "Or you'll die. 'I'm sorry, Officer, I didn't know he had a peanut allergy. If only we could have found the epi pen in time.'" I frowned theatrically and shook my head.

"Fine . . . fine. I had . . . Paul killed. Had Alice . . . kidnapped."

"Isn't confession good for the soul, Vinnie?"

He looked at me, gasped, and sank to the floor. "Oh, all right. I guess I shouldn't let you die." I took the cap off the epi pen, stabbed the needle into his thigh, and pushed the plunger. Vinnie's anguished expression softened into something approaching relief. He still gasped, but his breathing cleared up over the next minute.

"You bastard," he said.

"You don't know the half of it," I said. "We already talked to Margaret, Sal, and Chaoxiang."

"Who?"

"The man you derisively call Sam."

"What did . . . they say?"

"They're going to roll on you. You're done, Vinnie. They'll testify against you." I smiled at him. "I didn't even need your confession."

"What the fuck . . . was all this, then?"

I stood. "I wanted you to suffer for what you had done to Paul and Alice Fisher."

"You motherfucker." Vinnie stood, but the effort almost sent him sprawling to the tiled floor again. He recovered his balance and threw a shaky right cross at me. I blocked it and elbowed him in the face. He fell back to the tile and rubbed his jaw.

"Stay down, Vinnie. I have to make a phone call. Rich is going to come in and arrest you. You remember him, right? He's a real detective . . . with the police and everything."

"The confession you get won't hold up."

"I told you we didn't need it. I'm sure Alice will testify against you. Between her and your three former employees, you're going up the river for a while." I took out my cell phone and called Rich. "He confessed." Vinnie scowled at me.

"I'll be right in." Rich hung up. I put my phone away.

"I'll get you for this," Vinnie said.

"Better make it fast," I said. "Rich is only half a block up the road."

Vinnie walked to the counter as quickly as his wobbly legs would allow. He grabbed a knife from the block of fine cutlery on the countertop. "I don't need much time to cut you up."

I shrugged and took out the .32 from a small holster at my back. "Vinnie, didn't anyone ever tell you not to bring a knife to a gunfight?"

"You said no guns!"

"I had my fingers crossed."

"You son of a bitch." Vinnie looked at me, looked at the knife, then looked at me again. I saw a gleam in his eye.

"Don't do it, Vinnie. I'll shoot you if I have to."

"Will you?"

"And if he doesn't, I will," Rich said. He walked into the kitchen, his gun pointed at Vinnie.

"He tried to kill me," Vinnie said, pointing toward me with the knife. "He gave me poisoned food."

I shrugged. "How was I supposed to remember he had a peanut allergy?"

"He deliberately bought food cooked in peanut oil!"

"I saved your life by finding your epi pen, Vinnie. You might try being grateful."

"You might also try putting the knife down," Rich said.

Vinnie looked at me, at Rich, and back at me. "This thing between us . . . it isn't finished."

"But you are."

Rich spun Vinnie around, shoved him into the refrigerator, and read him his Miranda rights while putting handcuffs on him.

"I'll get out of jail one day," Vinnie said as Rich led him toward the front of the house.

"Maybe when we're in our fifties." I sat back down at the table.

Rich stopped and looked at me. "What are you doing?"

"I bought all this food. I might as well eat it. You want any?"

Rich shook his head. "You want to come downtown with me?"

"After I eat. You won't need me right away, will you?"

"I think I can manage without you."

"I just got you an arrest. It'll look very nice on your new detective record. Don't presume you can live without me." I started eating the rest of my pita sandwich. "I'll bring you a doggie bag if you want."

"Just come downtown when you're done, if your head will fit through the doors." Rich shoved Vinnie forward and guided him out of the house.

I looked down at my food. It hit me I sat in an old friend's house—an old friend who would be going to jail because of my handiwork. Now Alice Fisher didn't have to be afraid anymore.

Nothing could bring her husband back, but she could try to get on with her life and not have to worry about Vinnie and his people. I smiled. It felt good—all of it. I had helped someone who landed in a bad situation and didn't have anywhere else to go. I had made a real difference. My parents would be beaming. This was exactly what they wanted.

But it was only one case. If I wanted to get back into their good financial graces, I had to work more of them. The realization killed my good mood. Once word of what I did hit the media, I would have a lot more prospective clients to sift through. More fights with goons in alleys, more breaking into houses, more times looking over my shoulder for guns or black-jacks, more couples who can't communicate, more allegations of adultery.

It was enough to make me lose my appetite.

*CHAPTER 23*

I walked into the police station. Rich wasn't at his desk. I didn't think he would be. He probably had Vinnie in an interrogation room, trying to get him to confess and give a statement. After what I did to him, I doubted Vinnie would confess. He'd be defiant, and it wouldn't do him any good. His people agreed to roll on him. They were expected at the station at some point tonight, in addition to Alice Fisher. Vinnie could be defiant all he wanted. He was bound for jail regardless.

The interrogation rooms sat off the main floor. A viewing room was attached to each where interested observers could peer through the one-way mirror. I looked through the small window on the door to the first room and saw Rich and another detective talking to Vinnie. The next door led to the observation room. I opened it and walked inside. I was not the first observer; a large black man with a shaved head stood inside. He turned and looked at me as I walked in, then went back to watching the interrogation. Audio came in through two speakers hung on the wall above the glass.

"Make it easy on yourself, Vinnie," Rich said. "You know we have your people ready to roll on you."

"No, I don't know," Vinnie said. "You keep telling me. I don't know, and why should I believe you?"

"Because I'm telling you the truth." Rich sat in the chair opposite Vinnie. The other detective stood a few feet behind Rich, leaning on the wall. He had his arms folded across his chest and he spent most of his time staring at Vinnie. From what I could tell, he looked about ten years older than Rich. He had already surrendered the hair battle, eschewing a combover in favor of a short cut around his bald spot.

"So you say," Vinnie said. "You fucking cops ain't above lying to get a confession out of someone. Hell, your cousin tried to kill me."

My guest in the observation room glanced at me at Vinnie's comment but didn't say anything. "You have a bad food allergy, Vinnie. He saved your life, using your epi pen on you when he did."

"Whatever. I know what happened. I think you do, too, even if you won't admit it."

"We have cops collecting your people, Vinnie," the other detective said. "Your girlfriend is going to give you up. So will the big dumb Italian and the little Asian guy."

"What the fuck do you need my confession for, then?" Vinnie said. "You turn my people into canaries. Don't sound like I need to say anything."

"If you admit to what you did, the state's attorney might see clear to give you a lesser sentence," Rich said. "Kidnapping and murder are serious charges, and they're not the only ones you're facing."

"I'll take my chances."

The other detective started to say something else, but my fellow observer flipped the switch and killed the audio feed. "I saw you at the Walters," he said. "You were at Karen's exhibit opening."

"I didn't know her name," I said.

"I went to college with her. How do you know her?"

"I don't. My parents do. Being patrons of the arts makes them feel good, so they know their share of artists. They bought me a ticket, so I went."

"You're Rich's cousin." It wasn't a question.

"I am."

"He told me about you."

"Are you his boss?"

He shook his bald head. "No. He's not really in my supervisory chain. This is an interesting case, and your cousin has a promising career."

"He does?"

"He does." He turned to look at me now. This man who was not Rich's boss had about four inches on me, along with at least seventy pounds. Even though he looked to be in his late forties—the shaved head made it hard to tell—none of the weight appeared unnecessary. "I'm Lieutenant Leon Sharpe," he said, extending a burly hand.

I shook it. It felt like putting my hand into a car compactor. Sharpe knew he had a strong grip, but I didn't take him for the type to show it off and try to intimidate someone. "C.T. Ferguson."

"I know who you are."

"Should I be honored?"

Sharpe smirked. He did it without looking amused. "I see the files on everyone living in Baltimore who gets a PI license."

"I don't feel so honored anymore."

"Rich filled in some details for me."

"You mentioned he told you about me."

"He did. He said you're self-centered, reckless, you cut corners, have no interest in following proper procedure, don't care much about your clients, and care even less about the system and how it works."

"He's such a flatterer." Did Rich really say all those things about me? He hadn't been supportive of my decision to become a detective, though he never voiced an objection in those exact words. Only toward the end of the case did Rich soften his stance toward me.

Besides, I couldn't find fault with anything he said.

"He also said you're as smart as anyone he knows, you learn quickly, and you don't let something go when you're involved with it."

At least he found something positive to say. Sharpe continued before I could comment. "On top of it all, he vouched for your experience overseas."

"What do you mean?"

"Like I said, I saw your file. I thought what you did in China sounded like bullshit. Rich said it was legit."

I hoped I hid my surprise. If I hadn't, Leon Sharpe could pick at my embellished experiences and unearth a few problems. "Rich and I haven't always been tight," I said. "It's good to hear he's willing to put a good word in for me."

"You seem a little surprised."

"Like I said, Rich and I haven't always been tight."

"I hope he didn't sell me a bill of goods. I value Rich's opinion."

"What's the point, Lieutenant? You strike me as the type who forms his own opinions."

Sharpe looked at me for a moment, then nodded. "I am. Just wanted to see how you'd react."

"Learn anything?"

"Of course. Did you really try to kill Vinnie Serrano?"

"Vinnie has an active imagination. I brought food to his

house. I wanted to talk about the case. Rich and I flipped his people, and I wanted to give Vinnie a chance to confess."

"Why?"

"He's an old friend."

"So you took food to his house," Sharpe said. He had a way of asking questions without really asking questions. Alex Trebek would be displeased.

"Yes," I said. "Apparently, the restaurant uses peanut oil. I didn't know they did, and I forgot about Vinnie's peanut allergy."

"You forgot about it?"

"It's been a while since we were in school together."

"So Vinnie had a reaction to the food."

"Yes. He had trouble breathing, and he ended up on the floor. I found an Epi-Pen and gave him the shot."

"Why does he think you poisoned him, then?"

"I guess because I brought the food," I said.

Sharpe looked at me for a moment without saying anything. "I know you don't have to follow all the same rules we do. I know you don't want to follow a lot of the ones you're supposed to. At the end of the day, I care about results. I want to see good people go home happy and bad people caught and arrested. I'm willing to look past a few things to get those results. Within reason."

"I'll remember."

He walked past me and stopped at the door. "Make sure you do. Turn the sound back on if you want." Sharpe left the room.

I watched the door close behind him. Leon Sharpe would take an interest in my cases; I felt sure of it. Maybe it was because I was Rich's cousin, perhaps it was because of all the things Rich had to say about me, maybe he didn't have anything better to do. Regardless, I knew I would see more of him.

* * *

I DIDN'T BOTHER TURNING the audio back on. Vinnie could sink quickly by keeping up the defiance or sink a little more slowly by cooperating. If he didn't see the difference, it was just too bad. I tried to get him to confess. Hell, I even poisoned him to give him some motivation. Some people simply have no follow-through.

Before I left the police station, I saw Sal brought in wearing handcuffs. He didn't look at me as the cops led him toward the back of the precinct. I saw Alice Fisher as I walked out the door. She stopped and gave me a hug. "I'm going to tell the police everything I know," she said.

"Good," I said. "Make sure you say it again in court, if it comes to a trial."

"I will."

"Oh, and check your bank account. Vinnie sends his condolences."

She canted her head at me and whispered. "Did you siphon money from Vinnie's account into mine?"

"Does it matter? Paul's funeral is paid for, and you have enough money to start over somewhere else if you want to. Just make sure you don't wager with it." I turned to walk away,

"I won't," Alice said. "This whole mess has gotten me over gambling."

I hoped she told the truth.

* * *

I DROVE AWAY from the police station. The story would get around. I would probably have to talk to Jessica Webber again. Good thing we patched things up after I yelled at her and slammed the door in her face. Before I talked to any reporters, though, I needed to talk to someone else first—someone whose opinion of what had gone down would be more important than a journalist's.

Parking in Little Italy is easier during the week than on the weekend, and as the hour grows later, weeknight parking becomes better. I left my car half a block away from *Il Buon Cibo*. As I walked toward the restaurant, I saw lights on inside and at least one table with smiling patrons still eating their food. I entered, went past the vacant maitre d' station, and looked around.

Tony Rizzo was putting his coat on near his usual table. Two men with large arms and invisible necks stood near him. "Tony," I said as I moved toward the back of the restaurant, "have a minute?"

The goons glared at me, then looked back at Tony. "Warm the car up, boys," he said. "I'll be along in a few." The goons gave me a final glance, then walked toward the back of the restaurant. "I always have a few minutes for my friends, C.T."

"Glad to hear it. I'll try not to take up too much of your time."

"What can I do for you?"

I sat at the booth without being invited. Tony frowned at me and sat down, also. "It's about Vinnie Serrano," I said.

"What about him?"

"I had to take him down." I watched Tony for a reaction. He spent years meeting with people far more menacing and more important than I. But he liked me. He liked my parents. They were old friends. Tony might be friendly with a lot of the people he dealt with, but how many of them did he actually like? I figured it couldn't be very many. Tony didn't give any reaction except slight nods of his head I had to be watching to notice.

"I guess he became too much of a problem."

"Basically. He killed a man—the man who was working to pay off a debt his wife racked up."

"Bad business." Tony shook his head now.

"It certainly is. He and his people tried to cover it up, but I figured out what they did. Took a little while, but the evidence was there."

"How'd you get him?"

"Rich and I convinced his people to turn state's evidence on him. They each decided some leniency from the DA was worth more than whatever loyalty they had to Vinnie."

"Vinnie didn't inspire loyalty in his people. It's why I wouldn't let him work for me."

"He wanted to?"

"You shitting me? Of course he wanted to. He wanted the protection, the prestige." I felt Tony was overstating the benefits of being in his employ, but I decided against arguing with the man in his own restaurant. "I wouldn't have him. He had my blessing to do what he did, but nothing else."

"What about Sal?"

"Sal Who?"

"Sal, Vinnie's goon. He had a Chinese guy and an American girl working for him. Vinnie isn't the type to care about diversity. Was Sal one of yours?"

"You're a smart kid, C.T. You always were." Tony smiled, more with the corners of his mouth than anything. It looked wistful, almost sad. "Yeah, Sal was one of my guys at one point. He flunked out, so to speak. Vinnie snatched him up almost as soon as his dumb ass bounced off the pavement. I think he felt it gave him a little more legitimacy to have one of my people in his little organization."

I nodded. "I wanted to personally let you know what happened with Vinnie."

"I appreciate it."

"Are we cool?"

Tony smiled at me again. It was the same smile. I didn't feel any happiness and warmth. "You're a friend, C.T. Your parents are friends. Don't get me wrong, I'd go after you if it came to it. I hope I don't have to. But not over Vinnie. Fuck Vinnie. He got stupid and got caught. We're cool."

I let out a long, slow breath in relief. "Glad to hear it."

"Hey, tell your parents hello for me, will you? I haven't heard from them."

"Still?"

"I'm sure they're busy." Tony didn't smile this time, but he had a forlorn look about him, like he had been reminded of something sad.

"You know them, Tony. They're not busy with anything important. I'll see if I can get them down here."

"Great." Tony smiled for real this time. I could even see his teeth. "See what you can do. I'd love to see them again."

"I'll do my best."

"What else can we do?" He looked around the restaurant, then looked at me. "We through with our conversation?"

"Yeah, sure. I didn't want to keep you."

"Walk me out, will you? The boys will give me hell if I walk out by myself."

"Can't have people jumping you for your meatball recipe, can we?"

Tony chuckled. "No, we can't."

## CHAPTER 24

I STOPPED AT MY APARTMENT LONG ENOUGH TO PRINT A couple handfuls of pages. Then I drove back to the precinct. Rich sat at his desk, frowning at something on his screen. He looked up as I approached. The frown didn't soften. "What's up?"

"I heard you went to bat for me," I said.

A small smile appeared on Rich's lips, then vanished. "The lieutenant can ask a lot of questions," he said.

"Still, you didn't have to answer them like you did. I appreciate it."

Rich nodded. "Don't make a liar out of me. I'm giving you the benefit of the doubt here."

"I'd like to think I earned it," I said.

"You're starting to." Rich leaned back in his chair and scrutinized me. "Something's changed about you. Maybe it was your time in China; I don't know. You're different. More . . . focused. More down to earth."

"I had some time to think about things," I said.

To his credit (and my relief), Rich didn't push the issue. Instead, he inclined his head toward the papers in my hand. "What do you have there?"

"Printouts. I know you stuck up for me, but I also know you think what I did over in Hong Kong was bullshit." I tossed the small stack onto Rich's well-organized desk. It made it three hundred percent messier right away. "My friends and I—mostly me, but they pitched in—got some Americans out of the country, and helped Chinese dissidents hide from the government. Those are emails thanking us for what we did. Before I settled on doing this job, I read them over. I told you I had them, and they're real—not fake, not hacked. Read them. Then tell me it was bullshit."

Rich looked at the papers, then back at me. "Why are you giving me these?" he said.

"You think I'm not cut out for this job," I said. "Maybe I'm not. I don't have your experience or your instincts. But I bring other skills. I've helped people before. There's your proof. You vouched for me, and I'm grateful. You might as well know what you stood up for."

Rich sat in silence a few seconds. Like me, he rarely suffered from being speechless. "Thanks," he said after some more seconds had ticked by. "I'll look them over."

"Thanks for your help. I hope not to need it in the future."

My comment made Rich grin. "Let's not get carried away," he said.

ON MY DRIVE HOME, I called Jessica Webber and told her the story was in the bag. When I got to my building, she sat on my front steps. Her jeans fit her legs as if applied with patient strokes of a paintbrush. Her jacket, zipped to her neck against the cold, hid the low-cut top she probably wore underneath. She held a notebook and pen in her hands, and was busy writing when I approached. When I stopped in front of the steps, she jumped and almost came off them. She looked up. "You startled me."

"I was told I need to practice my stealth," I said.

She stood and closed her notebook. "You're off to a good start. Can we talk about your case?"

"Sure."

"Even before you called, I heard it all got wrapped up tonight."

"You must have a source in the police department."

"A good reporter has many sources."

"Let's go inside and talk." I opened the door and climbed the stairs to my apartment. Jessica went in ahead of me and I shut the door behind her. I walked into the office and turned the light on. She followed me in and sat in one of the guest chairs. I stood behind the comfortable desk chair and shook off my trench coat.

"This feels so official in here," she said.

"You can ask me some questions in the bedroom later," I said.

Jessica blushed as she unzipped her coat. As I expected, she neglected the top three buttons of her blouse. I wondered if she chopped the top three off all her shirts to resist the temptation of using them. "Maybe I will," she said. Jessica set her phone between us on the desk and opened her notebook again.

I sat in my chair. "Wow, a recording and a notebook. This really does seem official."

"I'll try to keep it comfortable. What can you tell me about the case?"

"Anything you want to know. Where should we begin?"

"What allowed you to put it all together?"

"I found the dots and connected them." She scribbled a few things, then paused to look up at me. When I didn't elaborate, she shrugged and kept writing.

"Anything else?"

"I followed the facts and followed the money," I said. "Those led me to conclude Paul Fisher had been murdered. I had to prove it, and I was able to assemble the evidence I needed to do it."

"Was it dangerous?"

"I got waylaid and abducted at one point, and I got in a few fistfights. Nothing I couldn't handle."

"Were you scared?" said Jessica.

"At a few points along the way, yes."

"Did you have to shoot anyone?"

"I'm not a killer, Jessica."

"You don't have to be a killer to shoot anyone."

"True. No one put me in the position to test your statement. For that, I'm grateful."

"You knew Vinnie Serrano prior to this case, didn't you?"

"Yes," I said, "we went to school together."

Jessica jotted things down sporadically. "How did it feel to take him down?" she said.

I shrugged. "It felt . . . necessary. Vinnie strayed way over the line. He needed to be stopped, and I was right there to stop him."

"It didn't feel good?"

I thought about her question for a few seconds. "Satisfying, definitely."

"But you helped someone. Paul's widow got out of a really bad spot directly because of you." She paused, so I nodded to acknowledge the fact. "It didn't feel good, to help someone like that?"

"It did. I try not to approach the job in such a way, though. Someone somewhere will always need help. Sometimes, I'll be the one to provide it."

"Do you ever think you'll *want* to do it?"

"You know I'll sound like an asshole if you run these questions in your story, right?"

She smiled at me. "I know how to write a story to make someone look good, C.T. Don't worry. The public won't think you're an asshole. I'm surprised you care so much how you're perceived, though."

"Like I said, I need the job. People have to want to hire me."

"They will."

I nodded. "I will leave the story in your capable hands."

She smiled. "Good. This case started as an adultery case before turning into a lot more. There's a lot of infidelity out there. Do you expect a bunch of infidelity cases?"

"Not at all. This was my last one."

"Your last one?" Jessica said.

"My last one. I don't really care who sleeps with whom, nor who gets upset about it. If anything, this case was a prime example couples should talk to each other more. All of this could have been avoided if the Fishers could have communicated with each other."

"Do you think Alice realizes it now?"

"She's not stupid," I said. "Of course she does."

Jessica talked to me for a while longer. She must have exhausted her insightful questions the last time she interviewed me. Maybe she decided this should just be a puff piece to help my business. I couldn't complain; I needed the business to keep getting money from my parents. When she ran out of questions, Jessica took out a laptop. "Do you mind if I type it all up here?" she asked.

"Never let it be said I stood in the way of freedom of the press."

"Or a deadline," Jessica said with a grin.

"Mine sounded more dramatic," I said.

She spent about forty-five minutes keying in everything, referring to both her notes and recording several times. I read articles online while she worked, then got up to make some tea. When I gave Jessica her mug, she looked up at me and smiled, then got right back to work. She spent some time reviewing and proofreading, making a few changes here and there. "I'm finished," she said. "Before I send this, do you have anything to add?"

"I'd love to get you out of those clothes," I said, raising my mug toward her.

Jessica blushed and smiled. "Patience, Mr. Ferguson. I'll leave that out of the story." She stroked a few more keys, clicked around with her mouse, then closed her laptop. "There. My editor will see it shortly. It should make the morning paper, and it'll be online."

"Excellent."

Jessica stood and sauntered over to me. I watched the sway of her hips with some interest. She swung one leg over me and lowered herself onto my lap. "Now we can talk about you getting my clothes off," she said.

* * *

WE DID MORE than talk about it. My bedroom floor ended up littered with clothes as Jessica and I ripped shirts, pants, and underwear off each other on our way to the bed. Once there, we both proved insatiable. We collapsed beside each other and fell asleep quickly.

The next morning, at the beastly hour of eight-fifteen, my cell phone rang. I felt like hurling the bloody thing across the room but decided to look at the caller ID first. I looked at the other side of the bed. Jessica had left during the night. Normally, such things woke me. I must have been tired.

"Hi, Mom," I said as I answered the phone.

"Coningsby, your father and I are so proud of you," my mother said. I could hear the happiness in her voice. It sounded like the same tone I heard her use when bragging to other parents about my grades.

"If you'll still be proud in an hour, can you call back then?"

"Coningsby!"

"Fine. Thanks."

"That Jessica girl wrote a very nice article about you, dear. She seems very sweet."

I decided against telling my mother Jessica was much more than sweet, especially with her clothes off. "Yes, Mom, she's very nice," I said.

"You should ask her out," my mother said.

"Mom! I'm doing OK. Can we go back to talking about the great job I did?"

"If you insist, dear. We read all about the case. It's a shame Vincent turned out to be such an awful person."

"He would appreciate you calling him Vincent, though."

"I'm sure he would. How did it feel to go after one of your old friends?"

"It felt like something I had to do. I hadn't seen Vinnie in a few years. We were never the best of friends."

"You can expect the news stations to come talk to you, too, dear. I forwarded the story to them in case they didn't see it."

Of course she did. "I'll check my messages when I actually wake up," I said.

"You're not awake yet?" she said.

"Mom, how many times have you known me to be up this early if I didn't have to get up for school?"

"I thought you might be working on another case already."

"I can't believe I haven't drained you of your optimism yet."

"You're doing good work, Coningsby. Your father and I are going to keep some of our optimism."

"You make me out to be more noble than I am."

"Well, in time, I think you'll come to like it," my mother said. "I wish it weren't dangerous, but this is what you've chosen." She paused. "Your father told me I would like helping people. I didn't believe him. But he was right. Altruism gets in your blood. You'll learn that the more of these cases you do."

"I guess we'll see," I said. "This was my last adultery case, though. People should sit down and talk to each other instead of running to detectives to sort out their messes."

"There's some truth to that. Well, you'll be pleased to know that your father and I have decided to give you a nice bonus for completing your first case. This should help you make a nice down payment on a house. We're cutting you a $50,000 bonus today."

Wow. I hadn't expected so much. "Very generous of you," I said. "Thank you."

"Don't expect it all the time, dear," she said. "This is merely to get you started and keep you interested."

"Mission accomplished."

"Go listen to your messages, Coningsby. You have some interviews to do and some new clients to talk to."

"I think all my new business can wait until after breakfast."

"I guess so," my mother said. "Good job, dear. Your father and I are very happy."

"Thanks, Mom." We both hung up. I was happy, too, but more with the amount being transferred into my account than anything. Already, I imagined ways I could spend it. I needed to be judicious, though, to save and invest enough money so I didn't need to do this job anymore.

For now, though, it was a living.

I went downstairs to make breakfast, drink some tea, and

check the answering machine, satisfied with case number one in the books.

They could only get easier from here, right?

## END of Novel #1

Hi there,

Thanks for coming along on C.T.'s first case.

Contrary to his concluding thought, they don't get easier. Where would the fun in *that* be?

Readers who grabbed all the books have commented how C.T. grows into his job—and grows up in general—over the course of the series. The process starts with some harsh lessons in his next case.

You can start reading *The Unknown Devil* today!

## THE END

Do you like free books? You can get the prequel novella to the C.T. Ferguson mystery series for free. This is unavailable for sale and is exclusive to my readers. Visit https://bit.ly/HKD2021 to get your book!

If you enjoyed this novel, I hope you'll leave a review. Even a short writeup makes a difference. Reviews help independent authors get their books discovered by more readers and qualify for promotions. To leave a review, go to the book's sales page, select a star rating, and enter your comments. If you read this book on a tablet or phone, your reading app will likely prompt you to leave a review at the end.

## The C.T. Ferguson Crime Novels:

1. The Reluctant Detective
2. The Unknown Devil
3. The Workers of Iniquity
4. Already Guilty
5. Daughters and Sons
6. A March from Innocence

7. Inside Cut
8. The Next Girl
9. In the Blood
10. Right as Rain

## The John Tyler Action Thrillers

1. The Mechanic
2. White Lines (summer 2021)

While these are the suggested reading sequences, each novel is a standalone mystery or thriller, and the books can be enjoyed in whatever order you happen upon them.

**Connect with me**:
For the many ways of finding and reaching me online, please visit https://tomfowlerwrites.com/contact. I'm always happy to talk to readers.

This is a work of fiction. Characters and places are either fictitious or used in a fictitious manner.

"Self-publishing" is something of a misnomer. This book would not have been possible without the contributions of many people.

- The great cover design team at 100 Covers.
- My editor extraordinaire, Chase Nottingham.
- My wonderful advance reader team, the Fell Street Irregulars.

Made in the USA
Monee, IL
14 April 2021

65814078R00156